WINTER

A LOVE STORY

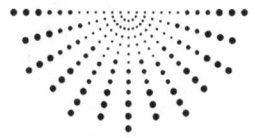

NORIAN LOVE

ISBN: 978-1-964019-08-6

ISBN: 1-964019-08-7

This is a work of fiction. Names, characters, businesses, places, events, and incidents are either the products of the author's imagination or used in a fictitious manner. Any resemblance to actual persons, living or dead, or actual events is purely coincidental

For my Family

The time we have to love in life is all we have to give.

To love and lose is what you choose should you decide to live.

— NORIAN

INTRODUCTION

Okay, before we get into anything else, let me say this: Winter: A Love Story – The Soundtrack is a straight-up banger. These artists put in WORK to bring the essence of this story to life. Whether you're reading, chilling, driving, or just pretending to clean, you need this soundtrack in your life. So, queue it up now. I'll wait…

You got it queued? Good. Now where were we? Ah yes.

I've come to love our chats at the start of each novel. It feels like just yesterday I was writing one for Money, Power & Sex. Rereading it now, I realize not much has changed—except, maybe, me. Over the years, you've seen me risk, hurt, laugh, and most importantly, grow. You've been with me every step of the way on this journey, one that challenges the corporate infrastructure and defies the so-called "status quo" of publishing.

Your support—whether you picked up this book from my site or simply offered a kind word—means everything to me. From the bottom of my heart, thank you. It's been beautifully humbling to discover just how many souls in this world rock with me.

The world feels more restless than when I last wrote a novel. There's a collective unease, and many of us are settling into routines that make us forget what's truly important. This book is my attempt to remind us all that as long as there is time, there's a chance to embrace life, love, and growth.

These characters enriched me deeply, and I walked away from their world feeling like I'd made new friends. I hope they do the same for you. And before I go, one more time—Winter: A Love Story – The Soundtrack. If you don't listen to it after all this hype, I'm judging you. Hard. Seriously, go check it out.

"Winter is the season that strips the world bare, reminding us that even in the coldest silence, there's beauty in resilience."

TIP OFF

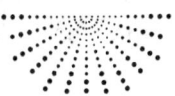

"Come on, Miri, we're gonna be late!" Winter Carter screamed at the top of her lungs.

"I'm comin', Momma." Miracle rushed down the stairs wearing a peach colored light coat over a cream turtleneck and matching leggings.

Winter examined her daughter. A sixteen-year-old girl with skin a shade of rich caramel, like warm honey under the sunlight. Even at her young age, her body had begun to blossom into womanhood, which had caught Winter off guard. Without thinking, she asked her, "First of all, when did you get a shape?"

Miracle rolled her eyes. "Momma, stop it. I'm a world class athlete, it was only matter of time."

"Well since the time is here, you're gonna need something heavier than that lil' coat you tryin' to look cute in."

"Dang momma I—."

"Better watch who you saying *dang* to, now get your you-know-what upstairs and get a proper coat! It's 43 degrees outside, Miri,"

Winter huffed at her daughter. She watched as Miracle scoffed and took off the jacket. At 5'11, her daughter was already six inches taller than her, but as she aged, she looked more like an older sister than her child.

Oh my God... my baby is turning into a woman.

Winter ignored the thought and looked at the picture sitting on the hallway table while Miri searched the downstairs closet. A moment from the eighth grade when her child was still innocent, wearing her favorite pink jacket with unicorns on the back of it. Winter smiled as she recalled the memory and walked over to help Miri as she ruffled through the closet. After sorting through a few things, Winter found the old coat.

"Miri, why don't you wear your unicorn co—"

"Hard pass."

"I see. So just who you trying to look cute for?"

"That is none of—Nobody, Momma, it's just... look, I'm a senior and I don't want to dress like I'm in eighth grade anymore."

"Just because you've skipped ahead a couple of grades does not make you grown."

"Yeah, but it does make me a senior, and even if I wasn't, who do you think would be wearing this at sixteen?"

Winter ignored her daughter and tried to put the coat on her. Miri shrugged away.

"Just try it on, I'm sure you can still fi—"

"Momma, it has a unicorn on it."

"You love unicorns."

"I do, but did you miss the part where I told you I was a senior. I can't be seen with a unicorn jacket on. You really want me to go out there and play myself?"

"I want you to be yourself."

"I am, but I got a rep to protect." Miri snatched the jacket from her mother and buried it in the back of the closet.

Winter processed her daughter's words, hoping they didn't mean what she thought they meant.

"Oh, so you got a rep! What kind of reputation do you have?"

"The kind of rep that is too cool to be wearing a unicorn jacket. Momma, please, this is hurting the brand."

Winter shook her head as she rolled her eyes. She pulled the unicorn jacket from the back. "Brand or not, you're not catching a cold, Miri. Your immune system is too co—"

"Momma! Ugh, why are you like this?"

"Why do I want to keep you alive? I don't know. I thought that's what all good parents did."

"Ugh! I can't wait to graduate so I can get out of here and go to U Conn."

"Well *U Conn* go upstairs and get you another jacket. You see what I did there?" Winter chuckled as her daughter rolled her eyes. Miri continued her protest,

"Well, can I put on one of your jackets?"

Winter paused, shocked. It was all the hesitation her daughter needed to shift through the closet again. After a spell, Miracle pulled out a black Jones of New York jacket, one Winter had bought last December, and hoisted it in the air.

Winter shook her head and said, "Miracle, I'm not gonna—"

"Momma, please? I'm the captain of the varsity basketball team, and we're about to do something special, I can feel it. I can't go outside wearing no dang unicorns."

Winter looked at the desperation in her daughter's eyes. She smirked. "Fine, but when we get back, we're gonna dig more into this 'rep' of yours and what social media platforms you are and aren't on with that phone."

Miracle kissed her mother on the cheek and put the jacket back in the closet, confusing her mother. Before Winter could ask, Miri explained, "Since you agreed to this jacket, I'm gonna assume that grace extends to all your jackets. Be right back."

Before she could respond, Miracle sprinted back upstairs, and after a few minutes came down in Winter's bubble vest and burgundy oversized turtleneck sweater with a matching beanie cap.

Winter had to concede; she was too old for a unicorn coat. She was entering the next phase of her life. She was a beautiful young woman.

Miracle looked timid, still unsure of her budding womanhood, seeking her mother's approval as she took each step towards the next chapter of her life. Miracle cleared her throat and asked with the uncertainty of the eighth grader that used to come down those stairs a question she could only ask her mother. "Well, how do I look?"

Winter paused. It was a moment she never wanted to forget, and she was grateful for time slowing down enough for her to capture it. Slowly, she walked closer to her daughter and looked into her big light-brown eyes. "I wish your dad could see how beautiful you look right now. He'd probably make a joke about buying a gun. But he'd be so proud."

The pair embraced as Winter wiped a tear of joy from her eyes and then pulled away from their hug. She stroked her daughter's cheek and said, "Tomorrow, we'll go shopping. It's time to replace your wardrobe."

"Finally!" Miracle screamed in excitement before catching herself. "I mean, thank you, Mom, thank you so much! I have so many ideas. How big is your credit limit?"

"Miri!"

"I'm just sayin', I need to know what I'm working with budget wise."

"You need to budget your behind into the car and quit worrying about my credit limit. In fact, stay out of grown folk business altogether."

Miracle rolled her eyes as the pair headed out of the door. The moment they opened the door, they were met with a chill in the air, forcing the pair to shiver.

The ground was covered in snow, which was unusual for Houston. For a city used to one snow day once a decade, it had now had a week straight of snow. Winter had even salted the ground earlier, but it was already freezing over again.

"Miracle, be careful running to the car."

It was too late. Miracle was already out of earshot running to the car, giggling hysterically. Winter shook her head and got in the driver's side of the silver late-model Audi sedan.

She turned to her daughter. "Do you have your seat—"

Miracle sighed. "Yes, Mom, I have my seatbelt on."

"Okay, I'm just asking."

Miri put in her earbuds, something that annoyed Winter, but she knew she'd been fussing enough already. She decided to just enjoy her own company. She listened to Preston Cole's Christmas album, one of her favorite new artists, as she headed to the Snowfest in downtown Houston.

Every year, the city would import snow to build a wonderland, and it had become a family tradition to visit. Except this year no imported snow was required, it was truly a white Christmas. She was excited about the carnival and the opportunity to support the local vendors, but she knew there was one place they had to go before they did.

As she parked the car, almost on cue, Miracle took out her earbuds and asked, "Momma, can we get a funnel cake first please?"

Some things never changed.

"Now wait a second, didn't you just make a whole fuss about how you're growing up?"

"What does that have to do with funnel cakes?"

"Well, like you said, you're a senior now. I wouldn't want it to ruin your 'rep.'"

"Momma, quit playin', good food is good food at any age," Miracle replied.

Winter laughed, admitting defeat.

The funnel cake shop would be their first stop. The fact was, she loved her funnel cake and hot cocoa just as much as Miracle did. She'd been looking forward to it all day, knowing it wouldn't be much longer before Miri wouldn't want to hang out with her mother. Winter wanted to savor this time and enjoy it with her daughter. She glanced at Miri, who was smiling in anticipation.

Winter turned to her daughter. "If you start to feel bad—"

"I'm fine, Momma."

"Did you take you medication?"

"Ugh, why are you like this? I said I'm fine. Now, can you act like I'm a normal kid and you're a normal mom for just a few hours?"

"Little girl, don't play with me. Now did you take your medication or not?"

"Yes. Now can we please just..." Miracle sighed. "You know what, just forget it." Miri pulled out her phone and started scanning the university of Connecticut's website.

Winter recognized she was probably working her daughter's nerves and decided to end the conversation.

The pair got out of the car and began to walk into the fair.

"Is Uncle Jaden gonna be here?"

"I think he is, but I'm not sure."

"I hope so, 'cause I needs my money."

"Money? What money does he owe you?"

"We bet twenty-five on the Rockets vs Lakers and he lost, then he went double or nothing for some strange reason and he lost again. So now, he owes me fifty bucks,"

Winter's mouth dropped wide open. She cut her eyes at her daughter. "What in the sports hell? Miri, I'm not raising no gambler."

"Mom, it's not gambling if it's a sure thing. This is Uncle Jaden. How do you think he got the nickname 'Choke'?"

"You better never let your uncle hear you call him that." Winter shouted as her daughter laughed at one of her uncle's more dubious nicknames. She rolled her eyes. "I don't know how you got this cocky, I swear."

"First of all, I'm not cocky, I'm confident. And secondly, if you didn't want me to be confident, you shouldn't have named me Miracle." Miri kissed her mom on the cheek as she chuckled.

Her daughter was full of life. Winter wanted her to be confident enough to use her voice now, because the world would spend the rest of her life trying to silence her. "You are going to do good things in this life, young lady. But somebody gonna pop you in that mouth one day."

"They can try, but remember, I'm a world class athlete." Miri smirked.

The pair continued through the entrance and looked around. The night was cool, and the ground was covered with snow. This was the place to be in the city, and Winter was glad to be there with her daughter.

As they turned the corner Miracle's eyes lit up. "Look, it's Uncle Jaden!"

2

HOME COURT ADVANTAGE

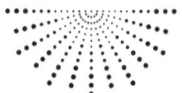

"Welcome back to Channel 6, I'm Rob Preston, sitting down with Jaden 'Smoke' Carter, former All-American college and Houston Rockets NBA star, who's now using his once-lethal hands to give back in a unique way. Jaden, could you tell us a little more about what you're doing here?"

"Thanks Rob. What many people don't know is that, although I grew up in Dallas, I'm a Houston native, and it was important to me to make sure that, with all the love this city has shown me, I find a way to return it, which is why I started the Helping Hands project, tackling sickle cell research in new, aggressive ways. It's a serious disease that affects millions of people, and I can't begin to describe the pain that not only the individual endures, but their families as well. I decided to make it my mission to help. My team and I have created a support network that includes top physicians, public transportation to and from appointments, and a cost-saving prescription app. On top of all of that, we're investing heavily into technology to research the disease to ultimately and hopefully find a cure in our lifetime."

"This cause must be really important for you to dedicate your own time to."

"Sickle cell disease took my brother, Malik's, life. He, and my mom, had an acute form called thalassemia. I never want a family to go through what mine had to."

"We all remember the last game the pair of you played together, ultimately your brother's last game, scoring a combined 78 points. But on a positive note, it looks like his legacy is living on. Your niece, Miracle Carter, seems to be on a tear though the Texas high school basketball league."

The words stung. There likely wasn't an easy way to approach it, but still, he resented the segue and fired back before his media training could kick in. "Not sure there's a positive takeaway from losing your brother and best friend, but yeah, Miri is doing great out there."

It was the kind of mistake a rookie would make, because he knew what the reporter would do with that kind of emotional response, however slight it may have been.

The anchor nodded and replied. "I'm sorry. I didn't mean to sound insensitive—"

"I get it, you were doing your job. We gotta talk about Miri. Yes, she's having a heck of a season. But I'd like to focus a little more on the facility—"

"And I promise we will, but we've just received a tweet on our social media page @6houstontv. A fan has asked you, 'What's up Smoke Carter, Houston is known for its superstar female athletes being discovered at a young age. Simone Biles and Brittney Griner are just a few. How does it feel for your niece to be alongside them as a H-Town legend?' Excellent question. Jaden, care to comment on that?"

He took a breath to compose himself.

He'd been in this position most of his life. Right on cue, Rob was doing what news analysts did so well, subtly swinging the conversation toward the popular story. He hated it. Still, he was on camera, and he would not discredit his brother's charity in any way.

With a deep sigh, he replied calmly. "It feels good. She's earned it, and proven that hard work pays off. Just like the hard work of the doctors, engineers, and tech gurus dedicating their lives to cure a disease that affects a predominantly African-American population, and if we can get back to talking about those people and the facility—"

"Sorry, Jaden, we've just received another fan tweet. Victoria_459 says 'Women's professional and college basketball is on fire. Do you think Miri is good enough to play on the college level when she'll only be sixteen once she enters the NCAA?'"

Jaden nodded. "Well, there's no question the game is faster, but Miri has a different gear and loves a challenge. But outside of her amazing play on the court, I'd also like you to know that our clinic has a doctor who has developed an amazing new method of testing, and we—"

"Amazing indeed. Before we go, we have one last question that reads 'Hi Smoke Carter, do you think the Lady Nets have a shot at winning the state title and how do you really feel about her breaking your record?'"

Jaden visibly sighed. There was no point in continuing the interview.

He looked blankly at Rob, then turned to the camera. "Records are meant to be broken, but I don't want to talk about Miri, and I can see that's what this is turning into. Instead I'm going to get back to helping the great people that are saving lives. Thanks for having me, Rob. For more information about the free clinic and our services, visit us at helpinghands.com."

Rob clearly received the message and did his best to salvage the interview. "That's right, go to helpinghands.com to learn more about Smoke Carter and his latest venture. Jaden, it's been a pleasure. This is Rob Preston reporting back to you in the studio."

Jaden ripped off his microphone as the camera cut, trying not to expose any more of his frustration.

The reporter walked over to him. "Listen Jae—"

"Before you say anything, let me say I know why you did what you did. All the stations are covering the Lady Nets and you couldn't pass up the inside scoop of having a conversation with her uncle. The question I need to know is if this was your idea or your producers?"

The reporter shrugged his shoulders and said, "What difference would that make?"

Jaden placed his hand on the reporter's shoulder and looked him in the eyes. "Because I don't want my niece to be around people who prioritize their own interests over helping sick people. Remember that when they win the state title."

Without another word, Jaden turned around and walked away. His message had been made clear. He'd make sure Winter didn't give Rob Preston or anyone at Channel 6 access to his niece.

There was no question that this was her moment, and he'd had enough of his own moments to know she was ready for it. Miri was a basketball sensation. Combined with a budding social media presence and an impressive performance all season, she'd become a star in her own right, rivaling his own notoriety. And the one thing he knew all too well was the sweet, yet deceptive, nature of fame.

He made it to his red Range Rover, got in the car and drove to meet the only people he cared to see. He tried calling his niece, but was sent to voice mail. The traffic to the Snow fest in Discovery Green Park downtown was horrendous but he managed to arrive in under an hour and quickly made his way towards the entrance. He called his niece again with no success.

As he pocketed his phone, he heard his name being called in the distance. "Jaden 'Smoke' Carter!"

He turned around, coming face-to-face with Miracle pretending to dribble an imaginary basketball around him. He grinned as she continued.

"You wanna know why they called this man Smoke? Because when there's smoke, there's fire. And if Jaden scored three in a row, it was gonna be a long night. Say, I hear your niece is dominating on the court. Some say she's even better than you."

"If she is, it's because she's stealing all my moves."

Miracle feigned ignorance. "What moves, Uncle Jae?"

"You know what moves. Don't think I didn't see you in that last game, blowing smoke off your hands."

"Gotta cool the guns down," Miracle quipped as she blew both of her hands in pistol fashion.

The two chuckled as Jaden responded. "Well, before you use those pistols on me, here's your bread." Jaden retrieved a few bills from his wallet and handed them to his niece.

Miracle whooped and pumped her fist in the air. "See, that's why I rock with you, Uncle Jae, I ain't gotta go beating down doors for my money."

"Then what do you call texting me like a bookie, 'bout sending goons to my house?"

"Okay, I may have been gloating a little."

Jae playfully shoved his niece in her shoulder to get her out of the way as she laughed at him, counting her money.

Miracle frowned. "Unc, you gave me sixty, you only owe me fifty."

"You keep the extra ten for that funnel cake I know you're gonna get."

Miracle walked over to hug and kiss him on the cheek. She pulled away, pointing towards him with a mock glare. "You're just hoping I gain weight so I won't break your record, aren't you?"

Jae let out a belt of laughter. "Miri, you might be good, but I was eating two hard-boiled eggs and oatmeal for breakfast every day, a protein shake for lunch and baked skinless chicken for dinner when I broke that that record. I'm not giving it up without a fight."

"So it's like that, huh?"

"When have I showed you it's not? Come on, now, they call me Smoke for a reason."

"Well, whatever, I'm gonna eat a funnel cake, and I'm gonna enjoy it. Just like you should enjoy your record while it last, because I'm coming for what's mine."

Jae nodded and smiled. "Well, there's a lot of basketball between now and then, so we'll see." He started towards her mother, who was approaching them from a distance. Miri continued her taunting. "Admit it, Uncle Jae, you secretly can't stand the fact that a girl is gonna break your state record for the most points scored in a high school season."

"False. I don't care if it's a boy or a girl. I hate the fact that she's technically a sophomore. Took me all four years to put that season together."

The pair laughed as Winter approached.

Taking notice of the money Miri was waving in the air, she snatched the money from her daughter's hand.

The teenager huffed. "Hey, that's my money!"

"Like I said, I ain't raising no gamblers," she retorted as she put the money in her purse.

Miracle looked to her uncle, silently begging for him to come to her aid.

Jae smirked, shrugged his shoulders. "Hey, she's your mom. All I know is my debt is paid."

It wasn't what Miracle wanted to hear. She groaned and rolled her eyes, hoping to appeal her mom's decision. "Well, the bet was for fifty and Unc gave me sixty. Can I at least get ten for the funnel cake?"

Winter considering her daughter's words with a frown, then pulled out some cash. "I'll give you twenty since it's Christmas." She turned to Jae. "Now, since that's settled, let me see if I can read the minds of the two most competitive people I know. Let me guess, you guys were talking about... the state record."

"Double up," Jae said. He met her hand in a Double up high five they'd been doing since college.

Miracle smirked. "Uncle Jae is mad that it took me half the time to do what it took him four years to do."

Jaden shrugged. "I'll admit there was a time I thought that record was gonna stand forever. But if it has to fall to anybody, I'm glad it's you."

Miri rolled her eyes. "Oh, don't think I'm falling for that sweet babyface act. I've seen you trash talk Kobe Bryant, I ain't buying it. The only thing that's gonna be sweeter than this funnel cake I'm about to eat is taking your record. But don't worry, I won't rub it in your face. I still gotta impress the many, many college scouts coming out to see ya girl." Miri brushed imaginary dirt off her shoulder.

Jae scoffed in reply. "So, to be clear, this is you *not* rubbing it in my face?"

"Oh, the levels of petty are deep, Unc. You're getting the friends and family discount."

"Let's not forget who taught you how to shoot."

Miracle stopped and grabbed Jae's hands, looking him deeply in the eyes. "You're right, and all kidding aside, I've been thinking of a way to honor my first and favorite coach."

"That's really thoughtful, but it's your moment, Miri."

"No, I'm serious. It's important to me to give cred where cred is due. So when the time comes, you mind calling Steph Curry's agent to see if he'll come to town?"

"Let my damn hands go!" Jae barked at Miri as he feigned putting her in a headlock.

After a minute or so, Winter's voice interjected. "Okay guys, that's enough of that. Jeez, every time the two of you get together, it feels like a basketball game," she said.

Jaden pulled away from his niece with a breathless laugh. "Your mom's right. Go get that funnel cake. Matter of fact, have two."

Miri rolled her eyes as she ran off to get in line. Jae watched Winter as she looked at her daughter in amazement.

"That girl is as tall as a giraffe and still runs like she did when I made chocolate chip cookies."

Jaden smirked as they started to wander through the rows of vendors. "To be fair, you make some damn good chocolate chip cookies."

"It's the vanilla."

"I thought a chef never gives away their secrets?"

"I'm just talking to you, Jae, and we both know you ain't about to bake a damn thing."

"For your information, I get busy in the kitchen."

"Yeah, eating."

The pair laughed before Jaden broached a more serious topic. "But speaking of the kitchen, Mr. Armand called."

He watched Winter become visibly frustrated. After a beat of silence from her, he leaned in. "Wyn?"

"Huh?"

"If you can *huh*, you can hear." Winter scoffed as he continued. "I don't get it, Short stack. You've been talking about opening up Villery's for years now, then almost like it was meant to be, the space literally connected to the bakery opens up—"

"I cannot take on the responsibility of a full-blown restaurant right now. I'm catching my you-know-what as it is with the bakery."

"Then hire some help."

"And when am I supposed to have time to do that?"

"Then hire someone to help you hire some help. You got the money because I'm the bank."

Winter tried to walk faster to skirt past Jae, but he quickly caught up to her.

"Look Wyn, all I'm saying is you're working hard and not smart. You opened the bakery to honor your mom and you've been talking about this as a way to honor your pops since I've known you."

"Jae this isn't th—"

"You're doing so good you don't even need the money."

"Come on, Jae, I—"

Jae raised a hand to stop her. "Just hear me out Wyn. You don't have to do it all. Hell, just on the real estate alone you can pick up a cool million in equity. But people are lining up around the block for your baked goods."

"I hear you. Can we not talk about this right now?"

Reluctantly, Jaden nodded. After years of friendship, he knew when to push and when to back off.

"Okay. Just know this ain't over. It's prime real estate in downtown Houston and these kinds of deals don't happen often."

"I know, Jae. And thank you."

Miracle joined them, a funnel cake in each hand. "Oh my god, these are incredible, Momma, you gotta try this." She closed her eyes and smiled, already high on sugar.

Winter looked over at Jaden, already anticipating his next words.

"You won't believe this, but your mother loved funnel cakes—"

She sighed. "Here we go. Jae, can't you tell a new—"

"You're either going to let me finish this story, or we're gonna talk about Mr. Armand's deal."

"You know, I always liked this story. Please Jae tell it to us. Again."

Jae turned back to Miracle and continued. "As I was saying, when she was pregnant, your momma craved funnel cakes. Your pops, always looking for an angle, tried to get your mom to make her own."

"Jae, we've heard this story a thousand times, can you—"

"Wyn, if you cut me off one more time..."

"Yeah, Mom, I want to hear the story. It never gets old. Go ahead and finish, Uncle Jae."

"So, your dad buys all the ingredients for the funnel cake, four different kinds of filling. Kisses your Mom, then goes to sleep on the couch."

"Jae..."

"Next thing I know, I'm getting a knock on the door and it's Malik. He's covered in all the ingredients, telling me I need to help him find a place that sells funnel cakes."

Winter pouted and folded her arms as Miri and Jae laughed hysterically. "I was six months pregnant and my ankles were swollen. I had just pulled an all-nighter at the bakery and this fool tells me to make my own damn funnel cake. So I did."

The trio laughed. Winter playfully punched Jae in the arm, who was on the verge of tears.

After gathering his breath, he said. "All I know is we drove for hours." Jae was about to continue when he notice a lanky, dark-skinned kid roughly his niece's age walk over to them.

"Hey Miri," the kid said nervously.

"Hi Clinton," she replied just as nervously.

Jae watched. A cocktail of giddiness and embarrassment was painted across her face as she continued. "I didn't know you were going to be here."

"Yeah, me and a few of the fellas decided it would be cool to come and hang out before the all-star game. Congratulations, by the way. Being the starting point guard on that team is major."

"Yeah, I... thanks. It's cool that you're here. I... would've come with my friends, but my Uncle Jae wanted to come, so I had to do the family thing."

The boy looked up and stammered. "You... you're Jaden Smoke Carter. Number 14."

"That's me."

"Shooting guard for the Rockets."

"Yep."

"You scored 67 points on LeBron James."

"It was 62, but—"

"You're a first ballot Hall of Famer."

"Kid, I need you to breathe."

The boy reached out his hand and as Jaden reached out to shake it, he moved next to him to shoot a selfie. Jaden, use to the attention, just smiled.

The kid turned to Miri. "Aw man, this is so cool. Miri, I didn't know Smoke Carter was your uncle. Smoke, can I have your autograph?"

Jae obliged, taking note of his niece's change in attitude, from sarcastic and rugged to bubbly and flirty. He met Winter's eye before they both gave the boy a once over.

"Miri, who is this lil' boy?" her mother enquired, overly sweet.

Miracle jolted as if only now remembering they were still there. "Uh....right, Mom, Uncle Jae, this is Clinton. He's our starting shooting guard."

Clinton smiled and added. "Yeah, growing up, Smoke was my favorite— "

"I'm sorry, young man, I was talking to my daughter when you so rudely cut me off," Winter admonished.

The young boy nodded solemnly. "I'm sorry, ma'am."

"But since we're here, I have a few questions for you. You go to Dawson High too?"

Clinton nodded nervously. "Yes, ma'am."

Miri tried to interject but Winter was like a dog with a bone. Her inquest was just beginning.

"How are your grades?"

"I have a 4.3 GPA."

"Do you plan on going to college? And if so, what do you plan on studying?"

"I'm going to the University of Houston to be a cougar, like Smoke, and I'm planning to study international law."

She was grudgingly impressed, but she pressed on. "How do you plan to pay for—"

"Mom, can we go ice skating?" Miracle interjected, deciding the inquisition had gone on long enough.

Winter glanced at Jae, who was giving her a look she didn't quite understand. She turned to her daughter. "Sure, baby. I thought you were staying off the ice before the all-star game, but just let me get a funnel cake and—"

"No, I mean... can I go ice skating... with Clinton and his friends?"

The words caught Winter off guard, but now she knew that Jae's glance was deliberate. She was missing something. "Well, sure... if that's what you want."

"Thanks, Mom!"

Without another word, Miracle ran off with Clinton, leaving Winter stunned and somewhat confused. She'd never seen her daughter behave that way before.

She glanced at Jae who was trying to suppress a smirk at her confusion. "Did I just miss something?"

"You did."

"What exactly did I—"

"When Clinton walked up, did you not notice how quiet Miri got?"

Winter's eyes widened. "So that wasn't just me? She *was* acting weird. Wait, you don't think..."

"Yep. Miri has a crush."

Winter was excited but also a little disheartened. All the signs were in front of her and she missed them. It was another reminder that Miracle was growing up.

Jaden looked around. "Well, since it looks like it's just gonna be you and me, let's go grab some—"

"Hey, baby, sorry I'm late."

He turned around to see who had interrupted him. It was Darren Bailey. His former college teammate.

3

FULL COURT PRESS

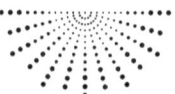

"**W**hat's up, Darren?" Jae reluctantly addresses Darren.

The man replied coldly, "What's good, Jae?"

The two men exchanged a fist bump and stood in awkward silence.

Winter picked up on the tension and turned to hug her boyfriend. "Hey, Darren."

He leaned in and kissed her, reaching for her hand. "Sorry I'm late. I got held up at the office."

"Ah, the life of an NBA junior executive," Jae quipped.

Darren was quick to pick up on the sarcasm in Jae's voice. "My title is Vice President of Operations. Don't worry, you can still use the court. That's if I'm not finding talent to win a championship."

"That's great, baby. How was work today?" Winter said, trying to diffuse the building tension.

"You know, the usual, dealing with athletes and their over-inflated egos. Speaking of which, Jae, I didn't know you'd be here."

"Darren, I know the concept of loyalty is foreign to you, but—"

"Guys, it's Christmas time. Can we pretend to get along just for a while?"

The two men took a breather. "Anything for you baby," Darren said, pulling Winter closer.

As they were talking, people were taking notice of them, pointing to Jaden. Winter, being his best friend since college, realized what that meant. "Let's start moving before Jae forms a fan club."

Jae chuckled as Darren rolled his eyes. Still, they moved away from the growing crowd.

Once they'd moved to a lesser populated area, Darren perked up. "Hey Jae, I saw your lil' spot on the news today. Congratulations, that's good stuff."

Jae blew heat in his hands together and to buy himself a moment. *I hate this fucking guy.*

He removed his hands and composed himself. "Thanks Darren, I'm just doing what I can to save lives. Appreciate your support."

With Yo' bitch made ass.

The silence resumed.

After what seemed like a lifetime, Darren muttered in Jae's direction. "So, you talk to any of the guys from the old squad? The reunion is coming up."

"Nah, can't say I have as of late. What about you?"

"I heard from Mike-Mike a couple of times. He's doing good. Got a coaching gig on the east coast at a division one school."

"That's cool."

Darren continued. "He told me he was trying to reach out to you, said you never answer his calls, so I covered for you and told him—"

"And why would you need to cover for me?"

"I didn't mean it like that, Jae—"

"I ain't slow, you always mean it like that, D."

"Guys!" Winter said, interrupting the two of them. Both men gazed her way as she pulled their shirts like a disapproving mother scolding her children. "This is the one holiday tradition that still means something to Miri, and when she goes to college next year, I want to look back on this moment and remember enjoying it. Darren, I asked Jae to come because he's been here every year and, as her uncle, it's important to her. I asked you to come because you are important to me. So, can we please just try to get along, for Miri's sake?"

Jae glanced at the two of them. He remembered a time where he and Darren had been closer. It had been years. But he couldn't forgive his brother's best friend for starting a relationship with his widow.

He let out a long sigh, his breath visible in the cold air. "Short stack, you know I'd do anything for Miri, but she's doing her own thing and, like you said, if I stand around too long I'll be signing autographs. So, no offense, but right now I'm more of a third wheel to your date. Maybe it's time to let this tradition die—"

"Hey, Wyn! Girl, sorry I'm late."

Jaden turned around to see Christina Waters, one of Winter's closest college friends and business partner.

Winter embraced her friend, whom Jaden noticed seemed to be thicker than the last time he'd seen her. *Did she get a Brazilian butt lift? This girl always been thirsty...*

As the pair released their embrace, Winter responded. "Christina! Girl, what are you doing here?"

"Girl, I was just in the neighborhood and then I remembered you said you were gonna be here, so I just popped by. Jaden, is that you?"

"Hi Chrissy," Jaden said as he gritted his teeth.

Did she say she was late? I coulda swore I heard... I know Wyn not trying to do what I think she's trying to do.

He realized straight away what was in front of him. He had to get out of there before it was too late.

Jae turned to the three of them and said, "You know what? Maybe I should go."

Before he could move, Winter blocked his path. "You know, I've been having second thoughts about your offer to help me with the expansion, but it didn't feel right without discussing it with my right hand. Now that she's here, maybe we can talk about it?"

"Oh, that's what you were waiting on?"

Winter shot her boyfriend and best friend a grin as she dragged Jae by the arm and pulled him out of earshot. "Alright, I won't play you. I set this up."

"Dammit, Wyn—"

"But I'm serious about the proposal. If you stay just for a little while, I'll strongly consider opening the restaurant and letting you give me more money."

"Just wins all around for me."

Winter barked out a laugh. "I'm serious, Jae. Miri is gonna be so disappointed. This has been a tradition all her life. Just stay for a little while."

Jae glanced back over at Christina and back to Winter. She smiled at his hesitation. "I mean, you were just saying how you felt like a third wheel. Now there are four of us."

As she said that, Darren and Christina approached.

"Yeah, we can make it a double date," Christina said as she latched on to Jaden's arm. He wanted to pull away, but before he could, Darren chimed in.

"Yeah, Carter. Besides, what else do you have going on?"

I really hate this fucking guy. He thought.

The truth was, this was all he had planned for the day. This was their tradition, and it was being ruined by the two outsiders. He wasn't going to let Darren's ego or Winter's poor matchmaking skills ruin his day. He raised his head and said, "You know what? Fine. Lead the way."

Christina squeezed him tighter as the quartet headed deeper into the festival. With each step, there was a wonderment of winter unfolding. The snow men were moving in one station. There were children sliding down ice slopes in another. There was ice skating and a bobbing for apple contest which was meant to test your endurance in the cold.

"Would you do that?" She asked.

"Hell no," Jaden remarked. "Would you?"

"Would who? Do you see any of us over there? No, those are Anglo-Saxon games in Anglo-Saxon weather. I'll stay warm, thank you."

Jaden chuckled at her wit. She was different than what he remembered from college.

He laughed as she continued. "Shoot, bobbin' for apples in this temperature, this is how you get pneumonia."

It wasn't long before Jaden was enjoying Christina's company and the ambiance of the group. Even Darren seemed to get on his nerves a little less. Yet as the quartet walked past the game area, Jae noticed Winter become more detached.

He watched her as she scanned the crowd. "Where is that girl?" he heard her mutter.

He leaned in closer to her. "She's over by the cotton candy stand."

The shock was evident on her face. With a grin, he replied. "Six foot seven, remember? I can cover a lot of ground from up here. Don't worry, she's having a good time, but not *too* good a time, if you feel me."

"As we should be," Christina chimed in, still rubbing his arms. Jaden glanced at Christina, then back to Winter, whose disposition changed as she realized Darren was watching their exchange.

Jaden rolled his eyes and continued to walk when Darren snickered. "Bag Boy still got the touch with the ladies."

"Bag Boy?" Christina questioned.

"Here we go." Jaden groaned.

"Oh, Jae never told y'all about the legend of Bag Boy?"

The four of them stopped. Jaden closed his eyes and shook his head dismissively. Christina, confused by the statement, turned to Darren. "Who or what is a Bag boy?"

Before Jaden could stop him, Darren told the story. "U of H had this tradition that the incoming freshmen would have to carry the starters' bags, and Jae was on the bench behind me so he had to carry mine."

"And as you can imagine, Darren was a prick about it," Jaden chimed in.

"Nah, you were being soft. Long story short, one day he gets this idea that he can challenge me to a shooting match. Well, I had nothing to lose, so I told him if he lost, he had to carry the bags for all the other guys on the team, even the other freshmen. Needless to say, I smoked him. No pun intended." The group laughed as Jaden thought,

I really, really hate this fucking guy.

Darren continued.

"Don't get me wrong, he was a hell of a player. Just wasn't on my level at that time."

Jaden chuckled. "Darren, I know that journey down memory lane takes you back to the best time of your life, so I'll humor you. That was a long time ago and no offense, you played four years in college. I played fourteen years in the NBA. We're not the same."

"I'm not saying I'm a better player, I'm saying I'm a better shooter. Because I know when to shoot my shot and when not to. And when I do shoot, I don't choke," Darren said with a quick side look toward Winter. His innuendo was obvious.

Jaden smirked. Their subtle jabs had escalated to the point of action, and he would not back down. Looking at the stalls around them, Jae spotted a Hoop Shot station. "Well, let's prove it." Jae said,

Darren raised his eyebrows, noticing the carnival basketball game. "I don't think you want that, Jae."

"Nah, I think I do. Let's play a friendly game. Say, first to ten?"

"Jae, I don't want to embarrass you in front of your date."

"See, I think you're scared. I tell you what, I'll only use my left."

Darren scoffed. "So you think you got it like that? Okay, I'm in, but let's put some cash on it. Say, a hundred a ball?"

Jae made a show of checking his pockets. "That's cool, I think I got a little spare change on me."

It was Darren's turn to smirk. Jae was flexing, and they both knew it.

Winter gasped. "Darren, that's a lot of money!"

"I got it, baby. Believe it or not, NBA executives get paid too. Some of us dribble the ball and some of us fill the seats. It's the difference between the talent in the circus, and the ringmaster. We all work for the circus, but some of us are just clowns."

Jaden grinned. He was getting under Darren's skin. "That might be true, but nobody comes to see the ringmaster. Now, are we playing or what?"

Darren took off his dark charcoal coat and blew his breath into his hands to warm them up. "Make it, take it, right?"

"Keep shooting until you miss, Darren. Won't take long."

Darren glared at him and asked the worker for a basketball. He took two dribbles, raised up and sunk the first shot effortlessly. "Easy money," he exclaimed as the ball spun through the net. He hit the next three until he finally missed one.

Jaden nodded and walked up to the machine. "Step aside, let me show you how it's done." Jaden threw the ball with his weak hand and felt the ball slip, resulting in an air ball.

A crowd that had formed around them, queuing for the chance to see Smoke sink a basketball. He could hear some of them snicker at his failure.

"Choking already?" Darren mocked.

Jaden rolled his eyes. "Just hurry up and miss so I can get the ball back."

Darren grinned and shot the ball. As predicted, he missed.

Jaden smirked and took the basketball, tying Darren, until he missed his fifth shot.

"Four up," Darren called.

The tension between them was palpable. The crowd around them had started a chant for Jaden, some pulling out their phones to record the contest.

"8-4, Smoke. You better end it now because if you give me another shot, it's over."

Jaden ignored him. If he lost, he risked being roasted on social media. He wasn't sure why he took the bet; he had nothing to prove to Darren. Yet here he was, doing the last thing he wanted to do: going back and forth with his ex-college roommate.

He shot the first ball in, followed by four more. He was about to hit the tenth shot when he noticed Miri had joined the back of the crowd with her friends. Her presence caused a temporary distraction, making him rush his shot and miss the game winner.

Darren pumped his fist in the air and looked at Jaden. "Still can't close when it counts, huh?" Darren teased as he took the ball and made the first shot. The score was 9-9 when Darren shot the last ball. The ball hit the backboard and fell into the net, the crowd gasping and cheering as the game came to an end.

Darren extended his hand, motioning for Jaden to pay up. Jaden took the cash out of his pocket and paid him the thousand dollars.

As Darren counted the money with a smile, he remarked, "Told you I was a better shooter, Choke." He winked.

Jaden glared at him, his competitive instinct taking over. "Double or nothing. I'll hit fifteen before you hit five. Same rules."

Darren smirked. "You're a glutton for punishment Carter. Easy money. You got a bet. Oh, and since I'm the king, I get the ball first."

Jae nodded in agreement. Darren shot the first two before missing the third. "Your turn."

Jaden sunk the first one without a problem. "One." He got the ball back to shoot again. "Two." He hit the next seven in a row. By now, a larger crowd had formed, and people were live streaming with their phones.

"Ten," he called. He turned to look at Darren, maintaining eye contact as he shot the last five. When each one landed, he spoke.

"We." *Swish!*

"Are." *Swish!*

"Not." *Swish!*

"The." *Swish!*

"Same." *Swish!*

As the last ball fell in, he lifted both of his hands up and blew the smoke off of them. "Ball game."

Their makeshift audience cheered at his victory, and Jae raised his hands in the air, whooping with glee.

A voice broke through the cheering. "Still got it, Uncle Jae!"

"Never lost it, never will. Where there's smoke, there's fire."

He gestured toward Darren, motioning for the money back Jae had just given him. "Don't worry about it, D, a kid reminded me tonight that I scored 62 points on LeBron. You never had a shot." he smirked as he put his arm around his niece. "You guys have a good time. I'm gonna go on a few rides with Miri."

He left without saying another word to Darren or Christina, satisfied with beating his former friend.

4

THE PICK AND ROLL

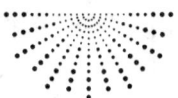

"Sorry I'm late," Winter called breathlessly as she entered her bakery, Winter's Wonderland, on the south side of Houston.

"Hey Wyn. Working a half day?" Christina joked.

Winter groaned, spotting a stack of boxes that were an eyesore for customers trying to enjoy their snacks in the dining area. She glanced over at Christina, who was working the register for the morning crowd. "They're the new pans you ordered. I was going to move them when I got a break."

The crowd was growing, and there wasn't a lot of time to move them. She decided to jump in and help her friend at the counter, where a line was forming. Around midday she moved to the kitchen to prepare for tomorrow's crowd, and a specialty order of pies that were requested for the Black Excellence gala in two days.

It wasn't until Christina walked in, getting ready to leave for the day, that she realized how much time had passed. "Girl, you've been a machine in here. You need a break," Christina said as she dipped her finger in one of the leftover bowls of raspberry filling.

Winter continued to knead the dough she'd been working on. "Oh, trust me, when this is over, I'm taking a long hot bath and having a glass of wine. Hell, maybe a bottle."

The two chuckled as Christina handed her the can of cinnamon sugar, Winter's unique blend specifically made for the topping on each pie. She noticed her friend paying close attention to how she sprinkled the can. "You know it's just cinnamon and sugar in this can, right?"

"You know, that's one thing that use to irk me about you in college. You were so damn good at presentation. Every time I try to make this, it never comes out tasting like yours. Like, how do you get it to sit right on top of the fluff like that and still be spread out enough to cover the pie?" Christina said, examining the can.

Winter shrugged her shoulders. "Now, you know every chef has their secrets."

"You know what, I'm not even finna play with you today. Don't act like I didn't graduate top of our—well, *my*—culinary class."

"You know you wrong for that, right?"

"For what?" Christina snickered.

Winter rolled her eyes. It had always stung Winter that her friend seemed to bring up her degree when Winter didn't graduate, but that was just the way Christina was.

Picking up on her friend's souring mood, Christina walked over and touched Winter on the shoulder. "Girl, don't act like that. You know I'm playing. I'm just saying I'm a chef, too."

"I never said otherwise."

"Well, between that salty attitude and that dry-ass response, you kinda did. Talking about every chef has their secrets."

"Whatever, Chrissy." Winter said. It was the one downside of working with her best friend. They had a great relationship, but every now and then Christina would work on her nerves. This was one of those moments.

Christina recognized this and decided to change the subject. "Look, my bad. I didn't mean nothing by it, okay? You know you my girl."

"I know. I'm off too. Miri's mouth is getting out of control and she's too damn tall for me to just pop her in it like I want to, so I'm a bit sensitive today. That's on me."

"It's all good girl, seems like it's a case of that going around. Speaking of which, what was all that BDE between Jaden and Darren?"

"BDE?"

"You serious right now? Big Dick Energy."

"Gross."

"Girl get your head out the pie crust and take a look around now and then."

Winter slammed the dough on the island and wiped her brow. "Well, as you can see, I have a business to run. I'm behind on every single order, and I have a child who thinks she's the one in charge. On top of her graduating two years earlier than I'd planned, and prom right around the corner, I don't have time for big dicks or little dicks or anything dick related right now. But as far as Darren and Jae go, they been like that since college."

Christie crossed her arms as a look of bewilderment fell on her face. "Hold on, you wanna run that back, sis?"

"Run what back?"

"That part about you not having time for anything dick related."

"What of it?"

"You and Darren haven't…"

"It's new."

"Oh, this is making so much sense now. Wyn, it's been two months and you haven't broken that man off none of your cookie?"

Winter shrugged unapologetically. "It could be two years. No one gets to eat this cookie until I'm ready. Besides, it's been long distance, so we're mainly just talking on the phone and if I'm honest, the only thing I want to do in the bedroom these days is sleep for six solid hours."

"So that's why he's trippin'? You haven't given up the goods, so he must think that you and Jae are doing something… are you?"

"What? Girl, no. Ugh. Y'all both know Jae is my brother-in-law."

"Brother-in-laws don't have dicks?"

"I'm gonna ignore that. Jae is Miri's uncle, and Darren knows I'm not that kind of chick. It was weird enough thinking about dating Darren in the first place, him being Malik's best friend and all."

"Yeah, I could see that being an issue."

Winter nodded. "I didn't know him that well in college. Once me and Malik got married, life started happening fast, and they lost touch. We really didn't know each other outside of 'hi' and 'bye' in college. So, we're taking things slow till he got this job back in Houston."

"So if that's no the issue, why do him and Jae got a problem with each other?"

Winter reached into the fridge to pour a glass of red wine for them both. "Jaden took Darren's spot as a starter, and if I'm being honest, his spot as a friend to Malik."

"Damn, that had to hurt. So Malik played on that team, too?"

"Yeah, girl, he's the whole reason Jae came to U of H. He didn't know his big brother growing up, and he wanted to connect with him. He could've gone anywhere, but he wanted to play with Malik. It was a big deal on campus."

"So the three of them on the same team? I didn't know any of this. I feel like I went to a totally different college."

"You went to do what you needed to do. I was the unfocused one. It's stupid, because Jaden doesn't like the idea that Darren is with me, because he feels like he's disrespecting Malik's ghost or whatever. I'm like, what, am I supposed to stay alone forever?"

"For real, like, ain't he one of the people that tell you that you need to get out of the house and meet people?"

"Exactly!" Some of the filling that Winter had been scooping into the pie shells splattered over her as she remembered her frustration with Jae. "Now I finally connect with someone and Jaden got a problem."

Christina scoffed. "Girl, you know men are territorial."

"They're both just worrisome. It's crazy, because they are so much alike."

Winter put the last of the pies in the oven before moving on to packing the pies that had cooled down. Her mind wandered to the two men, and how their competitive rivalry went all the way back to their college days. She remembered him being called Bag Boy back in the day, and how much grief the team gave him. Still, she knew to stay out of it.

Christina, however, had no such insight, and wouldn't settle until she had answers. "All I know is that Bag Boy comment set Jae off."

"That did hurt his feelings, but not as much as when Darren called him 'Choke'. That's the one that had us standing there watching a middle-age pissing contest."

The two women laughed as Christina handed Winter another box for the pie. "What's the story behind that nickname exactly?"

"Girl, maybe you did go to a different school."

"That's right, cause I was in the classroom trying to graduate—"

"Yes, you graduated, we get it Chrissy. But while you were doing that, this was one of the biggest deals on campus. Hell, in the city. Like, I can't overstate how big it was." Winter put the next pie in the box and continued. "You gotta remember, the University of Houston had never been on the map when it came to college basketball. Jae was their first real big-time player since Hakeem Oljuwon and Clyde Drexler. Throw in the background story of two brothers reuniting, and ESPN was on campus every weekend."

"Damn, I didn't know that."

"Yeah, having Jae commit to the team changed how recruits looked at the school."

"Girl, land this plane and just tell me what happened. You know I don't care nothing about sports, just about ballers."

Winter rolled her eyes and flipped her friend off before continuing. "So, you got this big-time star, Jaden 'Smoke' Carter and he's balling all season long. We're one game away from going to the college championship, and he's been on fire for three and a half quarters. We were going to the championship, no question. And then..."

"And then what?"

"Then suddenly, he was off. Making turnovers, costly mistakes, all in the last two minutes of play. We were down by one, and the ball was in his hands. All he had to do was hit the same shot he'd made twenty times that night. He missed, but the team got the rebound and kicked it back out to him. He missed again, but he got fouled. He goes to the foul line and misses three straight shots, which had never happened before. He was Steph Curry before Steph Curry. He hadn't missed two consecutive shots all season. That day he missed four. We lost by one point."

Christina shook her head. "Damn, I missed all of this in school?"

"You don't even know. So, the next day, ESPN had the worst angle, like he was scared of the moment or something, and one of these commentators called him 'Choke' Carter, and it stuck. He's been Choke ever since." She watched as her friend pulled out her phone and started to scroll. "Christina, what are you doing."

"Seeing how much he's worth."

"Were you even listening to anything I just—"

"One hundred and fifty million dollars! Oh, a bitch about to get pregnant for real."

"Christina!"

"Look, he might have been Bag Boy then, but he's definitely got that bag now, boy." She chuckled as Winter rolled her eyes. "Christina Carter. I like the sound of that."

Winter shook her head dismissively, causing Christina to toss her hands in the air and reach for her purse. Before she could grab it, Winter stopped her. "Christina, Jae isn't one of your celebrity fuckboys that will take you to Steak 48 and offer you a Plan B for dessert."

"First of all, I resent the implication that all I deal with are fuckboys."

"Kujo Rich?"

"Kujo was a good guy."

"Christina, Kujo Rich was a rapper who proposed to you after he got arrested for beating some poor guy's ass after he got caught in bed with said man's wife and wanted you to be an alibi."

"Allegedly. You know how the media be spinning shit."

Winter laughed. "Well, there's nothing alleged about the prenup he wanted you to sign that allowed him to have threesomes that wouldn't even include you. And don't even get me started on the time you were with Preston Cole."

"Damn girl, okay, we can't all meet our husbands in college. Some of us gotta grow."

"You know I don't mean no harm in what I'm saying, it's just... you know you're my girl, and Jae's like a brother to me."

"And you wonder why Darren's acting the way he is," Christina said dismissively as she folded her arms and looked at her friend.

A confused look crossed Winter's face. "What's that supposed to mean?"

"How many times has a girl swore up and down a guy was like a brother to her, but next thing you know he got her face down, ass up till the crack of dawn?"

"Christina Rene!" Winter's eyes widened in shock.

"All I'm saying is, Darren isn't wrong if he is feeling this way. I mean, if I was a dude, and I knew you were kicking it with a guy who had a hundred fifty mill in the bank...well, we're gonna have some problems."

Winter finished sprinkling brown sugar on a pecan pie before turning to her friend. "First, like I said, I'm not that kind of chick. I don't care about the money. Secondly, I appreciate Jae for stepping up when he can with Malik not being here. And lastly, if I really wanted him, I could have shot my shot years ago."

Christina gasped, her eyes widening.

Winter immediately regretted her words. Her best friend knew her well enough to know when she was holding something back. Winter sat quietly, staring away blankly. After a spell, she finally gave in. "Why are you looking at me like that?"

"Oh, so you just gonna sit there with a fresh cup of tea and not spill it?"

"There is no tea, I just—"

"Hoe, if you don't spill the goddamn tea! Don't act brand new to this."

Winter sighed. She garnished the last of the pies before conceding. "Me and Jae became friends sophomore year. We had a couple of classes together because I majored in sports medicine. I'd been working in the training facility and Jaden got hurt and started rehabbing a quad injury. He was dating Genesis Monroe, but they were on a break."

"Shut up! Genesis Monroe? The news anchor?"

"The one and only."

"Miss Live at Five?"

"Yes."

"She went to school with us too?"

"She did."

"That's a bad bitch."

"No lies told. I honestly thought they were going to get married, but they never worked out. At the same time, I had just broke up with Brandon Hightower."

"Wait a minute, are you talking about fine ass Brandon Hightower? Former running back for the Oakland Raiders?"

"Yeah, that asshole."

"Hold up, why on earth would you ever break up with that fine specimen of a man?"

"Because he wanted to share his specimen with anyone that batted an eyelash his way. He tried that shit one too many times."

"Do you know who he was cheating with?"

"I found some messages in his phone, but I didn't know who, and didn't care. I forgave him the first time. I told him if I even hear rumors of it a second time, it's over. He looked stupid when I confronted him the second time, so I dumped him."

"Wyn how do yo—"

"The point is, Jae was available and so was I. We were spending a lot of time together while he was rehabbing. He was kinda being a bitch about it, so I was pushing him, you know. Well, long story short, Jaden got better. He went back to the team and took us to the final four. The night before the game he was pumped, and he came by to ask me to meet him over at Cougars. You remember that sports bar?"

Christina was quiet, her silence confirming she didn't know.

Winter took off her apron and remarked, "My God, you really did miss all the best parts of college."

"Just tell the damn story."

"Well, Cougars was a little hangout spot the squad used to go to after a big game. Jae wanted me to be there, and I thought he was asking me out. So I got dressed up, made sure I looked cute and what not, but when I got there, he was already sulking from that bad game and he was talking to Genesis and they seemed to be hitting it off again. Then his brother Malik started talking to me, and the rest is history."

Winter put the pies in the fridge so she could clean up, but her friend wasn't satisfied.

"Wait, what do you mean, the rest is history?"

"I mean, I clearly got my signals crossed, 'cause he got back with Genesis and I got with his brother Malik, so, yeah, history." Winter shrugged, heading to the sink to wash her hands.

Christina strutted over and leaned on the counter. She waved her neon pink nails in Winter's face. "So, you never looked back on that?"

"There was nothing to look back on. The point is, he's a good guy and you're a good girl. But if he feels gold digger vibes, he's not going to stick around. I just want to make sure you're both happy."

"Let me tell you something: for a hundred and fifty million dollars, I'm gonna make sure that we both happy, you feel me?"

The pair chuckled before Winter suddenly stopped. She thought she heard a noise coming from the dining area. Her eyes widened as she looked at Christina. "Did you lock the door?"

"I... damn it, can't remember." Winter knew that meant she didn't.

She was about to walk to the front to see what was going on when she heard a loud bang. The sound of a large object hitting the ground scared the both of them in the dimly lit room. "Damn it, girl, why in the hell do you need to bake in these Sade lights!" Christina hissed.

Winter ignored her friend and yelled, "Hello? Is anyone out there?"

There was no response.

Bam! Bam!

The second burst of loud sounds made them panic. Christina, in a low, serious tone, whispered over to Winter. "Is Miracle supposed to come by?"

"No, she had a thing at school."

Bam!

This one sounded like a series of clashes.

She glanced over at Christina. "Call the police, now!"

Winter loved Houston, but she knew that, with all its majesty, there were still certain parts of town where you absolutely needed to lock your door at night, and her bakery was in one of those parts. There had been a few break-ins on the block over the last weeks.

The hairs on the back of her neck stood up as she imagined every worst case scenario. But they didn't matter—none of them were going to keep her from raising her daughter.

I need a weapon.

She looked around frantically for a knife but couldn't find one at hand. But the large, black iron casket skillet caught her eye. As she started towards the corridor with the pan, she remembered all the knives were in the dishwasher, which was near to where Christina was crouching. She pointed to the dishwasher and whispered, "Grab a knife."

Christina pulled out the largest knife she could find and stood back as Winter walked closer towards the door. A large shadow appeared under the door, heading their way.

5

FOUL TROUBLE

"Get out, motherfucker! The police are on their way! Help!" Winter screamed as she pulled open the door and swung the pot at the looming figure. The man dodged her attack, forcing her to tumble forwards. Regaining her balance, she turned around to swing again. The man grabbed her as she finally took a good look at the intruder.

"Wyn! It's me. Chill!" Jaden said as he held her hand, stopping her.

Her adrenaline was receding, but she was still furious. "Goddamn it, Jae! You scared the hell out of me! What was that damn noise, and why didn't you answer me when I yelled out?"

"Well, you had a bunch of boxes right against the corner and—"

"And your 6'7 ass bumped into it because you're just as clumsy as your niece," she scoffed.

Jaden shrugged his shoulders. "Why did you have the boxes of pans in the dining area in the first place? You know what, it's not my business."

Winter bustled past him to head for the door. Without turning around, Jaden called out, "Already locked it for you."

She turned around and gently hit him in the arm with the pan. Jaden winced. "Ow! What did you do that for?"

"I'm still mad at you. What are you doing here, anyway?"

"Wyn, you okay?" Christina yelled from the kitchen.

Winter turned around and walked into the kitchen, followed by Jaden. They saw Christina hiding near the stove with a knife in one hand and a cup of coffee in the other. Winter shook her head. "I have so many questions."

"Is it safe to come out?"

"It's fine. It's Jaden."

Christina popped up from her hiding area, put her makeshift weapons down and adjusted her clothes. "Jaden!" she exclaimed as she walked over, still fixing herself up. "What a pleasant surprise—"

"Hell no," Winter interjected as she walked over to join the pair at the island. "Like I said, I got questions. One, what happened to having my back? And two, why were you holding a knife and a cup of coffee?"

"I was going to throw it at him to blind him, then stab him."

"The coffee is cold, Chrissy."

"I didn't know that at the time."

Winter scoffed at her friend and rolled her eyes. "And what about having my back?"

"Girl, nobody told you to investigate the noise in the first place! Shoot, acting like a white girl in a horror movie." Christina chastised.

Jaden was laughing throughout all of it. He looked over at Christina. "That cup of coffee reminds me of that Coming to America scene."

Christina smiled and sidled closer to him. "Oh yeah? Well, maybe you can be my prince Akeem—"

"Okay, that's enough of that." Winter interjected. She looked at Jaden. "Back to you, Jae. What are you doing here?"

"Well, I was dropping off that paperwork from Mr. Armand. You just need to look it over, sign, and it's as good as done."

Winter walked over and snatched the paperwork. "I'll have Christina look over it in the morning. Now what was all that damn noise you were making?"

"I walked in, and when the door closed behind me, I think it shook your stack of boxes. They fell over. I was trying to pick them up, but I didn't realize the first one was already open and the pans fell out."

Christina threw her hands in the air. "I be telling her that, Jae. She trying to get us both killed. I'm saying, how hard is it to lock the door after your last customer?"

"Christina," Winter warned.

Jaden shook his head. "No, she's right. You carry cash, Wyn." She cut her eyes at him in protest.

"Alright, I'll let it go. You're just lucky it was me and not somebody ready to risk it all, because that little pot you were swinging wasn't going to hurt nothing but your feelings." Winter punched him in the arm, and again he groaned. "Look, Wyn, them little hands ain't hurting nobody either."

Winter was about to punch him again when Christina walked over to join the three of them. "Hey, Jaden."

Jae smiled. "Hey Christina, what's going on?"

"Listen, I just wanted to tell you that Darren calling you Choke was uncalled for."

"Uh… thanks, Christina."

"That was a tough game. You hadn't missed consecutive shots all year. It could've happened to anyone. It's just so stupid how these announcers are."

Jaden was somewhat surprised by Christina's insight. He settled in and continued the conversation. "Oh yeah? I didn't know you were into sports like that."

"Well, if you talked to me a bit more, you'd get to see I'm full of surprises." Christina said as she reached into a bowl of frosting and seductively licked a dollop from her finger.

"Definitely full of something," Winter mumbled under her breath.

Jaden tuned to her. "What did you say?"

"Nothing, just talking to myself."

"Cool. Anyway, I came to get Miri."

"From here? She said she was staying after school."

Jaden pulled out his phone. "That's weird. She told me she was working with you, which is why she couldn't practice."

"She said *what?*" Winter said as she snatched the phone to examine the messages between them.

The confusion on her face slowly morphed into anger. Jaden stood in silence as Christina said what they were all thinking. "She's probably with that boy from last night."

"Christina didn't mean that." Jaden said quickly, trying to disarm an already anxious Winter.

It was too late.

"I'm gonna call her." Winter said as she picked up the phone and dialed. The phone went to voicemail. She tried again, only to get the same non-response.

"I'll try." Jaden said in his diplomatic state. The phone went to voicemail for a third time, catching Jaden off guard.

"She didn't answer for you either?" Winter asked.

"No."

"Now I'm worried. If she's gonna answer anybody's call, it's gonna be Uncle Jae." Winter walked over and grabbed her purse. "Christina I need to go find my baby, can you lock up?"

Winter was headed full speed to the door when Jaden stepped in front of her. "Now wait a minute, Wyn, you need to take a breath. I'm sure there's a perfectly logical explanation—"

"Yeah, and when I find her, I'm gonna beat it out of her. Now, are you coming to make sure the charge is just attempted murder, or are you gonna meet me with the bronco after I do it?"

Jaden's phone dinged, and after taking a quick look at it, raised it to show Winter the screen. "Wait a second. It's Miri, she just started a live stream."

Winter rushed to take a closer look. The background was instantly familiar. "She's... at home?" Her confusion was trumped by the daughter's demeanor.

She looked relaxed—too relaxed. Her eyes were bloodshot red, and she was giggling nonstop.

Winter snatched the phone and examined it for herself. "Is she... high?"

"Wyn—"

Winter began to type furiously on the keyboard. "This heffa done lost her damn mind."

Jaden snatched the phone back before she could hit send. She jumped to steal it back, but his tall frame kept it out of reach as he read her message.

"Tell me you weren't gonna threaten to kill your daughter on social media."

"Jaden, give me the phone."

"Now, hold on, Wyn, you ain't my momma. Right now you need to take a breath and remember, your daughter is in the national spotlight. Whatever you think you want to say to her, you need to wait till you see her."

"You know I—"

"This isn't up for discussion," he said firmly. "She's trying to play basketball for one of the top colleges in the country. She doesn't know how close she's being watched, but I do. And we don't want to make things worse than they already are."

Winter took a breath and calmed herself. Jaden erased the message and typed one of his own. *Miri, I'm with your mom, get off the live and call me. ASAP.*

He hit send, hoping she would get the message, but there was a flood of her thirty thousand followers watching as she talked.

"What's good, Carter Crew? It's ya girl, Miri. I just wanted to say thank you for staying down with me. Today I got some news that kind of sucks, but my uncle taught me that sometimes politics come into this sport, and well... y'all know what it is. I ain't gonna say no names, but just know, when I see you on the court, it's gonna be a problem."

Jaden closed his eyes and shook his head.

"Don't do it, kid," he groaned.

"@baller83 asked how I feel about my shot at MVP with the news coming out today? You know that's a really good question. To me, MVP voting is more about favorites than about numbers, because if it were just about numbers, there would be no question it would be me."

The conversation was interrupted when Miri seemed to get animated from one of the comments. Jaden scrolled through them, finding one left by Shasha Wilcox. The All-American senior was the top-ranked in the nation until Miri's historic run, becoming a leading story of the high school basketball world. She said the one thing he knew would trigger his niece.

@swilcox3: Thirsty bitches riding coattails out here.

"Don't do it, Miri, don't take the bait." Jaden pleaded.

He and Winter continued watching the live in silence. Miri's eyes widened at the comment. *"Thirsty? Get on live and I'll show you thirsty."*

Jaden tried to type another message, but it was too late.

Shasha Wilcox had joined the live.

"What's up, Baby Choke? I mean Smoke. I see you trying to sneak diss. I just got on to see if you was gonna keep that same energy now that a real one is on the live with you."

Miracle scoffed. *"You can't be serious right now. When are you ever real? You spend half your time online hating me and the other half posting motivational quotes you don't follow."*

"Whatever you think I said about you, I'll say to your face."

"Well, I'm right here. Say what you said and stand on business," Miri fired back.

"Sure. Miracle Carter's overrated. #mediocore. The only reason you scoring all those points is because you ain't playing nobody."

"Oh, and I guess because you supposed to be the defensive player of the year, you must be somebody."

Shasha smirked. *"That's right, but unlike you, it ain't just about me. That's why we got the number one defensive team in the state. That's leadership. You could learn a thing or two with yo ball hoggin' ass."*

"Bitch, you guard every hole except the one between your legs. Don't come for me or I'll bury you."

There was nothing Winter or Jaden could do; the train had left the station. Instead, they were forced to sit and watch as Miri went into a full-blown rant as the chat filled with comments, each one more antagonizing than the last. It wasn't long before Jaden got a ping on his phone.

"Shit," he sighed.

"What is it?" Winter asked hesitantly, realizing the gravity of the situation.

"That was a friend over at ESPN. This has already gone viral."

The two girls on the screen continued to insult each other, each barb more disrespectful than the next, until finally Miri stopped the live.

It was nothing short of a disaster. Jaden looked to Winter and realized his niece's problems were about to get a whole lot worse.

6

DOUBLE TEAM

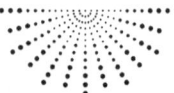

"Of all the reckless, irresponsible things you've done, this takes the cake, Miracle Ja'nae Carter. What were you thinking?" Winter yelled at her daughter.

Winter was furious. She'd wanted to know more about the marijuana, something that she clearly didn't know her daughter was into, but Jae had spent twenty minutes talking her off the ledge for the moment. The internet was already ablaze about the exchange. "Baby Choke" was already a viral meme.

She eyed her daughter, waiting for a reply. "Girl, you hear me talking to you!"

"Momma, I—"

"I don't want to hear it, Miri."

"But you just said—"

"Be quiet! I'm talking, you're listening! Hell, you were online, high as a kite, sounding like a '90s rapper trying to get a record deal, and throwing the opportunity you worked so hard for down the drain."

"Okay, I'll admit that it wasn't smart, but—"

Winter snorted. "You damn right it wasn't smart!"

"But Momma, she said—"

"I don't care what she said or didn't say. You got on that phone and you made a fool of yourself, plain and simple."

"I know, Momma, but—"

"Little girl, didn't I just say shut your mouth? Cause I ain't Shasha or Shashity or whatever that lil' girl's name is. I will break my foot off in your—"

"Okay, guys, let's all take a breath." Jae said, coming in between the two of them. He looked at the pair. "Winter, that vein is about to pop out of your head, so let's get you something to bake to calm you down. Miri, get the dough and while you do, please politely explain to your momma just what the hell you were thinking."

Winter didn't want to calm down, but Jaden was right: kneading dough was exactly what she needed to do right now.

As Miri gingerly pulled out the ingredients, Winter walked over and brushed her aside. She quickly threw the ingredients together and began to pound the dough viciously on the island. Miri turned to her uncle to plead her case, who just gestured towards Winter.

Miri took a deep breath. "B Hype Magazine came out today."

"And?"

"They had Shasha ranked number 1, and I was ranked number 2."

Winter folded her arms and looked at Jae, then back at Miracle. "So you out here cursing like somebody else raised you 'cause you came in second place?"

"Ugh! See, Uncle Jae, this is what I'm talking about! She's impossible."

Winter turned to Jae for direction. "Care to translate?"

He folded his arms, still digesting what Miri said. "The last five years, the number 1 ranked player in B Hype magazine went on to become MVP."

"So?"

Miri shrieked. "So? Momma, I worked my tail off this year. At this very moment, only four people have scored more points than me in a season in Texas history. One of them is in this room. They all won MVPs. My stats are better across the board, rebounds assists, steals, blocks, everything! And winning MVP this season almost guarantees I get into UConn."

"And you just threw all that hard work out the window with that stupid stunt you pulled, all 'cause you wanted to be Bob Marley with a jump shot. It was so reckless!"

"Momma, they already decided the rankings over the summer. And I know it's because she goes to a powerhouse school, and I go to the school closest to my house. Ugh! Uncle Jae, she doesn't get it."

"Oh, believe me, I get it very well. You're the one that don't get it. Everyone in the college and high school basketball world is watching your every move. Hell, the only reason I haven't gone upside your head is because the way I feel, your little yella ass would be bruised from head to toe, and I'm not going to jail."

Miracle huffed, fighting back tears.

Winter could tell Miri was hurting, but couldn't find words to console her.

"Excuse me," Miri said as she ran outside.

Winter stopped kneading the dough and hung her head worn down by the constant bickering between her and Miri lately.

"Jae, I don't know what to do."

"I'll handle it," Jaden promised.

He walked outside and found Miri was sitting one of the tire swings in the front yard. He approached her cautiously.

She scowled at first, but then glanced away.

He took a seat on the second swing. "It's been a while since you've been small enough to swing on this one."

"She doesn't get anything! I can't wait to get out of here."

"You know she's not wrong, Miri," he reasoned.

Miri scoffed at him. "'Course you're on her side. You've had a secret handshake with her since before I was born."

"What, the Double up? We just fell into that in college."

"I don't care about your stupid handshake. I'm just saying you two go back and forth more than me and her, and you're always on her side. I get that you're best friends, but sometimes she is just wrong."

"You're right about her being wrong. And if she was wrong, you know I'd be the first one to say something. But do you really think this is one of these times?" Miri sat silent as he leaned over and continued.

" I get it, but that's not why you're mad though, is it?"

He watched Miri wipe the tears from her eyes and decided to proceed with caution. "It sucks to have someone question your ability, doesn't it?"

Miracle folded her arms and huffed. "It's like, dang, I'm about to break a twenty-year-old record and all they want to do is talk about Shasha Wilcox. Then, the moment I defend myself, everyone is acting like I did something wrong."

Jae nodded and sat next to her. "You did, Miri. You decided not to handle it on the court."

"But Uncle Jae, I—"

"What's rule number one?"

Miracle rolled her eyes and let out a giant sigh that pushed her braided hair to the side of her face. "When it comes to ball, settle it on the court. But Uncle Jae you gotta understand—"

"You broke rule number one, Miri. That's where she got you."

"But Uncle Jae—"

"No buts. You were wrong. You know, the year I broke the record—"

"Oh, my god, Uncle Jae. I don't want to hear how you played one on one with Dr. Martin Luther King."

"Dr. King? Girl, how old do you think I—you know what? I see what you're doing and it's not going to work. You're gonna hear this story or deal with your mom."

Miri glanced toward the front window with a grimace. Her mother was standing inside watching them, arms folded, with a belt wrapped around one hand. She looked back at her uncle. "Okay, give me the story."

"As I was saying, freshman year of college, I left Dallas to come back to Houston and play with my brother, your dad. I was so preoccupied about getting to know my big brother I didn't realize that I'd have to compete for my spot, which belonged to Darren at the time."

"No offense, Uncle Jae, but is this going somewhere?"

"Chill out, I'm getting there. It frustrated me I wasn't getting the headlines, and no matter what I did, Darren was the guy everyone wanted to talk about."

"Uncle Jae, I'm just sayin', you gonna make your point by graduation or—"

"Cupcake, just listen," he sighed. "One game, he sat out for a small injury or something, and I finally got my shot. But he came to practice talking crap, and it really pissed me off, and when it was game time, I choked. I rushed all my shots and didn't play team ball. Totally threw me off my game, and he wasn't even on the court. And the thing was, I was better than him and we both knew it."

Miracle peered at him, understanding dawning on her face.

"I let him get in my head. I let the pressure get to my head, and by the time I snapped out of it, we were thirty points down. I thought that would be the worst thing that happened to me. But when I got off, the coach benched me for the rest of the season. And it wasn't because of my performance; it's because I wasn't playing team ball. The point I'm making is, you are about to make history, but so is Shasha Wilcox. She's trying to lead her team to an undefeated season, and you're the only thing that's gonna stand in her way. It's her job to get in your head right now."

Miri nodded.

"Listen, Miri, you're gonna have to embrace the fact that some people are going to treat having an undefeated season just as special as you breaking a scoring record, because they're both big for the sport. When you get on these social media live chats, when you go after anybody, you always have to remember you're not just speaking for you, you're speaking for your team. Hell, you're speaking for every little girl that wants to be just like Miracle Carter. You're a leader now."

Miracle nodded accepting the weight of his words as Jae looked off into the distance. After a spell, she said, "I didn't know it would go viral. Nobody cared who I was at the start of the season."

"Well, you're a star now, Cupcake. This is the last time the game will be pure for you. After you leave high school, it's all business. You gotta think more and react less."

"So you think I should apologize?"

"Oh, never that," Jae laughed. "Ball is still ball. You said what you said, now you have no choice but to prove it. But you know that already. I think a part of you wants to prove it to yourself too. I say, go show the world who Miri Carter is, and if you play the way I know you can, well, hell, that coach at UConn is gonna be sold."

Miri jumped up from her swing and hugged him. He'd said exactly what she needed to hear.

He hugged her back tightly. "Now you *do* need to apologize to your momma."

Miri groaned playfully. "I know."

"And it's a good chance I can't save you from that ass whoopin'."

"I know."

The two chuckled as they headed back inside the house.

Jae snuck a quick smirk at Winter to let her know that everything was fine. He stood by silently as Miri walked over to her mom and gave her a hug.

"I'm sorry. I made a mistake. You don't have to worry about me doing that again."

Winter kissed her daughter on the cheek and tightened her hold on her daughter. "Baby, do you know why I named you Miracle?" She felt Miri's head shake against her own. "Your daddy loved me very much, but there was nothing in the world he wanted more than a child. So, we started trying to have you, but as he got sicker, we found out that it would be harder—not impossible, but it was looking unlikely. But he never stopped wishing for a baby; we even started looking for surrogates as a backup plan. He got it in his mind we were going to have a kid one way or another. Even though we were young, we had a lot of options. And then, right when the doctors told us to stop trying, there you were.

"You were a miracle baby, and you've lived up to your name ever since. So I'm not worried about you. I'm just sad that I won't always be there to see the impact you're gonna make on the world with that bright light of yours people can't help but be drawn to."

Winter kissed her on the forehead, pulling back to look Miri in the eyes.

"I'm sorry, Mom."

"I know, baby. But not nearly as sorry as you're gonna be once you find out the punishment for smoking weed."

7

FULL-COURT PRESSURE

*M*iri stared at her phone in disbelief. Before the day's match, she'd succumbed to temptation and pulled up the video from earlier. The comment section was a war zone.

@BballFan123: Miracle Carter? More like Mediocre Carter. All that talk, but she can't even hold it together. MVP? Yeah, right.

@SportsJunkie: #ShashaAllDay. Miracle's a joke.

She clicked out of the app, her stomach turning. The viral clip of her rant was all anyone was talking about. It didn't matter how many points she'd scored, how many records she'd shattered this season. One mistake, one moment of anger, and it felt like the entire world had turned against her.

"Damn it," she muttered under her breath, pressing her palms against her eyes. She hadn't slept in two days, and every time she closed her eyes, she saw it all over again—her face, flushed with rage, spewing curse words at Shasha Wilcox on that stupid live chat.

A soft knock on her door snapped her out of the spiral. "Miri, you okay?" Her mom's voice was quiet, careful.

She didn't look up. "I'm fine."

Her mother stepped inside, sitting on the edge of the bed. She didn't say anything at first, just watched Miri, the silence pressing against them. "You know, I saw the video," Winter broached, her voice low, but not angry. "I've seen how people are talking about you."

Miri clenched her jaw. "Yeah, well, it's my own fault."

Winter let out a long breath. "Baby, we all mess up. But I need you to stop letting this get in your head."

Miri finally met her mom's eyes. "Everyone's saying I'm done. That I threw it all away."

"They don't decide that," Winter said firmly. "You do. You've got the end of the season and the playoffs coming up. That's where you prove who you are."

Miri swallowed hard, the weight of her mom's words heavy on her shoulders. "What if I choke? What if—"

"You won't choke. You never do."

Winter stood up, walking over to Miri's desk to pick up the framed photo of Miri as a little girl, holding her first basketball trophy. "You see this girl right here? You think she ever, for even one second, doubted herself?"

Miri smiled faintly. "She didn't know any better."

"She didn't care about what anyone thought," Winter said, setting the photo down. "She just played. You need to find that part of yourself again. Let the noise fade away."

Miri nodded, even though the pit in her stomach didn't ease.

After her mom left, Miri slipped on her sneakers and grabbed her basketball. She didn't know what else to do, so she headed to the backyard, where the hoop her dad had put up years ago still stood tall.

She started shooting. Shot after shot, some perfect, some bouncing off the rim. But she kept going, her muscles burning, her breath heavy. Sweat dripped down her face, and with every shot, she tried to push away the doubts.

Focus.

She was better than this. She was more than this moment, more than the comments, the video, more than the pressure suffocating her.

The ball hit the rim and rolled away. Miri bent down, her hands on her knees, panting.

A memory hit her— a recording of her dad's voice in her ear after her first championship game in middle school. "The game's always gonna throw something at you. You just gotta keep your head in it."

She picked up the ball again, steadying her breath.

"Keep your head in it," she whispered to herself, launching another shot. This time, the ball sank through the net cleanly.

For the first time in days, she smiled. She walked into the kitchen with confidence. It was almost game time. The pair got ready to head to the gym to face the Houston Elite Ballers.

The gym was electric with noise, every seat filled with fans, but it wasn't the energy of the usual home crowd.

Miracle could feel the weight of every eye on her, but none of them were rooting for her. The noise was suffocating; chants, boos, and insults aimed right at her. She knew why. She was persona non grata these days. The viral meltdown, the insults thrown online; everyone had something to say about Miracle Carter now. And none of it was good.

"Overrated!"

"Shasha's gonna end you!"

Various chants were thrown from the crowd. She wasn't even playing Shasha's team, and yet the venom from the online chat followed her across the gym.

Miri's heart pounded in her chest. Her hands were clammy, her body heavy under the weight of expectation. She needed to score thirty points tonight. If she didn't, her shot at breaking the state scoring record would be gone, and so would any chance of MVP. She could feel it slipping through her fingers with every second that ticked by.

The game started off brutal. The Houston Elite Ballers were known for their defense, and they weren't holding back. Her first possession? Their defender, Ashley Wilks, shoved her off balance before she even touched the ball.

It got to a point that every time Miracle touched the ball, the opposition doubled her, closing off her drives and blocking her shots. The ball felt foreign in her hands, like it didn't belong to her anymore.

Her first three shots? Clangs off the rim. By the fourth miss, the noise from the crowd got louder, the taunts stinging more than the ache in her knee.

"Come on, Carter, what happened to that jump shot?" Ashley called out, loud enough for everyone to hear. Her smirk was wide, her arrogance on full display.

Miri clenched her fists, trying to push down the rising panic. She was struggling to breathe, her chest tight. Sweat dripped down her face, but not from exertion—something deeper was clawing at her. Her vision blurred, her pulse pounding in her ears.

By the second quarter, she had only six points, and what felt like six more miles to go.

She winced as she caught an elbow in the ribs while fighting through a screen. The ref didn't call it.

She drove the lane again, determined to push through, but the defense collapsed on her. A rough shove sent her sprawling to the floor, the ball slipping from her grasp.

The gym erupted in laughter, and Ashley's team didn't even try to hide their grins.

"Get up, Miracle!" a voice from the crowd taunted. "Or should we call you Mediocre?"

Miri gasped for breath, but it wasn't just from the shock of the fall. Her chest burned, feeling tight, like it was caving in. She couldn't get air in her lungs fast enough, the familiar signs of a flare-up of her illness hitting her hard.

She stumbled to the bench, waving off the trainer as they rushed towards her. "I'm fine," she lied, even as her vision swam.

Coach Jackson didn't believe her. She walked over and examined Miri. "Get her to the locker room," she barked at the trainer. "Now!"

Miri tried to protest, but the words wouldn't come out. She felt herself being pulled toward the exit, the noise of the crowd a muffled roar in her ears.

The locker room felt like it was spinning. Miri collapsed onto a nearby bench, clutching her chest as she struggled to breathe. Her throat was tight, her body betraying her at the worst possible time. Tears brimmed in her eyes, but she refused to let them fall. Her hands trembled as the panic and pain mixed together, leaving her dizzy and weak.

The door burst open, and Winter was the first to rush in, followed closely by Jae. Her mother's face was etched with panic, her voice shaking. "Baby, what's happening?"

"I'm alright—"

"Girl, don't lie to me, you're having an attack." Miri's eyes followed her mother as she paced the room. "Damn it, this was a mistake. I knew you shouldn't have been playing! Your body can't handle this—"

"I'm fine!" Miri snapped, her voice cracking under the strain. "Stop saying I can't handle it!"

Winter recoiled, hurt flashing across her face. "Baby, I'm just trying to help—"

"You're not helping!" Miri's voice broke as she lashed out, her hands gripping the edge of the bench, tears streaming down her face. The pain was deeper than her physical condition. This pressure was in her own mind. "All season, all I hear is how I have to be perfect. I fight every game, every practice, every minute, and it's still not enough! The crowd hates me, even though they don't know me. Shasha's out there watching this, undefeated, and I can't even make a damn shot! My body's falling apart, and you want me to just give up?"

Winter pulled back, still wounded by her daughter's words, but Miri didn't stop.

"I don't need you telling me I can't handle it!" Miri shouted, the tears streaming freely now. "You think I don't know that? You think I don't know what people are saying about me? That I'm some kind of joke? That Shasha Wilcox and everybody else is out there waiting for me to fail?" She slammed her fist against the bench, sobs wracking her chest. "I can't win. I can't beat her. I can't even beat this team. I'll never be enough."

Jae stepped forward, arms crossed, his expression unreadable. "You're right."

Miri's head snapped up, eyes wide. "What?"

"You're right," Jae said again, shrugging as he leaned against the wall, arms crossed. "You ain't got it in you, Miri. Not today. Not with the way you're playing."

Miri blinked through the tears, fury rising. "What the hell are you saying?"

"You heard me. You got Ashley Wilks—who barely made the top ten in B Hype this year—out there running circles around you, and you're in here crying about how hard it is." He let out a sarcastic chuckle. "You're supposed to be breaking records? Looks like Shasha's about to break *you* instead, and she ain't even on the court."

Miri's heart thudded painfully in her chest. "That's not fair—"

"Fair?" Jae stepped closer, his voice low and sharp. "You think this game is fair? You think breaking records is easy? You want to be great? Then prove it. Because right now, you're proving Ashley, Shasha, your mom—hell, *everyone*—right. They said you were over-rated. They said you'd crack under the pressure. And guess what? You are."

The words hit like a punch to the gut.

Her fists clenched, and through the haze of pain and panic, something else started to rise.

Anger. Determination.

"You think I can't do it?" Miri whispered, her voice hoarse.

Jae's smirk widened. "I know you can't. Not tonight. Ashley's got your number, and you're too busy choking to even realize it. You definitely should be scared of what Shasha's gonna do to you, but hell, you're just a sophomore. It's kind of what's expected of you."

Miri shot up from the bench, fire blazing in her eyes. "You think I'm scared of her? You think I'm gonna let her take what's mine?"

Jae leaned in, his tone challenging. "You gonna show me otherwise? Or you gonna sit in here crying about how hard it is?"

Miri's breath was still ragged, her chest aching, but the fire inside her burned hotter than the pain. She wiped the tears from her face, standing taller. Her heart pounded. Her vision cleared. She still couldn't breathe fully, but his words had struck something deep inside her. She stared at him, her eyes narrowing. She turned toward the door.

Jae grinned, but didn't let up. "Oh, you're going back out there? I don't know, Miri. That crowd doesn't think you can pull it off."

"I don't care what they think," Miri said, her voice hardening.

Jae stepped in front of her and the pair locked eyes. In a steel-like tone, he said, "Good. Now go out there and shut them the hell up. The job is not done. Get to work." Without a word she nodded at her uncle. She was still having symptoms, but it didn't matter. She had a job to do and it wasn't done yet.

The gym exploded in noise when Miracle stepped back onto the court. The crowd still booed, still chanted *Mediocre*, but Miri blocked them out. She didn't feel the pain in her chest. She didn't feel anything besides the ball in her hands.

Ashley smirked as she approached. "Come back for more, Baby Choke?"

Miri didn't respond. The moment the ball was inbounded, she moved with laser focus. Ashley was on her hip, guarding her, but it didn't matter. With a quick dribble and a hard pivot, she lost Ashley and let the first three-pointer fly.

Swish.

The crowd fell silent for a heartbeat.

Ashley's grin faltered.

Next possession, she stole the inbound pass and set back up the offense. She drove hard, drawing two defenders. She passed the ball out to her teammate, got it right back, and nailed another three from the top of the key.

Swish.

The crowd had shifted. No more boos, no more taunts, just stunned murmurs.

The next time down the court, Miri didn't even wait for the defense to set. She pulled up from deep, way beyond the arc, and let it fly.

Swish.

The crowd was stunned now, the once-hostile atmosphere turning to awe.

Miracle Carter had found her rhythm.

Miri caught fire, hitting shot after shot, moving faster and playing harder than she ever had before. The Ballers' defense, once so stifling, couldn't keep up. With every shot, her point total climbed. 18 points. 21. 24. By the end of the third quarter, she had already closed the gap.

Miri smirked, she glanced at her uncle in the stands who gave an approving head nod.

She was back.

By the end of the quarter, she had racked up 24 points. Her team fed her the ball every chance, and she delivered.

The fourth quarter started. She needed just six more points to hit thirty, but the Ballers defenders weren't backing down. They doubled her every time she touched the ball, trying to smother her.

It didn't work.

With two minutes left, Miri stood at the top of the arc, the crowd on their feet, watching her every move. Ashely glared at her, but Miri didn't even blink. She took one dribble, stepped back, and let the three fly.

Swish.

The Lady Nets were in full control of the game, up by eight points, but Miri kept her foot on the gas. She needed thirty points tonight to make her chances of breaking the record easier. This was the time to get it.

With one minute left, Miri stood at the top of the arc, eyes locked on the basket. The crowd held its breath. Her defender pressed up tight, but Miri sidestepped, creating just enough space, and fired.

Swish.

Thirty points.

The crowd erupted. Miri had done it.

As the buzzer sounded, the gym exploded into cheers, the boos from earlier nothing but an echo.

Miri stood at center court, her chest still aching, but it didn't matter. She'd silenced them all.

She looked up into the stands, catching Jae's eye. He gave her a small nod, that knowing smirk still on his face.

Miri smirked back. She'd proved it. To herself. To the crowd. And to the world.

8
THE SIXTH MAN

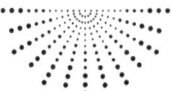

inter leaned against the wall of the gym, the smell of sweat and victory still fresh in the air. She exhaled slowly, the tension from the game starting to ease, though her worry for Miri lingered just beneath the surface. Her daughter had just pulled off one of the most remarkable comebacks she'd ever seen, but Winter couldn't forget the moment in the locker room when Miri had struggled to breathe, her chest tight with more than just pressure from the game.

Jae was standing nearby, his arms crossed, looking at Miri with that proud, half-smirk he always had. He'd done his usual magic—trash-talking Miri right back into focus—and Winter couldn't be more grateful. Even though they bickered, Miri and Jae had something special between them. Something that made Winter smile, even when she wanted to step in and protect her daughter from the world.

"You think you did something, huh, Unc?" Miri teased, leaning on her knees, still catching her breath from the game but full of that post-victory glow.

Jae shrugged, trying to act indifferent. "I mean, you got thirty points. I guess I had a little something to do with it."

Miri rolled her eyes. "A *little* something? Please, I would've hit those shots with or without your speech."

Winter chuckled softly, watching the two of them banter. There was something about these moments—when Miri could let go of the pressure, when she was just a kid again, teasing her uncle like everything else in the world didn't matter—that made Winter feel a warmth in her chest. These were the moments she lived for.

"Uh-huh, keep telling yourself that," Jae said, his smirk growing. "But we all know the truth. You needed that push."

"Psh, maybe," Miri replied, folding her arms and smirking right back. "But don't let it go to your head."

Winter smiled as the two of them exchanged playful jabs, their bond so much like siblings instead of uncle and niece. For a brief moment, everything felt right.

Then she heard footsteps behind her, and a familiar voice broke the moment.

"I've been trying to call you," Darren said.

Winter turned around, and there he was—tall, handsome, and with that look on his face that made her stomach flip, but something about the way his jaw was set told her this wasn't going to be easy.

"Hey, Darren." She stepped forward, softening her tone. "Sorry, I've been a little... distracted." She glanced toward Miri, hoping he'd understand. "Miri had an episode during the game. Her autoimmune condition flared up. I couldn't leave her."

Darren's eyes flickered toward Miri, who was still grinning at Jae, the moment of struggle during the game seemingly long forgotten. "I get it," he said, but there was something off in his voice, something Winter recognized. He was trying to be understanding, but it wasn't easy for him. His eyes lingered on Jae for a moment too long, and Winter knew exactly where this was headed.

"She okay now?" Darren asked, his tone measured but clipped.

"Yeah, she's fine," Winter said, trying to ease the tension before it could build. "She just needed a minute. Jae was there, and... well, you know how he is." She forced a smile, hoping Darren wouldn't push it. But she could already see the wheels turning in his head.

"Right," Darren said, his eyes narrowing slightly. "Jae was here."

There it was. The old rivalry, the unspoken tension between them. They'd both been college basketball stars, and even though that was years ago, it seemed like they could never quite leave it behind. Winter hated that.

"Look, Darren, it's not what you think," Winter said quickly, stepping closer to him, lowering her voice. "Jae's family. He's just here for Miri, you know that."

"I know," Darren said, though his eyes didn't leave Jae. "Just seems like he's here a lot."

Winter sighed. "He's her uncle. They're close. That's all."

Jae, for his part, pretended not to notice the tension, though Winter could see the stiffness in his posture. He wasn't going to let it go either. That was just who he was.

"Darren," Jae said, breaking the silence with a slow, deliberate smile. "You gonna stand there and stare, or you gonna congratulate Miri on her win?"

Winter shot him a look. "Jae..."

Darren's jaw tightened, but he forced a smile. "Congrats, Miri," he said, his voice a little too flat.

Miri glanced between the two men, sensing the tension immediately. "Uh, thanks," she said awkwardly, looking back at Jae for a cue on how to handle the interaction.

Winter stepped in, determined to diffuse the situation before it could escalate. "Listen, Darren," she said gently, placing a hand on his arm. "I know we had plans tonight, but after what happened during the game... I just really want to stay with Miri tonight. She's had a rough day, and I don't want to leave her alone. And having Jae around helps. Maybe we could take a raincheck?"

Darren's eyes softened slightly, but Winter could sense the disappointment. He nodded slowly, but it was clear he wasn't happy. "Yeah... sure," he said, trying to sound understanding. "We can reschedule."

Winter smiled, relieved, but also knowing how hard this was for him. She could feel the weight of the situation pressing down on her, the impossible balance between being a mother and having a life of her own.

"I'll make it up to you," she promised softly.

"Yeah," Darren said, forcing a smile. "I'll hold you to that."

He leaned in and kissed her cheek, lingering for a moment before turning and heading for the door. Winter watched him go, her heart heavy with the knowledge that this wasn't over. The tension between him and Jae, the complications of her life... it all felt so fragile.

When she turned back, Jae was watching her, his expression unreadable. "Raincheck, huh?" he said, arching an eyebrow.

"Don't," Winter warned, though there was a hint of a smile on her lips.

Jae held up his hands in mock surrender. "I'm just saying. I told you he's not a fan of the family reunion."

Winter rolled her eyes. "He'll be fine."

"Yeah," Jae said, smirking again. "If he can handle the fact that you'll always pick Miri first."

Winter sighed, knowing he was right. She glanced over at Miri, who was now scrolling through her phone, probably reading all the social media buzz surrounding her game. Her heart swelled with pride, but there was always that little nagging voice in the back of her mind, reminding her how hard this balancing act was.

"I just... I want both," she admitted softly. "I want to be a good mom and still have a life."

Jae nodded, his face softening for a moment. "You're doing the best you can, Wyn. Miri knows that."

Winter smiled, though the weight of it all still pressed down on her. "I hope so."

She glanced toward the door, where Darren had just walked out, and sighed again. One more thing to figure out. One more part of her life to balance.

The drive back from the game was loud and chaotic as usual. Miri rehashed every shot, play, and foul like she was giving a post-game interview, while Jae chimed in with his usual smart remarks, poking fun at her mistakes and exaggerating his role in her comeback.

Winter smiled, half-listening, but her mind was elsewhere. She couldn't shake the image of Miri collapsing in the locker room, gasping for breath, the fear that had gripped her when her daughter's body had betrayed her.

They arrived home, Winter heading to the kitchen and to pull out her baking utensils.

She didn't look up, but she noticed that the room grew quiet. It was obvious to everybody what she was thinking.

"I'm gonna go upstairs and shower, Mom." Miri said softly.

Winter nodded, still refusing to look up, fighting tears. She heard Miri run up the stairs, a sound she was accustomed to and, at this moment, was ever so thankful for.

She began to mix the dry ingredients to make a black cherry pie.

Jaden walked over and sat on the barstool closest to her, pulling out his phone without saying a world. Years of knowing each other meant he knew that space was what she needed, but she also didn't want to be alone.

Once she'd formed the pie dough, she broke the silence. "She's putting too much on her plate, Jae."

"She's fine, Wyn."

"Don't give me that. You saw what I saw. What if—what if I'm letting her push herself too hard?"

Jae didn't look up from his phone at first, but Winter knew he was listening. He always did this—let her freak out for a minute before he swooped in with his calm, steady logic.

Finally, he set the phone down and gave her a level look. "Winter, she's fine."

"She's not fine," Winter shot back, her voice sharp. "You saw her today. She could barely breathe. That doesn't remind you of anyone?"

"Of course it does."

"Well, what if something happened, I mean really happened, and I'd just stood there, cheering her on like everything was okay? Who does that?"

Jae sat up, his tone more serious now. "You didn't just stand there. You know what Miri's capable of, and so does she. This isn't like

Malik, Wyn. By the time you met him, his fate was already sealed. He was just really good at hiding it. With Miri, the treatment has come such a long way, and we know how to treat her symptoms."

Winter shook her head, the guilt eating at her. "I should've pulled her out the game the moment I saw her struggling. If she'd collapsed or—or worse, I would've never forgiven myself."

Jae got up from the barstool, crossing the room to stand in front of her. "Winter, listen to me. You did the right thing."

Winter looked at him, her eyes filled with doubt. "How can you say that?"

Jae's gaze softened, but his voice stayed firm. "You know that girl better than anyone. You know when she's hitting her limit and when she's pushing herself because she wants something bad enough. This wasn't about you pushing her. This was about Miri deciding she wasn't going to let her condition control her life."

Winter turned away, avoiding his eye and returning to her baking, placing the pie in the oven. "But what if it had? What if she'd—"

Jae cut her off gently. "Listen, Wyn, if anyone knows what she's going through, it's me. Malik died in my arms, remember? I'm not going to let anything happen to her. You're not going to let anything happen to her. But you can't wrap her in bubble wrap forever. She needs to live her life."

Winter closed her eyes, leaning against the wall, the weight of his words sinking in. She hated this; hated that she couldn't control Miri's condition, that her daughter had to deal with something so unpredictable, so dangerous. And hated, most of all, the feeling that she might be failing her as a mother.

"I know," she whispered. "I just—I can't lose her."

Jae stepped closer, lowering his voice. "You're not going to lose her. But you would've lost her in a different way if you'd pulled her off the court tonight. She would've hated you for that."

Winter looked up at him, her throat tight. "You think so?"

"I know so," Jae said. "Miri needed that game. She needed to prove something to herself. If you'd stopped her, it wouldn't have been her body that let her down—it would've been you."

Winter let out a shaky breath, running her hands through her hair. "I hate that you're right."

Jae smiled gently. "I usually am."

She swatted him half-heartedly. "Shut up."

He chuckled, but his expression softened again. "Look, I know this isn't easy. You're scared for her. Hell, I'm scared for her too. But Miri's tough. Tougher than most people give her credit for. And she's got you in her corner, so she's already ahead of the game."

Winter blinked back the sting of tears. "I just want her to be okay."

"She will be," Jae said, his voice steady. "You gotta let her live, Short stack. She's not a little kid anymore."

Before Winter could respond, the doorbell rang, startling them both.

Winter frowned. "Who the—"

She pulled out her phone, opening the front door camera app, and her eyes widened in disbelief when she saw who was standing on her doorstep. "No... it can't be," Winter muttered.

"Who is it?" Jae asked. She didn't respond.

"You have got to be kidding me," she muttered as Jae started to clean up her mess.

Jae, noticing the sudden change in her mood, leaned over to take a look at the screen. When he saw who it was, he burst out laughing. "Oh man, this is gonna be good."

Winter groaned. "My mom's here."

9
AND-ONE

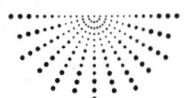

"So... you gonna let her in?" Jae asked, trying to hide the smirk that was unfurling on his face.

Winter rolled her eyes, already feeling the stress creep in. She suddenly turned to him with puppy dog eyes. "You let her in."

"The fuck I will. I don't live here."

"Jae, please—"

"Wyn, you can play that violin somewhere else, cause I'm not listening."

"Okay, okay. Rock, paper, scissors, best of three?"

Jae groaned. "One round... and I'm only doing this because I owe you from last week when I was ducking my agent."

"Deal!"

Winter and Jae had used the game since college to settle many disagreements, such as who went to class on a given day and who got to skip.

The pair stuck out their hands and locked eyes.

"Go." Jaden said.

They pounded their fists three times before revealing their choices.

"Ha!" Jae yelled in excitement. His scissors beat her paper. He pumped his hands in the air in triumph as the doorbell rang for a third time.

Winter huffed. "Damn it! Okay, I need to mentally prepare for this," she said as she fanned herself.

"Well, whatever you do, you better get to cleaning. Because this place is a mess."

Jaden chuckled as Winter flipped him the bird. She looked around the house, realizing there were half-empty water bottles on the coffee table, shoes by the door, and Miri's basketball gear scattered across the floor, not to mention there was a pie in the oven. It would be fine for anyone else who'd visit, but her mom had a way of noticing everything, and Winter wasn't in the mood for a running commentary on her "housekeeping".

"Shit," she muttered, rushing to gather up the mess.

"Wyn, I was joking—"

"Fool, shut up and help me clean this up before she starts her whole 'Oh, you'll never find a man this way, Winnie' speech."

Jae just laughed, kicking his feet up on the couch. "Nah, I'm good. Like I said, I don't live here, and besides, I like watching you scramble."

Winter shot him a glare, chucking a stray sneaker at him. "You are the worst."

Jae caught the sneaker with a grin. "Hey, you know out of anybody in this house, Ms. Denise loves me most. I'm not worried."

Winter rolled her eyes, this time flipping him off with both fingers, before hurriedly straightening up the pillows and throwing the scattered items into a closet.

Ding dong.

The doorbell rang again. She stuffed the rest of Miri's things in the closet and threw the basketball at Jae, who dropped the shoe to catch it. "Hey!"

"Shhh!"

She took a deep breath, trying to center herself before she opened the door. "Okay, here we go."

She swung open the door, and there stood Denise, all smiles, arms wide. "Well, look who decided to finally open the door. I know you live in a nice neighborhood, but this is still Houston, honey. Anyone could've shot me standing here on your stoop."

Winter forced a smile. "Hey, Mom."

Denise strode in like she owned the place, taking a quick look around the living room. "Hmm, nice to see you're keeping the place somewhat tidy."

Winter suppressed a groan. "I do what I can."

"Though knowing you, I probably shouldn't open that closet over there."

Winter glared at Jae. who was suppressing a chuckle. Her mother was right, and they both knew it was only going to get worse.

She was given a reprieve when she heard her daughter's footsteps. Miri bounded down the stairs, her tiredness momentarily forgotten when she saw her grandma. "Nan-Nan!"

Denise's face lit up as she pulled Miri into a hug. "There's my superstar! How's my future WNBA baller doing?"

Miri beamed. "Pretty good."

"Now, remember, when you get your first big check, what do I want?"

"A Lexus or a Land Rover."

"That's my girl!"

Winter and Jae exchanged a look, both silently bracing for whatever else Denise had in store. As much as Winter loved her mom, she knew Denise had a way of making things just a little... complicated.

Jae shot Winter a grin. "And here I was, just about to go home."

"You know what? Remind me to give Chrissy your home address."

Jaden playfully shoved her.

Winter's mom, Denise Harrison-Villers, was all smiles, her jet black bob making her look as young as she'd ever looked. Combined with her signature bold lipstick and eye-catching jewelry, she was a force of her own. All of it made her five-foot-four slender brown frame look as vibrant as ever.

She held Miri close, examining her like she was still eight years old. "Look at you! Getting all tall and beautiful, out here putting a beating on these girls and making me proud at the same time!"

Miri beamed. "Trying to, Nan-Nan. You just missed the game. You would have loved it—well, the second half of it, anyway. I dropped thirty points. I was lights out."

"And who says I missed it?"

Denise pulled out her phone and showed video of Miri hitting one of her three pointers.

Miracle's eyes lit up brighter than a Christmas tree. "You were at the game?"

"You know your Nan-Nan. I knows all, and I sees all."

The two embraced again.

Denise's eyes twinkled as she let Miri go and turned toward Winter, throwing her arms wide. "And here's my other superstar! How is the bakery going, honey?

Winter rolled her eyes playfully, but leaned in for a hug. "Hey, Mom, you didn't tell me you were coming."

Denise smirked, patting Winter's back. "Well, surprise, baby. Thought I'd pop in and check on my girls."

"How long are you staying? And why didn't you tell us you were at the game?"

"What's with the Spanish inquisition? Last I checked, I changed your diapers, not the other way around."

Behind them, Jae sauntered up to Denise with his usual swagger. "Hey, Momma D! How you doing?"

Denise's face lit up as she embraced Jae. "Jaden Carter. You always been tall, but you get more handsome by the day," she said.

Jaden stepped back and twirled her around in a spin. "Now, now, Momma D, you're the one over there looking like a whole meal."

"Well, you know how it is, honey. Gotta keep it... what do the young folk say? Demure."

"No one says that anymore, Mom."

"Yeah, Nan-Nan."

"Well, I'm bringing it back," she said as she pulled Jae into another hug, her affection obvious. "How's my second favorite Carter doin'?"

Jae laughed. "Doing great. Just trying to keep Winter here in line."

"Oh please, like that's possible," Denise teased. "Trust me, I raised her—you're fighting a losing battle."

Winter groaned. "Okay, Mom, can we not start already?"

They all made their way into the living room, where Miri flopped down on the couch, phone in hand, clearly exhausted but in good spirits. Denise sat with a satisfied sigh, like she'd been running the world all day and this was her well-earned break. Jaden and Winter took the seats unoccupied by the pair. Denise crossed her legs and looked at her daughter.

"So," Denise began, her tone loaded with curiosity, "what's this I hear about Darren?"

Winter groaned internally. Of course her mom would bring it up. "What about Darren?"

Denise waved her hand. "Oh, I just heard you're dating, and there's been some—shall we say, tension?—between him and Jae."

Winter's eyes widened. "Okay, how did you know I was even dating? Who told you that?"

From the corner of her eye, Winter spotted her daughter looking intently at her phone, studiously avoiding eye contact.

"Seriously, Miri?" Winter asked in shock.

Miri raised her hands in surrender. "Mom, it's Nan-Nan. I don't want that smoke."

Denise cleared her throat, drawing the room's attention back to her. "Avoiding the question, I see. But since Jae's right here, I'll just get it from the horse's mouth. Darren still got that chip on his shoulder cause you made him watch his senior season from the bench?"

Jae smirked, settling into his seat with the air of someone about to cause trouble. "You could say that."

Winter gave him a warning look. "Don't start."

Jae held up his hands innocently. "Hey, I'm just saying, the guy's had it out for me since college, even Momma D knows that. I can't help it if he's jealous."

"Jealous?" Winter echoed, crossing her arms. "You two just refuse to get along, that's all."

Miri, not looking up from her phone, chimed in. "To be fair, Uncle Jae, you are always around. Darren's probably just sick of seeing you."

Jae shrugged. "What does he expect? I'm family. He loves to say Leek was like a brother to him, why doesn't that extend to me? Besides, this ain't his first time watching me from the sidelines. He'll just have to get used to it."

Winter rolled her eyes. "Yeah, because that's gone so well so far."

Denise watched the exchange with an amused smile, then leaned forward like she was sharing a secret. "Maybe it's because the two of you have always been thick as thieves."

"I wouldn't say that, Momma D."

"Yeah, thieves is pretty harsh. Maybe grifters." Winter said, raising her hand toward Jae for a Double up high five.

Denise shook her head in amusement. "See, y'all at it again. Secret handshakes, inside jokes. I bet you played rock, paper, scissors to see who was gonna open the door."

Her comment made Jae burst into laughter, Winter threw a pillow in his direction as he conceded Momma D's point.

Denise leaned back and pointed towards the duo.

" You know, I've always wondered why you two never got together."

The room went still.

Winter blinked, certain she'd misheard. "Momma! Say what now?"

Jae raised an eyebrow, his grin creeping back. "Mama say mama sa mama coosa?"

Miri's attention snapped up from her phone, her eyes wide. "Wait, what?"

Denise shrugged, entirely unfazed by the awkward silence she'd created. "I'm just saying, Jae hasn't found anyone meaningful. Neither have you, Winnie. You two have been best friends since college. You're always hanging out, you're business partners, you finish each other's sentences. It just makes sense. But what do I know? I'm just an old woman with an impeccable fashion sense and a snatched waistline."

Winter felt her face flush as she groaned, long and drawn out. "Oh my God, Mom. See this is why I didn't want to open that door."

"Winnie, don't do that now. You're the one that told me your sophomore year that you and Jae had a chemistry."

"I was talking about our sense of humor—"

"Wait, you told your momma we had chemistry?" Jae interjected.

Winter fired back. "Not now, Jae."

"When was this? Where was I?"

"Jae, *not now*. Momma, why would you even bring that up?"

Denise pointed to the two of them. "Everyone can see it, trust me. The chemistry between you two is effortless."

Jae, recognizing the distress on his friend's face, couldn't resist teasing her. "Wyn, she's got a point. I mean, she's makin' sense."

Miri sat up straight, her face twisted in horror. "Ew! No. Just... no."

Denise smirked. "I'm just saying, Jae's been around more than any of these other guys. I thought maybe there was something more there." She wagged a finger at her daughter. "Don't act like it hasn't crossed your mind."

"Mom, stop," Winter said, her voice heavy with embarrassment. "Jae and I are just friends. Best friends."

"Best friends," Jae echoed with a wink. "With amazing chemistry."

Winter shot him a look. "If by chemistry, you mean the urge to punch you in the face sometimes, then sure."

Jae stuck his chin out and pointed to it, giving her a clear shot at him.

She drew back a fist, then picked up a pillow and threw it at him. Jae shrunk back in faux fear as Winter laughed at him.

Denise watched on with a smug look on her face, clearly enjoying the tension she'd stirred up. "Just as I said..."

"Dang it, Jae, you got her started." Winter said as she threw another pillow at Jae, who playfully shielded himself from the assault.

Miri, ever the voice of youthful disdain, scrunched her nose. "This is so weird. Please stop."

Jae chuckled. "Relax, kid. Nan-Nan 's been doing this for years. We both just like seeing Winter squirm."

"Speak for yourself, chile. I'm trying to get my baby down the aisle."

"Oh my God, Mom, stop please!"

Denise laughed softly, still watching them with that knowing look. "This is an underrated season for weddings, in my opinion."

Winter threw up her hands. "Mom, for the love of all things holy, can we *not*?"

Jae leaned back, grinning. "Hey, at least we're making Darren jealous. That's gotta count for something."

Winter groaned, covering her face with her hands. "You're both impossible."

Jae and Denise chuckled as Denise winked at him, clearly not done with her meddling. "Alright, I'll stop... for now. Now, let me turn my attention to my grandbaby. Miri, what's this I hear about you getting high as a kite online and cursing like you don't know the Lord on Beyonce's internet?"

Miracle tensed up, looking to her mother for help.

Winter shook her head dismissively. "Nuh uh, ma'am. You made this bed, you lie in it." She walked into the kitchen to pour a glass of wine, before reconsidering and bringing the whole bottle. She was going to need it if her mother was going to go into detail of every facet of their lives.

With all the discussion about Darren, she realized she hadn't thought to call Darren since arriving home. He'd seemed upset at the game. While she knew her mother's ribbing was good-natured, there could be a kernel of truth behind it. Maybe Darren really was jealous of Jae, which couldn't be good for the future of their relationship. Jae was sticking around whether Darren liked it or not.

"I'll work it out." Jae voice broke through the silence, snapping her back to reality.

She looked at him in confusion.

"The thing with Darren. I'll work it out, fall back if necessary. It's all good," Jae assured her.

He'd read her mind yet again.

She smiled in thanks and punched him in the arm. "Thanks, Jae."

The two exchanged a look, silently bracing for whatever else

Denise had in store for them. As much as Winter loved her mom, she knew Denise had a way of making things just a little... complicated.

10

TIMEOUT

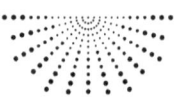

The smell of cinnamon, cloves, and freshly baked gingerbread wafted through the bakery, filling the air with the unmistakable scent of Christmas. The little shop was decked out for the holidays—wreaths hanging in the windows, string lights twinkling along the countertops, and a giant Christmas tree in the corner, decorated with red and gold ornaments. Winter was on her feet, apron dusted with flour, barely keeping up with the wave of customers lining up for their holiday orders.

She'd been at it since 6 a.m., juggling pies, cookies, and specialty cakes for the rush, and she was *exhausted*. But it was the kind of exhaustion that felt good—a reminder of how far she'd come. But it didn't feel like that at the moment.

The bakery was a madhouse. Christmas music blared from the speakers, barely audible over the sound of customers chatting, the clatter of baking trays, and the hum of the ovens working overtime. She was busy—*too* busy—but that was par for the course this time of year.

Flour dusted her apron, and her hair was tied up in a messy bun that she hadn't had time to fix all day. The rush of holiday orders was pushing her to the brink, and she still hadn't gotten to the most important thing she needed to do: signing the paperwork for the new bakery spot. It was sitting in the back, untouched, begging for her attention.

Jae strolled into the store, his usual laid-back swagger on full display as he squeezed past the line of customers. He spotted Winter juggling a tray of cookies and a roll of wrapping paper meant for gift-wrapping a few dozen special holiday orders.

"Don't you have somewhere to be?" Winter called out from behind the counter. "Like, I don't know, your actual job?"

Jae smirked. "Nah, figured I'd come in and help you, *again*, since you're doing that thing where you put off everything important."

Winter rolled her eyes. "I'm not putting anything off."

"Winter," he admonished, sidling up to the counter. "You sign those papers yet?"

Winter huffed, not even looking up. "Jae, do I look like I have time for that right now?"

Jae raised an eyebrow, glancing around the bakery. "Looks like you need to make time. Those papers are due, like, yesterday."

"I *know*," Winter said, her tone clipped, barely able to keep her frustration in check. She dropped the tray of cookies down a little harder than necessary. "I just—ugh, I'll get to it."

Jae leaned his elbows on the counter, arms folded. "You've been saying that for over a week now."

Before Winter could snap back, Christina appeared from the back, holding another stack of boxes. "You want me to put these out, or are we hiding them for Santa?"

Winter shot her a look that said, *not now*, but Christina was oblivious, too busy trying to keep up with the chaos.

Jae, still waiting for an answer, tapped the counter. "You gotta stop putting this off, Wyn. He's not going to hold the space forever."

"I know, Jae."

"It's literally the most important thing on your plate right now."

"I said I'll get to it!" Winter snapped, louder than she intended.

Christina, overhearing, paused as she stacked the boxes. "Wyn, if you need help with the paperwork, I can look over it for you," she

79

offered, her tone light, but with an edge of sarcasm. "Wouldn't want you to pull a muscle signing your name."

It was a good joke, but Winter wasn't in the mood.

"I don't need you to look at it, Christina, I need you to do what I pay you to do." Winter snapped, turning to her friend. "I can handle my own business. I just need everyone to stop asking me the same damn thing every five minutes."

Christina froze, eyes widening in surprise. "Okay," she said, her voice quieter, the hurt obvious despite her best effort to hide it. "I was just trying to help."

Winter sighed, her temper flaring again. "Well, I don't need help. I just need some space to breathe."

There was a beat of uncomfortable silence.

"Fine," Christina said, her voice steady but tight. "Well, let me know if you do need help."

Winter didn't respond.

Christina glanced at Jae, then back at Winter, before nodding stiffly and heading toward the door, her face set in an uncomfortable smile. "I'm going on break."

The door jingled as she left, and Winter exhaled sharply, wiping her hands on her flour-streaked apron. "Great," she muttered under her breath, already regretting snapping at Christina but too overwhelmed to deal with it right now.

Jae hadn't moved, watching the whole thing with that familiar look on his face—the one that told her he wasn't about to let her get away with her behavior. She ignored him and headed to the back room to focus on finishing her latest order.

"You know what you just did was fucked up, right?" Jae said, voice firm as he followed her.

Winter whipped around to face him, her frustration still simmering. "Excuse me? Do you not see how slammed I am? I don't have time for this right now."

Jae's face didn't change. "I see how slammed you are, and I saw you take it out on Christina. That's not cool."

Winter groaned, rubbing her temples. "Jae, I don't have time to apologize for every little thing—"

"That wasn't little, Wyn," Jae interrupted, his voice steady. "You embarrassed her in front of me and a shop full of people. She was only trying to help you."

"I'm under a lot of pressure right now, Jae," Winter said, throwing her hands up. "It's Christmas time, peak time for the bakery. I'm here to make money, and the only way that happens is by moving these cookies, cakes and pies. If you're not on my side, you're in my way. I don't have time to babysit you or Christina."

"Come on, Wyn."

Winter slammed a tray of cupcakes on the counter. "No, not *come on, Wyn*. I am so sick and tired of everyone telling me what I should feel. How to feel as a single mother, how to feel as a business owner, how to feel in a relationship. How to feel as a friend. I'm the only one being pulled in all these directions."

Jae stood silently as she paced the back room.

"My daughter hates me every other day, and for what reason? Cause I've been there for every cold, every fever, every stomachache, not to mention all of her appointments? It would be nice to hear a *thank you* from time to time. Then I'm supposed to come in here with a smile on my face and deal with people who complain about the slightest imperfection in the one millionth cupcake or cookie I've made this week, and I do it every. Single. Day."

"Wyn, I understand—"

"No, you don't, understand. Respectfully, you dunk a ball, I work. I'm a single mom. Hell I'm a woman and from what I can tell we're the only ones made to feel this way. We're expected to make breakfast, lunch, and dinner while working a full-time job. Then, somehow after that, turn into a closet nymphomaniac with whatever energy whoever we're dating thinks we got left, to entertain them because they're feeling sad, or lonely, or horny, or whatever the fuck they're feeling with one of their two heads that day."

"I didn't—"

"And we have to do it all with a smile, because heaven forbid we have a bad day, then you're an angry black woman and you hate all men."

"Short stack, just breathe—"

"I am *tired*, Jae." She sighed deeply. "I don't sleep. I don't eat. The only thing I do consistently is worry; about Miri, about this business, about if my relationship is going to work, and I am trying my damnedest to hold it together, but it's never good enough."

A tear fell from her eye as she took a deep breath and looked over at him. He was at a loss for words. She continued,

"You know, the one thing about having Black Girl Magic, being a She-EO, or whatever buzzword we're using these days, is that it dehumanizes you. Because if you want to know the truth, I'm not a superhero. I'm a goddamn human being forced every day to do superhero shit, and I am *tired*. When do I get to just be tired? When do I get to not be strong?"

Jae stayed silent. He didn't want to say anything for fear of saying the wrong thing. Instead, he walked over and hugged her.

Her weight collapsed against his frame as she began to sob openly.

He failed to find the words, his mind scrambled. Her crying intensified; he could feel the years of pain offloading onto him as he held her. His mind continued to race until he concluded it was best to say nothing. She was sharing her burden, and it didn't require a response. For now, holding her was all she needed, and he did so as the tears saturated his shirt.

As he looked down, she wiped the tears from her eyes. Their eyes connected in her vulnerability. It was time to find words, but he still had none. He allowed his heart to guild him as he said, "How can I help?"

The pair released their embrace as she reached for a tissue. "You can't… I just gotta get all this stuff baked by the morning."

Without another word, Jae walked over and picked up one of the aprons. Winter looked at him, confused. "Jae, what do you think you're doing?"

"I'm suiting up for the game, coach."

"What? No, hell no. You can't boil water, let alone cook."

"Well, Short stack, I may not know what it's like to be a woman, but I do know what it's like to be a teammate, and as your silent partner, I'm getting in the game. Now, I'm not as good as she who will not be named—" Winter grimaced at the reminder of her behavior towards Christina. "—but I can work my way around the kitchen, and I can follow instructions. Plus, if nothing else, I can bust down some dishes, so that's gotta take some of the load off, right?"

Winter wiped her eyes, her tears replaced by a smile of astonishment. "Are you saying you're gonna help me make these cinnamon rolls?"

"I'm saying the only way I walk out that door is if we walk out together."

"Jae, I don't know what to say."

"Tell me where the cinnamon is, and we'll get this thing started. Oh, also, how do you make cinnamon rolls?"

Winter smiled, and the pair exchanged a double five. "This is very sweet, but I'm not letting you poison none of my customers, Jae."

"Yeah, you're probably right." Jae took out his phone and start typing.

"What are you doing?"

"Huh? Oh, just sending a text. I'm gonna get on these dishes though."

He walked over and gave his friend a hug before starting to load the industrial dishwasher. After a spell, Jae spoke up, his voice low but pointed. "Look, I get that you're busy, and I get that you've got a million things to worry about. But Christina's your girl, and you snapped at her like she was the sole reason you're overwhelmed. Also, might I point out she was trying to help? You need to fix it."

Winter turned away, feeling the weight of what he was saying sink in. She knew he was right, but her mind was buzzing with a hundred things at once.

"I just..." She sighed, leaning on the counter. "I didn't mean to. Between the bakery, Miri, Darren, the paperwork..."

Jae softened, stepping closer. "I know you didn't. But she doesn't know that."

Winter stared down at the counter, her pulse still racing. "I'm just... so tired, Jae."

"I know," Jae said, his voice a little gentler now. "But don't take it out on the people who care about you. Christina's been with you since the start, and you know she's always had your back."

Winter nodded, guilt gnawing at her. "You're right. My bad."

Jae wrapped up loading the first load in the dishwasher before turning back to her. "Damn right I am. Now when this is over, call her, apologize, and make it right."

Winter gave him a half-hearted glare, but there was no fight left in her. "Fine."

Jae smiled. "Good. Now, get back to those cinnamon rolls before someone comes in here and thinks you're abandoning ship."

Winter managed a small laugh, shaking her head. "You're impossible, you know that?"

"Yep," Jae said, grinning. "But you wouldn't survive without me."

Winter wiped her hands on her apron, shaking her head again, but this time with a hint of a smile. "Yeah, yeah." She grabbed her phone, already thinking about what she'd say to Christina, feeling the guilt settle in her stomach as she prepared to fix the mess she'd made.

But before she could dial, her phone buzzed in her pocket. She pulled it out and saw Darren's name flashing on the screen. She'd missed a few of his calls earlier in the day.

Her eyes rolled. "Darren," she murmured, showing Jae the screen.

"Go ahead," Jae said, watching her carefully.

She answered the phone, her voice steady. "Hey, Darren."

"Winter," Darren said, his tone sharp, not bothering with any niceties. "I've been trying to call you."

"I know, I'm sorry. It's been crazy at the bakery with the holiday rush—"

"Yeah, I figured," he interrupted. "Are we still on for tonight?"

"What's tonight?"

"Remember you said you wanted to go to the nutcracker gala?"

Winter blinked, suddenly remembering they'd made plans. "Tonight? I—uh—I don't know. Miri's got practice, and I haven't gotten through half of these orders, and my help just walked out the door. Can I take a raincheck?"

There was silence on the other end of the phone.

Winter persisted. "Darren?"

"Yeah.. I'm here. Today is the last day of the festival."

"I'm sorry, Darren, I'm just swamped right now. I'll give you the money back for the ticket."

"It's not about the money, Wyn."

"Well, I'll still pay you back."

"You've been saying that a lot lately."

"I know it's just that I'm—"

"Busy, I know. I'll… let you get back to work."

"Okay, I'll call you when I leave here."

"Sure."

"Okay. Goodb—"

The phone hung up before she could say anything else.

She knew he was upset, but she couldn't worry about that now. The orders were piling up, and she'd just lost her help when she snapped at Christina.

She was elbow-deep in frosting a batch of peppermint cookies when the door jingled open. Winter braced herself for another wave of orders to come from the front counter, but instead, her mom waltzed into the back room, all smiles, with her Chanel bag in one hand and a matching scarf wrapped tightly around her neck.

"Hey, baby!" Denise called out, looking as lively as ever. "The cavalry has arrived."

11

THE ASSIST

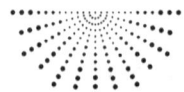

"Mom. What are you doing here?"

Jae raised his hand. "Well, I know I couldn't help you, so I figured I'd call in reinforcements."

"And I'm glad he did, because judging by the way your face is scrunched up, I figured you can use the help."

Winter sighed with relief. "Mom, you are a *lifesaver*." She hugged her who suddenly brought calmness to her raging storm. Jae took that as his cue to leave and quietly slipped out so the two could have some alone time. After a brief moment Denise said.

"You know that Christina girl has always been jealous of you, right?"

"Mom, don't start."

"Okay, okay, not my monkey, not my circus. Now, let me see what you've learned."

Denise set her bag down, took off her scarf, and grabbed an apron, immediately starting to pull out ingredients and holiday-themed decorations.

Winter instantly felt better. Her mother was the only person she'd never have to explain a recipe to because she'd taught her everything.

In fact, although she'd never admit it, her mother was the better of the two.

Denise scanned the waiting area out front, then turned back. "I know it's crazy in here, but it looks great! The place is packed! You must be doing something right."

"Yeah, if by 'right' you mean losing my mind in the process," Winter muttered, wiping her forehead. "It's been non-stop since Thanksgiving."

"Well, that's a good thing," Denise said with a smile, tying on an apron. "But don't forget to breathe. You've got this."

They quickly fell into a rhythm, working side by side as they filled orders and chatted, Denise's upbeat energy helping to lighten the mood a little. Winter had to admit, as much as her mom could get on her nerves, she was a rock when it came to pitching in when it counted.

A lull hit, giving them a brief moment to catch their breath.

Denise glanced at Winter, who was scribbling on the latest batch of order slips. "So, you smooth things over with Darren?"

Winter snorted. "No, I made it worse."

"And what about Jaden?"

Winter froze for a moment, her hand stopping mid-scribble. "What about him?"

Denise gave her that look, the one that said, *You know exactly what I'm talking about.*

"He's a good man, Winnie," Denise said, rolling out dough for sugar cookies. "Don't let him slip through your fingers. I mean it."

Winter sighed. "Mom, Jaden is my best friend. We've known each other since college."

"Exactly. He's always been there for you, if you want me to be blunt about it, I'm not sure why you're wasting your time on Darren."

"I'm not listening to this," Winter said.

"You don't have to," Denise pointed out, arching an eyebrow. "You and Jae have something real. Don't be blind to it just because you're scared of mixing business with pleasure."

"Scared?" Winter repeated, trying not to roll her eyes. "You didn't raise me to be scared. I'm not scared of anything."

Denise smiled, cutting out cookie shapes. "If you say so, honey."

The afternoon rush came and went. Winter was exhausted but refreshed. She couldn't help but smile.

"What's that look about?"

"Nothing, just... it's been really stressful lately, and I'm just glad to have the mommy and daughter time."

Denise hugged her daughter. "I had a great time too, honey."

"Of course, we could have more mommy/daughter time if you moved back—"

"Oh, no, you don't."

"What?"

"Winter, I love you. You're my youngest child, which makes you a baby by default. I need you to hear me and hear me well. It's my turn to live my life."

"But Momma—"

"But nothing. End of discussion. I swear, none of your siblings put pressure on me."

"They think it."

"Even if they do, they don't say it, not to me at least." Denise put down the towel in her hand and stepped closer to her daughter to hold her hand. "Listen, Winnie, I have been raising kids more than half of my life, most of it alone, and I did a damn good job with the four of you. It's my time now. I'm still young and healthy enough to see the world, so that's what I'm gonna do with my time. If you need me, I'll be on the first plane home, but you just keep posting on Facebook what my granddaughter is doing, and when I want to see it for myself, I'll pop into town."

"But Momma, can't you just—"

"This isn't a debate, it's a decision that's already been made." She kissed her daughter on the cheek and resumed cleaning the counter.

She wanted to protest, but her mother was still her mother. There was a line of respect she wouldn't dare cross.

"See, this is why you need to get you a man."

"Momma, I already have a man, and—"

Denise carried on, seemingly not hearing her. "Someone to keep you warm on these cold nights, because while a lady does enjoy a good toy doing a cold stretch, ain't nothing like the real thang."

Winter's jaw dropped in shock. "Momma!"

"And by 'thang' I mean dick."

"Mom!"

"Girl, tell the truth and shame the devil. You ain't getting enough dick cause if you were, you wouldn't be trying to hold Miri hostage and get me to move into Spinsterville with you. No, honey, you need some grade-A dick. A shellacking is what we use to call it."

"Good lord!"

"And we both know Darren ain't it. He don't look like he can find the hole, much less know what to do with it. Nah, he's compensating. Always trying to prove himself. No, honey, you need the kind of dick you can feel in your stomach three hours later."

"Oh my god! Can we please just stop—"

"Preferably rich, young, handsome, athletic, and generous, with a kind heart and carrying what I imagine is a... girthy package to unpack. So, someone like Jae."

"Denise!" Winter screeched. She looked to her mother as if to say, *explain yourself.*

Denice arched an eyebrow. "Girl he's your friend, not mine. I'm a woman with eyes, and from what I can see, the basketball rim ain't the only thing hanging. Besides, you're gonna need company once Miri goes away to school."

Winter scoffed. "Momma, I'm proud of Mir, she's smart, and she's a good kid, but she knows she can't go anywhere."

"And why not?"

"Because she's sick, and Houston is the best place for her."

"And since when has any sixteen-year-old girl done the best thing for them? Listen, Winnie, if you don't think she's strongly considering going to UConn, you are makin' a huge mistake."

"Then it's my mistake to make." Winter cut her eyes at her mother, watching as she gathered her thoughts.

"Winnie, I don't mean to interfere in your parenting, but it seems to me she's considering a full scholarship offer from one of the best colleges in the country."

"Momma, Miri's just talking. She only says that when she's mad, but she ain't going nowhere. She's gonna stay here for at least a year, maybe two, to help me with the bakery. We decided that years ago. Like you said, it's in her blood."

Denise shook her head, eyes widened in shock. She stepped closer to Winter. "You really don't see it, do you?"

"Miri just gets in her feelings from time to time. She'll come around."

"Winnie, I'm sorry to break it to you, but that girl is far from being impulsive or emotional. This is her *plan*, honey, like when you decided to marry Malik, and I thought it was a bad idea. She's just trying to prepare you, because in her mind, she's leaving. If I were you, I'd open my eyes to brace for impact."

Before Winter could respond, the front door swung open, and Christina walked in, the paperwork for the new bakery spot in hand. Winter tensed immediately, remembering their exchange earlier that day.

Christina walked gingerly to the island and reached in her purse. "Hey," Christina said, holding up the papers. "I went over the forms. Everything looks good—just need your signature."

Winter wanted to apologize, but between her mother's conversation and her previous outburst with Jae, the words escaped her. Instead, she wiped her hands and nodded. "Thanks, Christina. I'll get to it."

Christina hovered for a second, glancing between the two women. "So, what are you two talking about?"

Denise, never one to hold back, grinned and answered before Winter could. "Oh, just talking about Jaden. I'm telling Winter not to let him go."

Christina raised an eyebrow, her lips curling into a smirk. "Really? You two? Together? Well, that'd be something. Maybe that's why she went off on me in front of him."

Winter shot her a look, sensing the sarcasm behind Christina's comment. "What's that supposed to mean?"

Christina shrugged, the smirk still in place. "Nothing. Just... it's Winter's world, we're just all supposed to cower in it, I guess."

Something about the way Christina said it—so casual, yet so loaded with meaning—set Winter off. She was already on edge, and she'd had enough of the passive-aggressive digs. "What is your deal, Christina?" Winter snapped, crossing her arms. "You've been acting weird for weeks. If you've got something to say, just say it."

Christina blinked, caught off guard by Winter's sudden outburst, but she quickly recovered, folding her arms. "My deal? I don't have a 'deal', Winter. I just think it's funny how you've got everyone wrapped around your finger, acting like you're the only one who matters."

Winter's eyes narrowed. "Excuse me?"

"You heard me," Christina said, her voice laced with bitterness. "You're always so busy, so important, and everyone else is just here to make sure you don't fall apart. Must be nice, is all I'm saying."

Winter felt her temper rising. "*Nice?* Are you serious right now? I've been busting my ass in this bakery—*our* bakery—for years, and you're acting like I haven't done a damn thing for you."

Christina's eyes flashed. "Oh, you've done plenty, and you never take a moment to not remind me. I'm just saying, maybe it's time I stop following your lead and figure things out for myself."

"Following my lead?" Winter repeated, her voice growing louder. "Christina, I've been carrying you! You've been riding my coattails since college, letting me handle everything. Even around here, like... I love you, but you don't do *anything* without needing me to hold your hand!"

Christina's face went red, but she stayed quiet for a moment, clearly embarrassed and hurt. Finally, she shook her head, letting out a humorless laugh. "You know what? You're right. I don't need this. I don't need you. You want me to go figure things out for myself? Fine. I will."

Without another word, Christina turned on her heel and stormed out of the bakery, the door jingling loudly as it shut behind her.

The silence that followed was heavy. Denise, who had been watching the exchange quietly, let out a low whistle. "Well... that escalated quickly."

Winter exhaled, her anger fading into guilt almost immediately. She'd gone too far, and she knew it. "I didn't mean it," Winter muttered, rubbing her forehead.

Denise placed a hand on her shoulder. "You might not have meant it, but you said it. You're going to have to fix that."

Winter nodded, but she didn't move. The weight of her words hung in the air, and she knew she'd crossed a line. But part of her still bristled at Christina's attitude—there had been tension between them for a while, and it felt like it had all boiled over today.

Denise gave her shoulder a squeeze. "Don't let that stew too long, baby. Fix it before it gets worse."

Winter swallowed, her mind already racing with how she was going to make things right. But at that moment, she couldn't shake the nagging feeling that maybe Christina wasn't the only one who needed to figure things out.

12

BASELINE DRIVE

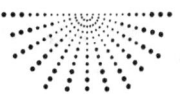

The bakery was busier than ever, the scent of cinnamon and vanilla swirling through the air as the holiday rush kicked into high gear. Winter moved through the chaos like she was on autopilot, her mind still buzzing from her recent argument with Christina. She hadn't shown up to work, which wasn't like her, but Winter expected that would be the case after their exchange. Thankfully, her mom was at the counter, chatting up customers with her signature charm, expertly balancing holiday cheer with the hectic pace. It felt good to have her around, and even though she was still struggling to find balance in her life, at this moment she felt like she wasn't alone. Her orders were ahead of schedule since her mother was an early riser and started almost half of the orders before she got to the bakery. She wanted this tentative peace to last as long as possible.

"Mom," Winter said, setting down a fresh tray of sugar cookies, "I don't know how I'd get through this season without you."

Denise waved her off, grinning as she boxed up an order. "Oh, please, baby. You know I live for this. Besides, that so called friend of yours—"

"Don't start, Momma. You already said I was wrong, and I own that."

"I'm gonna leave it alone, cause you grown. But there's an old saying: 'don't mix business with family and friends'. Now, what's next?"

Before Winter could answer, the bell above the door jingled, and a delivery man entered, his arms laden with roses. She blinked, eyes widening as she took in the sheer volume of red blooms.

"Delivery for Winter Carter?" he said, setting down the massive bouquet on the counter.

"That's me," Winter said warily, glancing at her mom, who raised an eyebrow in amusement.

"Well, someone certainly loves you," Denise teased, admiring the roses. "I've never seen this many in my life."

Winter's cheeks flushed as she read the card: *Winter, I would give you a hundred roses every day if we could spend every night together. Let's make today the first day of that promise. Can we start fresh? I'd love to take you out tonight. Darren.*

She felt a pang of guilt over their recent tension, and a smile crept onto her face as she reached for her phone, dialing Darren's number.

He answered on the second ring, his voice warm. "Winter."

"Hey, Darren," she said softly, glancing over at her mom, who was watching the exchange with thinly veiled interest. "I got your flowers. All one hundred of them. They're beautiful."

"Good," he replied, relief evident in his voice. "I know we've both been in flux, and I wanted to make things right between us."

"Well... maybe we can start fresh tonight?" Winter suggested, her heart fluttering slightly. "I'd love to go out with you."

Darren chuckled. "I'd like that. I have a meeting till five thirty. I'll pick you up around seven?"

"Perfect," Winter replied, hanging up and turning to her mom with a grin.

Denise smirked, her hands on her hips. "Well, look at you, getting all dolled up for date night. It's about time."

"Oh, hush, Momma," Winter said, but the smile lingered. "Now I just have to figure out who's going to take Miri to her college combine... Momma, can you—"

"Nope, not gonna happen."

"But Momma, you just said—"

"That I was happy for *you*. That did not mean I was open to add extra work for *me*. I've done my Winter duty for the day. This is all I'm doing."

"All I'm asking is—"

"Figure it out, Winnie."

As if on cue, the door opened again, and Jae strolled in, giving Winter a nod. "What's good, fam?"

Winter grinned, her shoulders relaxing. "Jae, I'm so glad you're here. Can you take Miri to the combine tonight?"

"I mean, that's not a problem, but—"

"What?"

"It's just that you're usually such a helicopter mom, no offense. I figured you were going to the combine. So I kinda made plans. With Chrissy."

"Oh, so she can answer your calls, but—You know what, never mind."

Jae raised an eyebrow, a teasing smile playing on his lips. "Oh, you going on a date?" he asked, nodding to the huge bouquet on the counter.

Winter rolled her eyes and shrugged.

"He hit you with a hundred roses, so you gotta give him your... tulips."

"Jae, shut up."

"And here I thought we had chemistry, Momma D," Jae said playfully, continuing their joke from the night before. "Don't worry, I'll switch things up with Christina and take Miri to the combine."

Winter smiled and hugged her friend. "Are you sure? I don't want to put you in a bad spot."

Jae chuckled. "Nah, I've got this. What's the point of being a rich uncle if you can't do rich uncle stuff from time to time? Miri knows the deal at my house. Just try not to get into too much trouble."

"Oh, please," she shot back, crossing her arms. "You're one to talk. Chrissy is gonna—"

"Well, my work here is done, so I'm off," Denise said as she grabbed her purse and kissed her daughter on the cheek. She walked out the door, but not before pinching Jae on his backside.

Jae left to pick up Miri, and Winter locked up and began the drive home, which gave her time to finally think about her relationships.

She wanted to call Christina, but she knew it was too soon; they both needed space to sort through their feelings. But at least tonight she'd be able to work on another relationship that had been neglected.

The house was silent when Winter walked in. It had been so long since she'd had the house to herself. *Maybe I can relieve some stress before the date.*

She walked into her bedroom and pulled her rabbit vibrator and lubricant from the bedside table, a grin on her face. She was already growing moist in anticipation of the toy on her clit.

As Winter stripped down and lay on the bed, she turned on the toy and began to imagine what would happen tonight with Darren. Before she could move the rabbit down her body, the device cut off.

What the hell?

She tried the device again, with no response.

"No, no, no! Please don't do this to me."

The battery was dead.

"Fuck!" she yelled, throwing her head back against the pillow in frustration.

She let out a deep sigh, looking down between her legs. "Girl, you need some dick."

This only cemented her decision: she was going to fuck Darren tonight.

She put the toy back and poured herself a glass of red wine in preparation for the evening. While she was disappointed that the evening hadn't started as she'd wanted, she took solace in known he could satisfy the itch that needed scratching. And she was going to ensure it.

"Well, I might as well get some cooking done."

She turned on her Christmas playlist, and Donny Hathaway's *This*

Christmas blared though the surround sound in her home, the TV on mute on the counter.

She was halfway through prepping the ingredients when she caught a glimpse of someone familiar on the TV screen.

"Is that... *Miri?*"

She cut off the music and found the remote. Miri was at the combine, a scrimmage game for coaches from colleges to observe the players. She saw Genesis Monroe interviewing her daughter.

Winter immediately pulled out her phone to call Jae.

"Yo. Getting your back blown out yet?"

No, unfortunately. "Shut up, Jae. What are y'all doing?"

"Miri is running a couple of drills. What about you?"

"I'm... cooking."

"What? Now I'm jealous."

"Don't worry, big head, there's gonna be tons of leftovers. I figured since we're getting that restaurant space, I need to start dusting off a few recipes for opening day."

"Now that's what I'm talking about. Double up."

"I see your ex is there. That's still a bad bitch."

Jae laughed softly. "Yeah, it's good to see her."

"So?"

"So, what, fool?"

"You gonna try to rekindle that?"

"Wyn, get off my phone."

"Jae, I'm serious—"

"I'm hanging up now. Bye."

"Jae."

"Bye." Without another word, Jae disconnected the phone.

Winter resumed making her meals, knowing that conversation was far from over.

LATER THAT EVENING, Winter stood in front of the mirror, smoothing the fabric of her velvet dress. It hugged her curves in all the right places, a deep, rich shade of lavender that highlighted her ginger brown skin tone. She wore a simple gold necklace, just enough to catch the light, and her hair fell in soft waves around her shoulders.

She was nervous—excited, but nervous. It had been a long time since she'd decided to take things to the next level with anyone, but Darren seemed worth the risk.

At precisely seven, the doorbell rang. Winter took a deep breath and a large gulp of her second glass of wine, steadying herself before opening the door.

Darren stood there, holding a small gift bag, his eyes widening as he took her in. "Wow," he said, barely hiding his admiration. "You look incredible."

She smiled, feeling the warmth of his gaze. "Thank you. You don't look bad yourself."

"Are you ready? We have reservations at Fogo de Chão in about—"

"Actually, I was hoping we could stay in tonight," Winter said as she grabbed his hand. Darren was reluctant as she pulled him inside and headed towards the dining room table, but his demeanor quickly changed.

"You did all of this?" he asked, amazed at the spread, taking a seat at the candlelit table.

"Well, Jae has been on me about opening the restaurant, so I figured why not test some recipes on my most important customer?" she said with a grin, before she continued pointing to the menu options. "We have honey-baked salmon, and roast beef wellington. There's also my famous roasted whole chicken, that's the one sliced on a platter over there. For sides, I made twice-baked mashed potatoes, asparagus, and this jalapeño macaroni pasta salad I've been tinkering with. Now, I didn't make the desserts—I just brought them home from the bakery—but you have two options: strawberry cheesecake, and my favorite—the pineapple upside down cake."

Darren pulled her in closer and kissed her on the neck. "This is incredible. Way too much food, but incredible."

"Thanks. I had some energy to burn off. Don't worry though. I saved some for you," she said, before diving in for another kiss, this one with more passion. "Bon appetite."

The pair shared a quiet dinner, amongst the candles and wine. The moment Darren tasted the salmon, he exclaimed, "This is the best thing I've ever eaten in my life." He would go on to say the same about everything he tasted, each reaction more exaggerated than the last. Winter knew he was trying to get in her pants, but she also appreciated the vote of confidence.

When he put his fork down for the last bite, he said, "Malik always told me you could bake, but how did you get this damn good in the kitchen?"

The mention of her late husband in such an intimate atmosphere shocked her. "He... um, I..."

"Damn. I'm sorry, I didn't think—"

"No, it's okay. Um, it's actually not about Malik. My dad taught me how to cook. He was a chef."

"I didn't know that."

"Yeah. He worked as a head chef for several restaurants in Houston for over twenty-five years. One day, he was closing up shop and then a fire broke out in the building next to him and well... He didn't make it."

"Wow, I'm so sorry. That had to be hard."

"Yeah, I don't talk about it much. Honestly, you might be the first person I've told that much to outside of family."

"Well, I'm honored. Wait, does Jae know?"

"Of course, he's family."

"Oh, right..."

Winter notice Darren's tone. The night was going well, she didn't want to jeopardize it.

"You know what let's take this over to the couch."

Darren visibly appreciated the gesture.

After settling next to each other, he wrapped his arms around her, pulling her close. She leaned in, feeling the heat between them, letting herself relax for the first time in what felt like ages.

They began kissing heavily, Darren rubbed her breast though her dress and she decided to give him a little more. She slipped off the top of her gown, and placed her hand on his stomach to feel his abs, He gently pushed her hand down in the direction of his dick and she started to rub the bulge of his package.

Nice. She thought

But then, just as things were heating up, he pulled back slightly, smiling as he looked her in the eyes. "You know, Winter," he said, his voice low and serious, "you've always been so sexy to me. My cock is hard right now thinking about you."

Winter's eyes flickered with something between amusement and disbelief. The line sounded so forced, so awkwardly out of place, that she had to hold back a laugh. She managed a small smile, but inside, the spark was starting to fade.

"That's sweet," she replied, searching for a way to steer the conversation elsewhere. "Really sweet."

He moved in to kiss her again, but she was already pulling back, her mind racing. She wanted to feel something for him, but now all she could think about was how forced everything felt.

She cleared her throat, sitting up. "Actually, I should probably check on Miri. I'm not used to leaving her this long."

Darren frowned, clearly disappointed. "Jae's got her, right? She's fine."

"Yeah," Winter said, reaching for her phone, "but I just want to make sure. You know how she gets."

He sighed, trying to mask his frustration. "Right. Of course."

"I'll only be a second," she assured him, but as she glanced back at him, she could see the look in his eyes—he was already slipping away.

She made the call, giving herself a moment to catch her breath. By the time she'd hung up, Darren was standing and gathering his things, his expression carefully neutral.

"I should probably get going," he said, his tone light, but his eyes said something else.

She hesitated, watching him. "Darren, I'm sorry. I didn't mean to cut things short..."

He gave a tight smile. "It's fine. Really."

Winter walked him to the door, the tension between them thick and unspoken. As he left, he gave her one last look, a hint of something final in his eyes. But before she could fully process it, he was gone.

She closed the door and leaned against it, exhaling heavily. This night hadn't gone the way she'd planned—not by a long shot.

And as she looked around the now-empty room, she couldn't help but feel that something important had just slipped through her fingers.

13

THE SHOT CLOCK WINDS DOWN

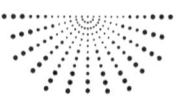

*W*inter sat at the counter of the bakery after closing, absentmindedly stirring a cup of tea that had long gone cold. She glanced at her phone, scrolling through the messages she'd left Christina over the past few days, all unanswered. She knew now that Christina probably wasn't coming back to work anytime soon.

It was strange to feel this kind of void, this empty space where Christina had been. They'd built the bakery together, side by side, and now it felt like she'd lost a limb.

After a moment of hesitation, she scrolled through her contacts and found Shana's number. She hadn't spoken to her friend in a while, but if anyone could understand, it would be her.

She took a deep breath and hit "Call". The phone rang twice before Shana's familiar voice answered. "Wyn!" Shana exclaimed, sounding as bright and warm as ever. "I can't believe it! How long has it been?"

Winter felt herself relax, a smile spreading across her face. "I know, it's been way too long. How are you, Shana? Are you still in the city?"

"Still here, still hustling," Shana replied with a chuckle. "But enough about me. What's going on with you? I know you didn't just call for small talk."

Winter laughed, knowing Shana could always read her like a book. "I guess you're right. I needed a little therapy session. I've been going through it over here."

"Oh, I'm all ears," Shana replied, her tone warm. "Lay it on me."

Winter took a deep breath. "So, you remember Christina, right?"

"From college?"

"That one. We had a huge falling out. She was running the bakery with me, and now... she's just gone. We were about to expand into a full restaurant, and I feel like I'm in over my head."

Shana's tone grew sympathetic. "Oh, Winter, I'm so sorry to hear that. You two were inseparable. What happened?"

"It's complicated," Winter said, rubbing her forehead. "I said some things I regret, and she's not answering my calls. And the restaurant, it was supposed to be our thing. Now it's all on me, and I'm just... I don't know. Lost, I guess."

"Girl, give yourself some grace," Shana said gently. "Dreams aren't easy, and this is a big one. But I'm proud of you. And hey, Jae finally talked you into it, huh?"

Winter smiled despite herself, feeling a familiar warmth at the mention of Jae. "Yeah, he's been pushing me. I'm glad he's still in my corner. You know, he's been there since day one, back when we thought we could conquer the world with nothing more than ramen and ambition."

"Of course he is," Shana replied with a knowing laugh. "You two were the problem kids. I remember y'all always had that little secret handshake—what was it called?"

"The Double up," Winter replied, grinning as she remembered. "We made it up that summer he was rehabbing his hamstring, and I was trying to get into culinary school."

"Was that sophomore year?"

"Yes, girl, before I met Malik. He'd come by with an endless appetite, and I'd try out every recipe I could think of. We were on a mission that summer to get what we wanted out of life, and everything was against us. Double Up became our motto. It was our way of saying, 'I've got your back'."

"See? That's why people always thought there was more between you two," Shana teased. "I know I did."

Winter laughed, feeling a slight blush creep up. "You and everyone else, apparently. But Jae's always been like a brother to me, which is why this thing with Darren is so hard. I mean, he'd never say nothing, but I know it bugs him we're dating—well, at least trying to date."

Shana paused. "Darren? Darren Bailey? Malik's best friend?"

Winter sighed. "Yeah, and I know how it sounds, before you even start. It's a mess, honestly. But I thought I'd give it a shot. He's great, it's just... I don't know if it's right."

"I heard he was working for the Houston Rockets now. That's Jae's old team."

"Right, so you can imagine how much fun that is."

"You know how to find a baller, don't you? But let's be real. Men are territorial, and Jae and Darren are both alpha males. Darren's gonna have a problem with any man being around as much as Jae is regardless. As far as Jae goes let's' be honest, you're sleeping with his brother's best friend, you gotta expect that to rub him the wrong way."

"Well, he won't have to worry about *that* for a while."

"Hold on. What does that mean?"

Winter realized she'd said too much, but it felt good to get some of this off her chest. "Shana, are you sure you have time? I don't really want to bother you with this."

"I got a patient right now, but they can wait. This is getting too good to get off the phone. You were saying…"

She conceded and decided to just unpack all she was thinking. She sat on a nearby stool and told her friend about the rest of her dilemma. "Okay, girl, so I call Darren over. We've been talking for a minute, so I'm thinking it's time to do the deed, you feel me?"

"So y'all haven't done the humpty dance?"

"We couldn't even get on the dance floor."

"What happened?"

Winter took off her apron. It was good to talk to her friend. They'd always been close, but life had kept them apart. It felt good to just talk without tension or repercussion.

She nibbled a piece of blue cheese that was nearby and continued. "So, we'd been taking it slow, and yesterday he sends me flowers, it was really sweet and I said, 'you know what, screw it', and by 'it' I mean him."

"Okay, sounds good so far."

"I haven't had any since Leek and—"

Her friend gasped over the phone line. "Wait, you haven't had any since Malik?"

"Girl, I got so many toys, every time I pull one out, I'm just waiting for a talking giraffe to show up singing a jingle. But that's not the point. So, I get it ready—like *ready* ready, Fenty on deck, lashes done, hair on point, smelling like an invitation to breakfast the next day."

"Oh, so it's going down."

"Yes, girl, the bakery is open, full service. He don't even know what he's in for, because, like I said, it's been a while for me, and the more I think about it, the more excited I'm getting, you feel me?"

"Sounds like my kind of night so far."

"So he gets there, he's looking good. We got reservations to Fogo, but I done whipped up a few things us to eat before... dessert."

"Alrighty now."

"So we stay in, we eat, he's saying all the right things. After dinner, we start going at it, and it's starting to heat up, right? He's got my top halfway off, and I see his bulge through his slacks."

Shana snickered. "That's always a good sign."

"You'd think, so I do that thing, you know, where you put your hand on his stomach because you wan' him to put it on his dick. Sure enough, he pushes my hand down there and I start rubbing it. Package confirmed, this is looking very promising."

"Sounds like this is gonna be a great night. So what happened?"

"Well, out of nowhere, he just says.... my *cock* is so hard for you right now."

Shana paused, taking it all in. "He said what?"

"You heard what I said."

"Oh, hell no, you can't be serious."

Winter sighed. "Yes, girl. Instant dryness."

"He said *cock?*"

"I couldn't believe it either."

"See, that's because he's an athlete. He's probably used to busting down Becky's, 'cause that's their word."

Winter laughed lightly. "You feel me? So now we're still going, but I'm saying to myself, what kind of black man says *cock?*"

"As you should. If nothing else, we are some strictly 'dickly people."

"Right? And I'm trying to stay in the moment, but now that's all I'm thinking about. Mind you, he's still groping me, and it's not registering. The moment is gone."

"So what did you do?"

Winter grimaced, recalling the moment. "I threw my baby under the bus, told him I had to check on Miri, and he bounced."

The pair laughed. After a spell, Winter said, "I need to fix this, too, don't I?"

"If you want to keep your man, yes, you do. Just call him today. See if you can go by his office and give him some of that Gawk, Gawk 3000."

"What? No, girl, I am not sucking his dick the first time I see it."

"Well, you're gonna have to do something, because a good-looking man like that, cock and all, ain't waiting around forever."

"Ugh! This sucks. And by 'this', I don't mean me."

"Well, I've put this patient off long enough, but before I go, I'll leave you this question to ask yourself. In your heart of hearts, is this the man you want to spend your time with once Miri leaves the nest? Because from where I'm sitting, it sounds like you're hesitant. You need to figure out why."

"I... I guess I never thought about it that way."

"Trust your gut, Wyn," Shana said gently. "I'll let you go, but let's catch up soon. And remember, you're not alone. You've got this."

"Thanks, Shana," Winter said, smiling as she hung up. She thought about her friend's words, and if there was any truth to them. She was ready to move on, but was Darren the right person to do that with?

Just then, the bakery door swung open, and Jae walked in with Miri, whose face was red and blotchy.

Winter's heart sank. "Miri, honey, what happened?"

Miri wiped her eyes, frustration written all over her face. "The coach pulled me aside today. He said UConn is interested in me, but asked if my health would hold up for the rest of the season."

"What? Jae, can they do that?"

"Not officially, but this is Division 1 sports." He replied. Miri continued. "He said they have questions about my 'reliability', and I just know Shasha Wilcox has something to do with it, because they were all over her at the combine."

Winter moved to her daughter's side, wrapping her arms around her. "Oh, Miri, I'm so sorry. That's not fair."

Miri pulled away, blinking back fresh tears. "I've worked so hard, Mom. And now they're acting like I'm broken, all because of something I can't control."

Jae stepped forward, his hand on her shoulder. "Hey, you're anything but broken, Cupcake. UConn would be lucky to have you. And if they can't see that, it's their loss."

Winter watched her daughter, heart aching at the pain in Miri's eyes. "Have you thought about U of H? They'd be thrilled to have you, and you'd be close to home."

Miri's gaze dropped, her voice barely a whisper. "I've thought about it."

"Well, between me and Jae as alumni, I don't see you having a problem going there. I'll call my friend over at admissions and—"

"I didn't apply yet."

Winter felt a jolt of surprise. "You haven't applied? But why—"

Before she could finish, she felt Jae's arm on her shoulder. She got the message. *Now wasn't the place or the time.* Taking his cue, she went silent.

Miri shook her head, her shoulders tense. "I wanted to focus on UConn. I thought... if I put everything into one dream, it had to work out."

Jae gave Miri a reassuring squeeze. "It's just one option, Miri.

There are plenty of schools that would love to have you. UConn is great, but it's not the only path."

"Baby, why don't you go in the back? I've got some eggnog and gingerbread cookies fresh out of the oven."

Miri's tension seemed to erode at the prospect of one of her favorite holiday treats. Without another word, she grabbed her gear and walked into the back room.

Winter took a deep breath, wondering if she'd been putting too much pressure on her daughter without even realizing it. But before she could say anything more, Jae turned to her, his tone lightening.

"So, Short stack," he said, "How'd date night go with Darren? Tell me he didn't mess it up."

Winter let out a sigh, rolling her eyes. "It was a disaster. I mean, we talked, and I thought we were finally on the same page, but then he got all weird, said something corny, and the whole thing just... fell apart."

Jae's eyes widened, clearly surprised. "That's funny, because when I dropped Miri off at practice this morning, I saw him. He was on the phone, laughing and talking to someone. I figured it was you."

Winter froze, her heart racing. "He was... laughing with someone?"

Jae nodded. "Yeah, he seemed pretty relaxed, honestly. I just assumed you two had a good night."

Winter clenched her jaw, a sinking feeling settling in her stomach. Who had he been talking to? And why did he seem fine, when she'd spent the whole night feeling like everything was unraveling?

She tried to shake off the feeling, forcing a smile for Miri's sake as she returned with the cookies. But deep down, a part of her wondered if she'd been fighting for something that wasn't worth the struggle. She needed to know. "Jae, you mind dropping Miri off at home? There's something I need to take care of."

14
TURNOVER

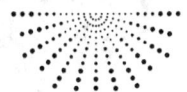

"Hey Darren, listen, I know you're upset. I'm so sorry about the other day. There was this mess with Miri, and I just lost track of everything. Call me later, okay? Please, I'm worried about you... I'm worried about us. And I'm going to fix it, okay? Call me. Bye."

Winter hung up the phone, her fingers lingering on the screen for a moment. She sighed, leaning her head back against the seat of her car. The tightness in her chest wouldn't ease up, and no amount of calling or apologizing was making it better. She'd left a cheesecake at Darren's place earlier—a peace offering—and she hoped that it would soften his anger. But deep down, she knew it wasn't enough.

Still, she pressed on. She called again as she exited the car going to his front door with the cheesecake. "Pick up... please," she mumbled to herself.

His voicemail greeted her for the second time. "Hey Darren, I just wanted to leave you a cheesecake offering... Come on D, I know you're there, because you never go anywhere. I made that strawberry whipped cheesecake you love, and maybe we can share a slice?" There was nothing. She sighed and continued the message. "Look I wanted to apologize again for recent events. I've been in my head lately, but I promise I'll do better, and I appreciate your understanding. I miss you, and I'll be at the shop tomorrow if you want to talk. Bye."

She hung up, feeling empty. It didn't matter how many words she threw at the situation—something had broken, and she wasn't sure how to fix it. She pulled out of his driveway and decided to stop by the coffee shop near his house, a spot they frequented when he was in town. She walked in and she ordered her usual triple chocolate mocha latte, trying to avoid the swirl of emotions that had been brewing all morning. When she turned around to find a seat, her breath caught in her throat.

"Darren?"

There he was, sitting casually with a cup of coffee in front of him —and across the table, another woman. Winter's heart skipped a beat, her stomach dropping.

Darren looked up, a faint smirk on his face as he met her eyes. "Winter? I'm surprised you recognized me."

Winter walked closer as she felt her blood start to boil. "What's this?"

Darren glanced at the woman and then back at Winter, shrugging. "This? This is me moving on with my life. Or did you not get the voicemail where I said that you clearly have more pressing things going on than this relationship, so it's best we go our separate ways?"

She swallowed hard, feeling the weight of his words crush her. "I told you—I don't check my voicemail."

"And I told you, I don't text. I call, like a grown-up. So that's not my problem." He stood up and excused himself from his would-be date. He stepped closer to Winter for privacy, who was clearly struggling to process it all.

"I'm not sure what was going on yesterday, but I don't want any part of that. I called you a couple of times to talk about it, and got nothing."

"Well, I haven't checked voicemail in a few days. There's a lot going on—"

"There's always a lot going on with you, Wyn, but none of it ever includes me," Darren said, pulling her outside of the coffee shop. He looked around, making sure no one was listening, before continuing. "Listen, you're a great person. We both know that, but I need someone I can build a life with. Not someone who has to find time to fit me into theirs. I wish you the best, but I know what I want, and I can't spend any more time wondering if you want the same."

Winter's head spun. "This is... unreal. Who is that chick?"

"Save me your fake moral outrage," Darren said, stepping closer. "If you must know, she's someone I met on a dating site I recently joined."

Winter's heart raced. "So just like that, you're done?"

"Done with what exactly, Winter? What do we actually have? I can't believe—You want to get into this now? After months of this cat-and-mouse game? After weeks of me asking to talk about the distance I've been feeling?" He paused, his voice sharp. "*Now* you have time?"

Winter's throat tightened. "No, I don't have time, but I'm willing to make time. For you. Because you're important."

Darren's gaze softened slightly, but only for a second. "And that's the rub. I'm sorry, Winter, but time is the one thing I no longer have."

He turned to leave, but Winter grabbed his arm. "Darren, if you'd just—"

"Just what, Wyn? What's going to change?" Darren looked deep into her eyes, waiting for her answer. But she had nothing to say—because she didn't know how to change things. Not with Miri, not with the bakery, not with Christina missing in action, and Darren knew it.

He nodded, hurt in his eyes. "That's what I thought. Listen, I'm not a priority to you, and that's not okay anymore. I'm not into sharing women with their basketball buddy."

Winter's face twisted in confusion. "What? Are you talking about Jae? What does he have to do with any of this?"

Darren scoffed, his tone cold. "More than you'll ever admit. He comes before me, before any man that could ever walk into your life. Hell, maybe even before Malik."

"That's a lie, and you know it!" Winter fired back, feeling the sting of his accusation.

Darren looked her dead in the eyes, his voice low. "If you were given an ultimatum today that you had to live without me or him, tell me you'd choose me, and I'll stay."

Winter froze, the words caught in her by surprise. She wanted to respond but her voice betrayed her. She couldn't answer.

The hesitation was enough for Darren. He shook his head, backing away. "Have a nice life, Wyn."

Winter watched him walk back inside, feeling brokenhearted and humiliated. She imagined storming in after him, throwing her drink in his face—but that wouldn't fix anything.

Instead, she walked back to her car, simmering in the pain of rejection.

"Fuck that."

She drove back to his house and picked up the cheesecake she'd left on his doorstep. She turned around and drove back to the coffee shop, spotting his car.

Winter picked up the cheesecake from the passenger seat, walked straight to Darren's car, and smashed it onto the windshield, smearing it everywhere until her frustration subsided.

"Now I feel better," she muttered under her breath, a laugh bubbling to the surface at her pettiness. She got back in her car and sped off just as he walked outside to find the mess.

She drove around aimlessly for a while, trying to clear her head, but her thoughts kept spinning. Darren had made it clear that he was done, and no amount of cheesecake or apologies could change that.

She glanced down at her phone. Christina still wasn't answering her calls either, and she didn't have the stamina for another fight.

Her thumb hovered over Jae's number. Maybe talking to him would help settle her nerves, bring some clarity.

She hit dial, and after two rings, Jae's voice came through, warm and familiar. "Hey, Short stack, what's up?"

The sound of his voice alone made her want to cry. "Jae..." Her words caught in her throat, and she fought back the wave of emotion rising in her chest.

"Whoa, hey, what's going on?" Jae's voice was suddenly serious, concern evident in every word.

Winter let out a shaky breath, wiping at her eyes. "I just—I can't believe it. Darren broke up with me, Jae. Just like that. I tried talking to him, tried to fix things, but... he's already moved on. He said I was never there for him, that I always put everything before him."

Jae was silent for a moment, then said, "He actually said that?"

"Yeah." Winter bit her lip, trying to hold back another wave of tears. "And then he threw you in my face, like somehow, you're the reason we didn't work out. He thinks I care more about you than I do about him."

Jae let out a soft sigh. "Wyn, you know that's not true. I mean, not the way he meant it, I'm your friend. Darren just couldn't handle the fact that you have a life outside of him. That's on him, not you."

"But maybe he's right," Winter whispered. "I've been so caught up with Miri, the bakery, the restaurant, and everything else... maybe I didn't give him enough. Maybe I don't know how to love someone the way I'm supposed to."

"Hey, don't do that," Jae said firmly. "Don't blame yourself for this. Darren didn't make you a priority either. If he had, you wouldn't be feeling like this right now. And trust me, you know how to love, Wyn. You've just been trying to balance a thousand things at once."

Winter sniffled, feeling a bit of relief in his words. "I just don't know how to do this anymore, Jae. Love, I mean. Since Leek died, it feels impossible. I want to feel passion again, to feel alive, but every time I try, I end up feeling like this."

"You'll find it, Winter," Jae said softly. "I know you will. And you've got Miri and me. I'm not going anywhere."

She smiled despite herself, grateful for the steadiness he always brought. "Thanks, Jae. I don't know what I'd do without you."

"You'd survive, Short stack," he teased. "But I'm glad you don't have to."

They talked for a few more minutes, his voice easing the weight on her chest. But as she pulled into the driveway of her home, that familiar heaviness crept back in. The house felt like a refuge and a prison all at once.

"Alright, I'm home. I'll talk to you later, Jae."

"You know where to find me. Double up." he said before they hung up.

Winter climbed out of the car, hoping to leave the tension of the day behind her. But as soon as she opened the door and walked into the house, something felt wrong. The air was too still, too quiet.

She opened the door, dropped her keys on the table, and made her way up the stairs, freezing when she reached the top.

Miri's door was ajar, and from the hallway, Winter saw something that made her heart stop. Miri was on the bed, making out with a boy, his hands under her shirt. They were far beyond where they should've been—second-base territory—and Winter's blood boiled. It was Clinton, the boy from the other night.

She kicked in the door.

"What the hell are you two doing?!" she shouted, storming into the room.

The boy hopped up, which only made Winter more uncomfortable, as his erection was pushing against his pants.

He scrambled to find his shirt. "Mrs. Carter, I'm—"

"If you don't want me to grab my cooking knives and chop off that thing you're trying to put in my daughter, I suggest you get the hell out of my house right now." Winter then turned to Miracle, who was still making sure she was presentable.

"Mom!"

She glared at her daughter, who was still scrambling to put on her shirt properly. "Girl, if you don't shut your mouth right now, I'm gonna ruin $8,000 of dental work."

Clinton was still buttoning his pants. "I—uh—I'll go," he stammered, grabbing his shoes and making a run for the door.

Winter scowled at him as he left, then turned her furious gaze to her daughter.

"Mom what are you doing here?" she responded nervously.

Winter cocked her head. "Is that all you have to say?"

"Nothing happened."

"Well, from the looks of things, that was about to change shortly."

"You were supposed to be on at work."

"I was coming home to see if you wanted to come with me to fill your prescription, but now I see the only remedies you were interested in is some vitamin D."

"We weren't gonna have sex."

"Then why were your titties hanging out?"

"Oh, I don't know, Mom. Because I like boys?"

"Little girl, now is not the time to play with me. What the hell were you thinking?" Winter screamed, her voice shaking with rage.

Miri jumped up, her face flushed with embarrassment. "Mom, you're overreacting. It's not what you think—"

"Not what I think? I walk in here, and your titties are out. I'd say it's exactly what I think."

"Fine. So what? It's natural to want to have sex, and before you say you don't, just know these walls are thinner than you think. I know you're the real reason we keep running out of batteries."

The words caught Winter off guard. Perhaps Miri wasn't as innocent as she'd thought.

She was going to fire back but caught herself. "You know what. I'm going to calm down, and I need you to do so too, because I don't want you to have an atta—"

"See, there it is right there."

"Miri—"

"I'm one of the best athletes in the history of Texas sports, and you won't even get upset when clearly, I was wrong. I don't need your pity, Mom."

"So what? Do you want me to strangle you? Because I'll do it."

"I want you to do something, anything, to make me feel like an actual kid, instead of one of your soufflés." Winter shook her head confused by her daughter's response.

"What is going on with you, Miri?"

Miri's eyes filled with tears, her voice shaking. "I just... I'm tired,

Mom. I'm tired of you treating me like I'm fragile! You're always on my back about my health, about everything. I'm not Dad!"

Winter's heart clenched, the mention of Miri's father hitting her like a punch to the gut. "Miri... I'm just trying to protect you. You don't understand how dangerous this could be."

"No, you don't understand!" Miri cut her off, her voice rising. "You think you know more than me because you're an adult, but you don't. You're perfectly healthy, so that's how you see the world. You have no idea what it's like to be in constant pain and to know that, no matter what you do, one day something will happen that there's nothing you can do about."

"Baby!"

"You think I don't know? Dad was 26 when he died, and I'm 16. I'm always in pain, Mom. Always! And the worst part is, even on my best days, I know already how my life ends. I bust my ass in the gym, and I'm dead tired every day, because if I don't, the disease gains ground. I'm always in pain because I'm fighting for my life. You're not. So, with whatever time I have, I want to live! I don't want to be a shut-in like you, hovering over me, reminding me every day that something's wrong with me! Running your stupid little bakery! That's *your* life, not mine."

It happened in an instant.

There was no thought behind it, just a reflex.

Winter slapped her daughter across the cheek.

The remorse kicked in immediately, and she tried to console her daughter, but Miri held her cheek and shrugged away from her mother.

"Well at least now you know I'm not fragile."

Winter's breath caught, her chest tightening with every word. "Miri, I'm not trying to keep you from living. I just... I don't want to lose you."

Miri's face hardened. "Well, guess what? You're suffocating me. That's the real reason why I don't want to go to U of H. And that's the real reason I won't apply. I want to get as far away from you as possible."

The words hit Winter like a sledgehammer, knocking the wind out of her. "Miri... don't say that."

Miri's eyes were blazing, her voice cold. "It's the truth, Mom. I need space. I need to breathe. And I can't do that here with you watching my every move."

Winter stood there, frozen, as her daughter's words echoed in her mind. She watched Miri storm out of the room, the sound of her footsteps reverberating down the stairs.

Winter sat down on the edge of the bed, her heart shattered into a million pieces.

She had lost control of everything—her daughter, her relationship, her best friend. Everything was slipping through her fingers, and she didn't know how to hold on anymore.

Tears filled her eyes, but this time, she didn't try to stop them.

15

BENCH WARMER

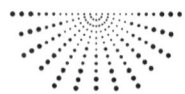

*W*inter's house felt unusually quiet—empty, even. Since the blow-up with Miri, everything had gone cold. Miri was staying with Jae for the rest of the holiday break, hoping to clear her mind before the big game against Shasha Wilcox's team. Winter knew Miri needed space, but it didn't make the silence any easier to bear.

Denise had also left, claiming she needed to visit her sister in Dallas. But Winter suspected it was more about escaping her daughter's relentless stress and mess.

Winter had tried to focus on the bakery's orders, but once she'd returned to her empty house, her thoughts drifted back to the argument with Miri. The words Miri had shouted still stung: "I want to get as far away from you as possible."

Everyone is tired of me, she thought bitterly.

She was moping when the doorbell rang. She got up to answer it, hoping it was one of the many people she'd rubbed the wrong way.

"Oh, it's you, Jae. Come on in." Winter slouched back to the couch.

"Woman, have you even bathed?" Jae said as he looked around. Her place was far more disheveled than normal.

Winter fired back. "Yes, I took a shower."

"Is that all you've done?"

"Where is my daughter?"

"She's with Clinton. I figured those two could use some privacy, so I got them a room."

Winter picked up a pillow and threw it at Jae, who began to chuckle. "That's not funny, Jae."

"Relax, Short stack. I got eyes on her. She's at agility training, and when she gets home, I've given Esme her holiday bonus early to keep an eye on her."

"Is she ready to come home?"

Jae was silent, confirming what Winter already knew. She buried her face in her palms.

Suddenly, she felt a pillow hit her in the head. "We're not doing that. Get dressed, we're going shopping."

"Jae, I don't—"

"Wasn't a question, Short stack. You got fifteen minutes to get dressed, or I'm carrying you out of here in your pjs. You got a restaurant to open. Now get up."

Winter wanted to remain reluctant, but she knew when Jae made his mind up, he was relentless, so she finally agreed. Soon enough, they were walking through the Galleria shopping district, stopping at various kitchenware stores to pick up supplies for the new restaurant.

Winter trailed behind Jae, half-heartedly pushing the cart as they navigated through the kitchenware store. Jae was on a mission, picking up items and dropping them in the cart with a decisiveness Winter wished she had right now.

She picked up a heavy stainless-steel pan, inspected it briefly, and then set it back down.

"You really gonna pass on that one, Short stack?" Jae teased, his voice light but his eyes attentive.

Winter shrugged. "I don't know. I mean, I want the best stuff for the restaurant, but I don't know why I'm even doing this. Everything feels so forced right now. Miri doesn't want to talk to me, Christina's gone, Darren's... you know. And now my mom's probably sitting on a beach somewhere, relieved to be away from me."

"I can relate to them. I've only been with you for an hour, and I want to get away from you."

Winter stopped, blinking in surprise. "Wait, what?"

"Well, you want to play your sad song, and since you're on the violin, I figured I'd hop on the drums and add a little rhythm." Jae smirked, enjoying her shock. "Seriously, Short stack, you're having a major pity party right now. I thought you were the one who never backed down."

Winter's lips twitched, a reluctant smile breaking through. "You're really an asshole, you know that?"

Jae grinned. "Now that's the fight you need. Remember how fearless you were back in college? On the quad, handing out flyers for that bake sale you threw together overnight? You had this fire in you, Wyn."

She looked away, feeling a mix of nostalgia and regret. "I guess I've lost that part of me."

"No," Jae said firmly. "It's still there. You always knew the bakery was just the start of your empire. You've always wanted more. That's why you're opening this restaurant," Jae said, tossing in a set of cutting boards. "You're doing this for your dad, right? This restaurant was always the endgame for you, not just the bakery. You owe it to yourself—and to him—to see it through."

Winter paused, letting his words sink in. "Yeah, it was always about Daddy. Every time I cook, I feel like I'm honoring him. But it's hard to stay motivated when everything else is falling apart."

Jae stopped and looked at her, a seriousness in his eyes. "I get that, but you've got to keep moving forward. This is bigger than just you. It's for him, for Miri... for your dream."

She nodded slowly, feeling a familiar ache in her chest. "I just wish Miri was excited about it. I thought opening this restaurant would inspire her, show her that no matter what, we keep fighting."

Jae grabbed a fancy set of steak knives and turned to her. "Miri's got her own battles, but she'll come around. Right now, she's trying to prove something to herself. You know how you were in college, hustling to raise money for your culinary classes? That same fire is in Miri—it's just pointed at basketball."

Winter smiled wistfully. "I guess you're right. I was pretty unstoppable back then, wasn't I?"

Jae grinned. "You were a force of nature. I still remember you hustling to sell cookies outside the library, wearing that ridiculous apron over your sorority hoodie."

"Oh God, I forgot about that apron," Winter laughed, feeling a hint of her old self returning. "I still have it, buried in my closet somewhere."

"And you should wear it on opening day," Jae said, playfully nudging her. "Get back to that fearless girl on the quad. She's still in there. You've just got to let her out."

She chuckled, finally letting herself feel a spark of hope. "You're right. I can do this."

"Damn right you can. One problem at a time," Jae replied. "And after the big game, you and Miri are going to patch things up. We're having a family night at my place. Old '80s movies, no cooking allowed, just plenty of takeout. I'm talking *Coming to America, The Last Dragon*, the whole nine yards. It's the perfect way to patch things up with Miri."

Winter's eyes brightened. "That's a good idea, Jae. She loves those movies, even though she pretends not to."

"See? I told you, I'm basically Uncle Phil in this situation," Jae joked. "I'm gonna make sure we all work this out, one way or another."

Winter's smile widened. "I don't know what I'd do without you."

He gave her a warm, lingering look. "You'll never have to find out."

"Double up."

They exchanged their high five and continued shopping. Winter felt a renewed sense of purpose. Jae's steady presence was pulling her out of her funk, as always.

Just as they were wrapping up, Jae turned to her with a sly smile. "Oh, by the way," he said, as if it were an afterthought, "I put your name in for the alumni New Year's Eve dinner gig."

Winter's eyes widened. "You did *what?*"

Jae's grin widened. "You got it unanimously. I figured it'd be the perfect way to kick off the new restaurant, so that's why I dragged you out shopping today."

She stared at him, disbelief and excitement warring in her expression. "Jae, this is huge! Why didn't you tell me sooner?"

"Because you weren't in the right headspace," he said simply. "But now you are. I wanted you to be pumped for this. It's your moment, Short stack."

She felt a rush of joy, a sudden surge of energy. "Thank you, Jae. This could be exactly what I need to make this happen."

"That's the spirit," Jae said, giving her another Double up. "Now let's pay for all this and get out of here."

WINTER AND JAE carried their bags into the bakery, laughing and joking about their wild college days. It felt like old times—a welcome break from the stress of the past few weeks. A knock on the front door, despite the bakery being closed, interrupted them. Winter cracked the door open a few inches.

"Ms. Carter?" the man asked.

Winter nodded, unsure of why he was asking for her. "Yes?"

"I'm Henry Adams, the agent for the property owner of the building you were considering for your restaurant," he said, offering a business card.

Winter felt her heart skip a beat. "Oh, yes! Is there an update? I was just about to finalize everything."

The man's face tensed slightly. "Well, that's what I'm here to discuss. Unfortunately, the space next to your bakery is no longer available."

Jae's eyes narrowed, but Winter's heart dropped. "What do you mean? I thought everything was ready for me to sign."

Henry looked uncomfortable. "I understand, but the lease was signed by another party two days ago."

"Two days ago?" Winter echoed, suspicion beginning to sink in.

"Who... who signed it?"

Henry hesitated. "I'm not at liberty to disclose that information, but I thought you should know as soon as possible."

Winter felt the world spinning around her. "I don't understand. I was literally about to sign the paperwork. I was just waiting to get some things in order."

"I'm truly sorry, Ms. Carter," Henry said, looking genuinely regretful. "My client is a fan of Smoke, I mean Mr. Carter and wanted to hold out but couldn't wait. There were no guarantees without the paperwork, and someone else came prepared."

Winter's legs felt shaky, and she had to steady herself. "This was supposed to be my expansion," she murmured, more to herself than to anyone else.

Jae stepped in, his voice tight with frustration. "There must be some kind of solution. Is there another property nearby?"

Henry shook his head. "Not one with the same specs or location. I'm afraid this was the prime spot."

Winter's eyes filled with tears. "But this was for my dad. It was everything."

Henry looked genuinely remorseful. "I'm sorry, Ms. Carter. I wish there was more I could do." He was about to walk out of the door when he stopped.

"One important note. Mr. Armand, the original owner, only sent out one listing with the paperwork. That was to you. That's the paperwork he got back."

"I don't under—"

Her eyes widened.

There was only one person who could have signed the paperwork.

The person she asked to look over it. The person who'd been avoiding her for a week.

"Are you telling me that Christina Washington is the new owner of that location?"

"I've said all I'm legally allowed to say. But if I were you, I'd give her a call."

As he walked away, Winter stood still, her face pale.

Jae gently placed a hand on her shoulder, pulling her closer. "It's okay, Short stack. We'll figure something out."

She shook her head, her voice choked with emotion. "No, it's not okay, Jae. This was my one chance, my dream, and I let it slip away. I can't believe I messed up this badly."

Jae pulled her into a tight hug, his voice steady. "You didn't mess up. You're trying to do everything all at once—be a mom, run the bakery, have a life. This is just a setback."

Winter leaned into his embrace, feeling the warmth and reassurance she desperately needed. "But it's such a big setback, Jae. How am I supposed to come back from this?"

He pulled back, cupping her face gently. "Because you're Winter Carter, and you don't give up. You didn't then, and you won't now."

Jae wrapped an arm around her shoulders, trying to comfort her. "We'll figure this out, Short stack. We always do."

But Winter wasn't sure she could this time. As she stood there, surrounded by the tools of her father's legacy, she felt more lost than ever.

16

REBOUND

*J*ae and Miri sat on the bench outside the gym, waiting for her practice to start. Miri was restless, tapping her foot and shifting her weight like she was ready to run onto the court right then.

"She's suffocating me, Jae. She's just unbearable," Miri groaned, her frustration spilling out. "Mom doesn't trust me to make my own decisions. It's like everything I do is wrong."

Jae nodded, giving her space to vent. "I get it. There's no question your mom's been on edge. I haven't seen her like this since, well…"

"Losing Dad?"

Jae nodded at he sipped the bottled water. "Not yours, but hers."

"She never talks about Grandpa. No one does."

"I think because it's hard for her to open that door."

Miri sat silently then looked at her uncle. "Do you know what happened?"

"I do, but it's not my business to tell."

She looked at him insistently. "Please, Uncle Jae. Everyone treats me like a kid but you. I'm old enough to know what goes on in my family."

Jae took a deep breath and smirked. "You know I can't say no to those dimples."

"It's an unfair advantage I'm this cute, I know. So are you going to tell me or not?"

Jae stood up and paced for a second, Miri following close behind. He turned and snatched the basketball out of her hand. "Okay, I'll tell you."

"Yes! See that's why you're the coolest, Unc," she said, pointing at him exaggeratedly.

"But two conditions. One, you can never, ever tell your mother I told you."

"That's fair. And the second?"

"You make peace with your mom after the game."

"Oh, come on, Uncle Jae, that's not—"

"Those are the conditions. Take 'em or leave 'em, kid."

Miri considered quietly for a second, and then said, "Deal."

Her eagerness was a tell. Jae shook his head. "Nope I don't believe you."

"What? Uncle Jae, come on."

"Nope, you got the same look on you, the same one when you're lying." He reached his hand out. "Secret handshake."

"Are you ser—"

"Miri, I need to know you will not say a word to anyone. Just like that time I didn't say a word about who broke that window."

Miracle chuckled and sighed. "Okay, okay. You were pretty clutch that day. She still thinks it was the neighbors' kids with the soccer ball."

"Exactly my point. So we got a deal?"

Miri nodded in agreement. "Deal."

The pair exchanged their secret handshake that not even Winter knew about.

After the complex ritual, Jae spoke. "Talking about your grandpa isn't an easy subject for your mom. We had a few classes together freshman year, back when I was going to class, and apparently your grandpa had just saved up enough money to open his restaurant, which was a big deal considering he had a few kids in school and he worked as much as he did."

Jae paused, hesitant to continue.

"Uncle Jae?"

"Right. So, his last night working, the building next door caught on fire. Your grandpa ran into the burning building to save a woman and her kids."

"Wait... so he was burned alive?"

"No, he made it out, but died of smoke inhalation about an hour later. Wyn was devastated, but you know your mom. Instead of dealing with it, she spent that summer cooking, and then she changed her major from sports medicine to culinary arts. The rest is history."

Miracle gasped as she processed Jae's words. The story was heavy, and he knew it.

He continued. "All that to say, when it comes to you, she's just worried, and rightfully so, Miri. You've been through a lot, not even counting the autoimmune stuff."

"Yeah, but she's treating me like I'm gonna break at any moment. My dad was your brother, and you've never treated me like that."

"That's because I know you're made of tough stuff. She's never had to guard you on the court."

The two chuckled for a spell.

Miri retorted, her voice taking on a melodramatic tone. "I know Mom has had a lot of trauma, but that's her life. I gotta live mine, and... I just can't live like this, Unc. I need to breathe."

Jae put an arm around her shoulders, pulling her into a side hug. "Look, I know she can be overprotective, but it's only because she cares about you more than anything else. She's scared of losing you, the same way she lost your dad... and quite honestly hers."

Miri's eyes softened for a moment, but she quickly brushed it off. "Yeah, well, I'm not either of them. Like you just said, I'm tougher than that."

Jae smiled. "I know that. But I don't care how tough you are, kid, you were wrong for the other day. It's still your mom's house, and there's gotta be a level of respect. The situation with Clinton? Not the best move. You've got to understand where she's coming from."

Miri rolled her eyes. "I know, I know. It was stupid, and it wasn't supposed to go that far, I swear. But I'm sixteen; I'm gonna mess up sometimes."

Jae chuckled. "That's true, Cupcake. But maybe next time, keep it PG-13."

She snorted, half-amused. "Fine. Honestly, you don't have nothin' to worry about. My mind is on the court. I'm fuckin up—I mean, messin up—the Mighty Jack Yates Lions." She said in air quotes.

"Ah, yes... Shasha Wilcox's team."

"I want to embarrass her, Unc, for trying to mess up my chances with UConn."

"Don't do that, Miri," Jae warned, his voice taking on a serious tone. "You don't need to prove yourself against her. You just need to play your game. Don't let her get in your head."

"Easier said than done," Miri muttered. "If I don't put up at least twenty-nine points, I don't get the record, and they have some serious defenders. I want to break the record, though. I need this. I need to show the world."

"I get that," Jae nodded. "But pace yourself. You're on the verge of something great, and you can't let your ego get in the way. Let the game come to you."

Miri sighed, taking his words in. "You're right. I just... I wish it wasn't so complicated."

"That's life, kid," Jae said with a small smile. "But remember, the family's rooting for you. After the game, we're all gonna hang out, watch some old '80s movies, and eat junk food. You, me, and your mom. We're going to work this out."

Miri hesitated, then nodded. "Okay, okay. I'm in."

Just then, a passerby called out from across the street. "Hey! Choke Carter! You're a bum!"

Jae's face remained neutral, but Miri's eyes flashed with anger. "What did you say? Your momma's a bum!" she yelled back, ready to confront the heckler.

Jae grabbed her arm gently. "Let it go, Miri."

"But Unc—"

"Let it go."

Miri took a breath, and after a spell, she said, "Doesn't that bother you? You're a Hall of Famer." she asked, her frustration palpable.

"It used to," Jae admitted. "But not anymore. See, Cupcake, you're about to find out something very important: people only remember the mistakes. They forget everything else."

Miri looked at him thoughtfully. "You've been through a lot, haven't you? With my dad, the injuries, everything."

Jae's face softened. "Yeah, I have."

"I understand why you came back to Houston… but why didn't you get out of here? They don't appreciate you."

"Not everybody is like that guy."

"But Jae, you turned down millions of dollars. That last contract the Knicks offered you was at least 100 million more than what the Rockets offered you. Why did you stay?"

"Because money isn't everything. I was able to watch you grow up and help you become a better baller than I ever was. You can't put a price on that. I'm right where I need to be. Staying here wasn't a sacrifice—it was a choice. You, your mom, all of this… it matters."

Miri smiled, and for the first time that day, her shoulders relaxed. "We're lucky to have you, Uncle Jae."

Jae grinned. "Right back at ya, Cupcake. Now, go make us proud."

"Oh, don't worry, I'm about to break off Shasha Wilcox. What are you about to do?"

"I have a lunch date."

"Oh! Snap. Uncle Jae 'bout to get a little action off the court, huh?"

Jae laughed. "You need to stay out of grown folks' business. Go practice. Love you, kiddo."

The two exchanged a hug and Jae left.

The drive wasn't long. He tried to call Winter, but she wasn't available. It wasn't long before he arrived at Le Colonial, an exclusive restaurant in the River Oaks area of Houston.

Jae walked in and sat at a private table, checking his watch. His date was always pretty punctual.

He was approached by a group of men, signed a few autographs for some fans, and had a mojito as they talked about the upcoming season.

It wasn't long before the woman he was waiting on walked into the restaurant.

Christina looked both wary and curious. Jae stood up and greeted her with a hug, which she held on to longer than he cared for. Still, he went with it as she pressed her chest against him and gazed at him seductively. He released her and pulled out her chair politely. "Hey, Christina. Have a seat."

Christina took a moment to scan the room, noticing the suited men at the adjacent table. Jae introduced them casually. "This is Bob, Rick, Mike, and James. They were just leaving."

All the men shook her hand and then got up and walked away.

No sooner than they left did a waiter come out with several appetizers that he'd ordered. The candlelight flickered, bouncing off her deeply melanated skin. He could tell her guard was up, so he decided to soften her.

He leaned in and said, "You look amazing, Christina."

"Thank you. You smell wonderful."

"I appreciate that. I'm glad you're here," Jae said softly.

Christina's eyes narrowed. "I gotta admit, I was surprised to get a call from you."

"And why's that?"

She rolled her eyes and scoffed. "Boy stop, I'm sure you know about this thing with me and Wyn."

Jae leaned forward and gently grabbed both her hands. "The way I see it, what y'all do on your time is your business. What we do on our time together is *our* business."

Christina smiled from ear to ear as she responded. "You know, I kinda thought we had some chemistry the other day, I just didn't know how things would work out with us since me and Wyn are on the outs."

"I could feel that. Why did it go down that way?"

A palpable tension crept onto Christina's face.

He leaned in and gave her a once over. In a low, seductive voice, said, "I think we both know why I called."

Christina's defense fell as she smiled and leaned in. "I'm feeling you, Jae."

"Look, we both know Wyn has her ways. I don't want to add insult to injury if you start coming around in the next few weeks."

Christina nodded as she held his hand briefly, then leaned back. "It was time. After the way she treated me—and not just that day, but in general, sometimes you just gotta know your own worth, you know?"

"True. So you'd been feeling this way for a while?"

"I guess…What's this about, Jae? I thought you were here to talk about seeing where this can lead."

Jae leaned forward, his tone direct. "I lied, I'm sure it's not the first time a man has done that to you. I invited you here to give you a chance to do the right thing."

Christina scoffed. "I can't believe I fell for this shit."

"Chasing dollars and not using sense is always a bad move."

"I'm out of here."

Before she could move, Jaden pulled out a blue folder. "That would be a mistake."

Christina paused, and he sat the folder on the table. "And what's the right thing, exactly?"

"To give Winter back what belongs to her."

"You mean, what belongs to me?"

"I got that paperwork for Wyn. You took that paperwork and signed it without her knowledge. We both know this."

"All's fair in love and business. This was business."

"And so is this." He slid over the folder that his lawyer had drawn up. "Here's a new agreement where you sign the property over to its rightful owner, Winter Carter."

Christina raised an eyebrow. "Ain't this a bitch. And if I don't sign?"

Jae's expression remained calm, then leaned in closer. "You

remember those men I introduced you to earlier? They're old friends of mine. Bob is one of the top civil attorneys in the country. In fact, he's the one who drafted this up for me. His biggest rival is Rick, next to him. Mike's firm tracks digital footprints and forensics of companies, and James is a former police chief who now heads the biggest investigative firm in the state."

Christina's eyes flicked to the men around the room, then back to Jae. "So, what? You brought muscle to intimidate me?"

Jae shook his head. "No, Christina. We're here to play golf, but it's important for you to let you know exactly what you're up against. That file you're holding could have all your personal records, your shopping habits, your health information, your creditors, basically anything and everything I want to know about you. I settled on this form. The people in this room keep this city running—both the parts you see and the parts you don't. I called you here as a courtesy, but don't think for a second that I won't use every resource I have to protect the people I care about."

Christina started to gather her things, ready to leave. "Respectfully, Jaden, my business with Winter ain't got shit to do with you. Now, unless you're trying to run me some dick, we ain't got much else to talk about."

But before she could leave, Jae's voice turned cold. "Christina, sit your ass down. Now."

The command in his voice was undeniable. Christina froze, then slowly returned to her seat.

"You're sitting with some of the most powerful men in Houston," Jae continued, his voice low but intense. "You were invited here, by me. Don't mistake my calm demeanor for weakness. I'm a big fucking deal in this city, and you? Well, you're a small fish that's wandered into the ocean." He leaned closer, his eyes locked onto hers. "I'm giving you a chance to swim back to your pond before I send the sharks."

Christina's face blanched, her confidence faltering for the first time. "What do you want, Jae?"

"I told you what I want. Sign the property over to Winter at cost,"

Jae said firmly. "I'll even sweeten the pot by twenty percent. That should be enough to start your business, and you won't need to interfere with hers ever again."

Christina opened her mouth to argue, but Jae cut her off. "And before you think about stalling, understand this: that dick you keep talking about? I'll tell you, it's not as big as my bank account. I could tie you up in court for years. So, sign it now, or anytime between now and the next time, I meet with these gentlemen. Your choice."

Just then, Carlie, the mayor's assistant, approached the table. "Mr. Carter, the mayor's ready for you."

Jae nodded and stood up, looking down at Christina one last time. "Gotta run, Christina. I've got a golf game to win and a campaign contribution to discuss. Try to get off Fuck Around Lane, before you get to Find Out Avenue. You don't want to go there."

He turned to walk away, leaving Christina to process the gravity of the situation, before turning back briefly. "You don't have to sign today. Enjoy the lunch. They have a grilled shrimp pasta that's from the heavens. I've already taken care of the bill. Now, if you'll excuse me, my boys and I are about to go kick the mayor's ass."

The message was clear. Although he was about to play an 18-hole game of golf, when it comes to Winter and her business, Jae wasn't playing games.

17

DOUBLE DRIBBLE

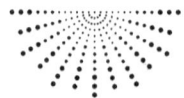

*J*ae pulled up to Winter's house, honking twice. Miri was already sitting in the back seat, earbuds in, preparing for the big game. She was determined, focused, and ready to take on Shasha Wilcox's team. They sat as the heater warded them from Houston's latest cold front.

"I can't believe it's this cold."

"Oh, this is basketball weather!" Jae said with excitement. "I used to say, when it's this cold, that's when the real ballers heat up."

"Facts. I can't wait to get out there and bust that heffa's ass—"

"Language."

"My bad. I'm just excited."

"I know, I'm not trippin', but your momma will be."

"You right. Let me reel it in now."

He hit the horn again. Still there was no sign of Winter. "I can't believe they got you playing two days before Christmas." Jae said.

"I know. It's fate. I get my gift early; my name in the state record, and giving that hoe a big fat L right in time for the holidays."

Jae turned around and glared at his niece.

"What?"

"I just said *language.*"

"No, I meant the garden tool."

He shook his head with a smirk and turned back around. "You got one more game to get the record in. Just play to win. The record will come."

"I hear you… but it would be sweet if we blow them out."

"You got the team to do that with. Where is your mother?" He hit the horn again.

"We're gonna be late, Uncle Jae."

"We're not leaving your mom, Miri."

"Then she needs to hurry up."

At that moment, Winter appeared at the door, smiling widely. "Hey, y'all!" she called out, practically skipping toward the car. She flung the back door open and plopped down with exaggerated enthusiasm, pulling Miri into an unexpected hug.

"Oh, my baby! My Miri! I've missed you soooo much!" Winter exclaimed, holding her daughter tight.

Miri wriggled in her mother's arms. "Mom! Let go! We gotta go, now!"

"Where's Ms. Denise? She's not coming?" Jae interjected.

Winter shrugged. "She's stuck in Dallas at her favorite kids' house. I guess I was working her nerves."

"Looks like it's just us. Can we leave now, please?" Miri said, slightly annoyed.

Jae nodded and put the car in drive. He watched from the driver's seat, he dimmed his eyebrows.

Something was off with Winter—way off. Her movements were a little too loose, her eyes slightly glazed, and her grin unusually wide.

Winter finally released Miri and leaned forward between the seats, her voice a bit too chipper. "So, how're my two favorite people in the world? We're gonna kick some serious ass today, aren't we?" she said, leaning to the side to ruffle Miri's hair. "Are we ready for this, or *what*?"

Miri pulled back in disgust. "Mom, what are you doing? Stop!"

Winter laughed, seemingly unbothered. "I'm just excited, honey! It's game day! Big, big game day!"

Miri gave her mom a puzzled look but shrugged it off, chalking it up to Winter being overly enthusiastic. As Jae started driving, Winter kept talking—about everything and nothing—her voice oddly cheerful and words a bit too drawn out.

"Jae, I was thinking, maybe after the game, we could go get ice cream or something. It's been *forever* since we had a family outing," Winter said, giggling at her own suggestion.

Miri glanced back, raising an eyebrow. "Mom, you're acting weird."

"Am I? I'm just happy! Can't I be happy for my baby about to dunk the ball on her nemesis Shasha's face?" Winter asked, her smile almost unnaturally wide.

"I guess..."

Winter pulled her daughter in closer. "Listen, when you get the ball, I want you to dunk it in that little hoe's face."

Miri looked at her uncle. "So, she gets to say it?"

"I... just want to get to the game." He was starting to worry about what was going on with his best friend.

Jae kept his eyes on the road, keeping an eye on Winter through the rearview mirror. He knew something wasn't right, but Miri didn't seem to notice; she was too focused on the game.

As they arrived at the gym, the parking lot was already buzzing with fans and players. Miri grabbed her bag, opened the door, and hopped out. "I'll see you guys after warm-ups," she called, closing the door behind her.

As soon as Miri was out of earshot, Jae turned to Winter, his voice low and firm. "Okay, Short stack, what the hell is going on?"

"What? I'm just—"

"You're high, aren't you?"

Winter's grin faded slightly, replaced by a guilty look. "Maybe a little. I had an edible this morning."

"You can't be serious."

"No, Jae, I'm not serious, I'm *high*. That's the point." She giggled at her own wit.

Jae's eyes widened in disbelief. "I'm not even going to touch the levels of hypocrisy you're standing on at this moment, since you were just on Miri's ass about this exact same thing. But how do you think you're gonna fare sitting in the gym for a whole game while stoned?"

"Well, you really gonna be mad at what I got in this cup, because I promise you it ain't water." She grinned as she pulled out a small pint of New Amsterdam vodka out of her purse .

Jae's eyes widened. "Wyn!"

"Boy, leave me alone. I'm pre-gaming," she said as she poured the vodka into her Stanley cup already filled with ice.

Jae fired back. "It's a high school basketball game. You're a mom. Any of this registering?"

Winter leaned back in the seat, her shoulders slumping. "Look, Jae, it's been a rough week, okay? I just needed a break from everything, even if it's for a few hours."

Jae ran a hand through his hair, frustration evident. "This isn't happening. You're gonna be passed out by halftime."

"Wrong again," Winter chuckled as she pulled out her mixer. "See, I figured if I add Red Bull to this, I'd stay awake."

"Ain't this bout a bit—"

He composed himself took a breath and softened his tone. "Listen Wyn, I know you're going through a lot, but you've got to pull it together, at least for the next few hours."

Winter took a deep breath, forcing a more sober expression. "Jae. I mean this with all sincerity: fuck that, I'm getting lit. Now, you can have some of this vodka or you can have several seats, but what you will not do today is kill my vibe. Oh, snap! That's what we need to be jamming right now. Alexa, play 'Bitch, Don't Kill My Vibe'!"

"There isn't even an Alexa—you know what, I'm going inside."

Jae got out of the car and opened the door.

"Jae, where are you going?"

"I'm gonna do what you should be doing: watching the game. Go ahead and get white-girl wasted."

He started to walk off, Winter trailing behind him. As the pair entered the gym, Winter began dancing to an imaginary song in her head, sipping on her mixed cocktail.

The atmosphere in the gym was electric. The bleachers were packed, and the tension was palpable as Miri's team prepared to face off against Shasha Wilcox and the Jack Yates Lions. Both teams were undefeated, and the stakes were high—this game would determine rankings for the playoffs. One of these teams was no longer going to be undefeated.

As the teams lined up for the tip-off, Shasha caught Miri's eye. "ESPN is here tonight. You ready to get embarrassed today, Carter?" she sneered, her voice low but cutting.

Miri's jaw clenched. "Fuck you," she whispered within earshot of Shasha, who smirked.

She glanced over at her uncle, who was sitting courtside, to see if he could read her lips. His glare in her direction indicated he could. She shrugged at him, at the same time noticing her mother dancing in her seat.

She's really acting weird... is she...? Nah.

She couldn't worry about that now. She couldn't be worried about anything. It was game time.

The referee tossed the ball, and the game was on. From the start, Shasha was relentless, sticking to Miri like glue. The trash talk continued every time they were close.

"You gonna shoot from there, Carter? Bet you miss."

Miri fired off a quick shot, hitting nothing but net. "Bet you shut up, it's about to be a long night for you, Suckcox—I mean, *Wilcox*." she retorted, her frustration building.

The game was evenly matched for a while. Miri heeded her uncle's words and played team ball, trying to ignore the constant berating from her rival.

She drove the lane for a layup only to get blocked by Shasha from behind. "You ain't got it, Carter. UConn my ass. This is my house! The only con out here is you."

"Trick, shut up and play ball."

It wasn't long before the game became a one-on-one showdown between Miri and Shasha, with Miri determined to outscore her rival. Every time Shasha scored, she'd taunt or bump Miri, frustrating her to the point where Miri started taking more shots, sometimes forcing them. A few went in, and the crowd would roar, but more than a few missed, leading to turnovers that hurt her team.

Shasha wasn't letting up with each mistake. "Damn, another brick, Carter? How's that record gonna feel if you lose?" she taunted.

Miri looked at her and threw an elbow to her ribs, hoping the ref didn't see it.

He did.

Chirrppp!

"Foul, on number 13."

"What? Are you kidding me? Come on ref, she's been jawing and fouling all night! Are you blind? Are you just on their payroll?" she yelled in frustration.

Chirrppp!

"Technical foul, number 13. One shot."

The crowd, predominately for the Jack Yates Lions, erupted. Miri's face was set in stone as she tried to block out the noise. The scoreboard was close, but Miri's actions cost her team three points as Shasha hit her two free throws and one technical shot. They were now down by four.

It didn't matter; she was determined to get those points back.

She hit the next open shot, only to be blocked the next time she went up the court. It didn't matter. She had 29 points and was tied with the state record any more it would be hers. Yet Miri wanted it all, she was determined to get the record *and* the game. She continued trying to force her way through the defense, ignoring her teammates' open looks.

Her desire to break the state record and show up Shasha was consuming her, throwing her off her usual game.

"What you gonna do, Baby Choke? Your uncle can't save you now. Not from this ass whoopin'."

She tuned out the opposition in her mind. It was her job to shut them up, and the state record would definitely do that.

With two minutes left, Miri hit a three-pointer from the corner, setting the new state scoring record. The crowd erupted in cheers, but the joy was short-lived.

Shasha's team took advantage of Miri's focus on individual glory, throwing a fast inbound pass to a wide open player on the other team who hit a three, negating her comeback. It was the heads up play that widened their lead. There was only a minute left now, and the Lions were in full control.

They played keep away for the next play, to run out the clock. Miri had won the individual battle but had lost the war.

The final buzzer sounded. Jack Yates Lions: 72, Houston Lady Nets: 68.

Miri stood there, hands on her knees, trying to catch her breath. She had broken the record, but the bitter taste of defeat was hard to swallow.

Shasha approached her, a smug grin on her face. "Congrats on the record," Shasha said. "I'll take being perfect, though. See you at state, if you don't... Choke."

Miri glared, but said nothing. She felt a mix of pride and disappointment, but slowly her uncle's words were settling in. Shasha had won, in more ways than one. She'd gotten in Miri's head, making her personal victory less fulfilling as she looked into the eyes of her frustrated teammates. The loss was hitting her harder than her achievement.

After the game, the coach made note to mention the selfish plays of the team. Miri knew it was directed at her.

She pulled it together for the post-game interview from ESPN, but the longer she stood on the court, the more she wanted to be anywhere else.

This was Shasha's moment, and Miri had gift-wrapped it for her with a bow.

As Miri exited the locker room, she looked at her mother who seemed to be a bit more solemn, but it was the gaze of her uncle that caught her eye. His expression said it all.

She headed toward them with her head low. "You don't have to say it, Unc, you told me it would happen. Coach told me, too. I'm sure the news is gonna tell me until playoffs. I screwed up."

They walked silently together to the car, where Jae finally spoke up. "I'm proud of you for breaking that record, that's special. Congratulations."

"Then why do I feel like crap?"

"Because you're a winner who just lost. Do you know *when* you lost this game?"

"Yeah, about ten minutes ago."

"Nope. You lost it when you got on that live. She was in your head and has been living there rent-free ever since."

Miri looked down, knowing what was coming.

"You were a ball hog tonight," Jae continued. "You let Shasha get in your head, and you put your own goals above the team's. That's not how you win."

Miri's eyes filled with tears. "I know, Uncle Jae. I just... I wanted to prove something to her. She made me feel like I wasn't good enough."

Jae softened, pulling her into a hug. "Miri, how many times do I have to tell you that you've got nothing to prove to anyone but yourself? You're beyond talented, and you've got heart. But basketball is a team game. There's no 'I' in team."

She nodded, her voice thick with emotion. "I know."

"Don't sweat it. You're gonna learn from this, and *when* you win the state title, and you get the scholarship to UConn, I'll get on the live and talk trash with you. We're getting back in the lab to make sure of it. It was close, but the world saw what I saw tonight. You're a miracle."

His words of encouragement forced a smile on her face despite how she was feeling. "Thanks, Unc."

"Always, feel better?"

"I'm getting there."

"Good," Jae said. "Now, let's get out of here. We've got some things to do."

As Jae drove, Winter, still giggly from the edible, realized he wasn't driving towards his home for their '80s movie. "Where are we going?" she asked, looking out the window.

"You'll see," Jae replied mysteriously.

They eventually pulled up to the bakery, and Jae led them around to the adjacent space—the one that Winter thought she'd lost to Christina.

Winter, who was quickly sobering up, was confused. "Why are we here, Jae?"

"Well... there's something you need to see."

He unlocked the door and the three of them walked in.

Winter's eyes widened as she stepped into a fully-furnished restaurant space. The décor was exactly how she'd imagined it—elegant yet welcoming, with warm colors and cozy booths. Through the double doors leading to the kitchen, she could see sleek, state-of-the-art equipment.

"I know you'd been having a rough go of things, and you won't admit it, but I know you were stressing because you didn't know what you were going to do about the alumni dinner. Well, now you don't have to worry about it." Jae announced, grinning from ear to ear.

Winter was speechless, tears welling up in her eyes. "Jae, how—when did you do all this? What about Christina?"

Jae looked proud. "I already told you, I'm on my Uncle Phil grind. I worked out a deal with her. She'll be around to sign over the paperwork by the end of the week."

"Jae, I don't know what to say."

"There's nothing to say. I didn't want you to lose your dream, so I made sure it happened."

Denise suddenly appeared from the kitchen, a big smile on her face. "I supervised, of course. Someone had to make sure he didn't mess up your vision."

Winter laughed, her voice cracking with emotion. "Momma! I thought you were stuck in Dallas."

Denise winked as she strutted closer to the trio. "Well, I might have told a little fib. But I figured this was worth it."

Winter hugged both Jae and Denise, overwhelmed by gratitude. "This is… too much… it's more than I ever dreamed of."

Jae put an arm around her shoulder as she wiped her tears. "You're back in the game, Short stack. We don't give up on our dreams around here."

He extended his hand. Winter smirked as they exchanged their Double up high five.

Denise looked amused. "I think I'll let you three have the rest of the evening. I'm feeling generous tonight—mostly because I've been having a blast spending Jae's money."

Winter grinned, both from her overwhelming joy and maybe a little from the edible. "Go ahead, Mom. We'll manage."

Denise waved them off playfully. "Go on. Enjoy your night."

As Winter, Miri, and Jae walked out, they felt a renewed sense of hope. The road ahead wasn't going to be easy, but with family by their side, they were ready to face it—together.

18

ISOLATION PLAY

*W*inter leaned back in Jae's passenger seat, watching the familiar streets pass by as they headed to his house. The game had been a whirlwind—Miri breaking the state scoring record, yet the sting of defeat still hung in the air. The drive was mostly quiet, filled with the kind of exhaustion that came after high stakes and emotional highs. But she couldn't get over the notion that Jae had put the restaurant together.

She turned to him and smiled. "You are such a dork, you know that?"

"Yeah, yeah. I feel the same way about you, Short stack," he teased as they pulled up.

As they stopped in Jae's driveway, Winter's eyes widened at the sight before her. She loved Jae's house, but it was never more vibrant than at Christmas time. She took in the stunning blend of modern and traditional architecture, sitting proudly at the end of a long, winding driveway lined with twinkling white lights.

"Red and white, huh?"

"Look, I played for the Cougars and the Rockets. What other colors are there?"

"You get no argument from me. The Delta in me will always love it."

The two chuckled.

A tall, elegant Christmas tree stood visible through the living room window, adorned with gold ribbons, silver ornaments, and a large star at the top. The porch was wrapped in festive garlands, with oversized nutcrackers standing guard at the front door.

"Wow, Jae, you really went all out this year," Winter said, a hint of awe in her voice.

He shrugged, smiling. "Esme did most of the work, honestly. I just pay the bills."

They all stepped inside, and the warmth of the house welcomed them instantly. The scent of cinnamon and pine filled the air, mingling with the faint sound of classic Christmas carols playing softly in the background. A roaring fire crackled in the fireplace, and the space was filled with cozy couches, thick rugs, and tasteful holiday décor.

Esmerelda, Jae's long-time housekeeper, appeared from the kitchen, wiping her hands on her apron. "Dinner's all set up, Mr. Carter," she said warmly.

"Thank you, Esme," Jae replied. "You can head out whenever you're ready. I'll take it from here."

Esmerelda nodded, giving Winter and Miri a warm smile before she left. "Enjoy your dinner, Ms. Carter. Miri, good game tonight?"

"I got the record. But we lost."

"Well, I'm sorry you lost, but congratulations on the record. Make sure this cheapskate pays you, *ya sabes como puede ser tu tio*," she said, looking at Jae.

"*Si, señora*," she replied. Jae rolled his eyes.

Winter, picking up on the conversation, turned her attention to Jae. "Y'all made another bet?"

Jae shrugged and fired back. "We made it right before we came and picked you up today."

"I told you that—"

"You said a lot of things... want to talk about them all with Miri, right now?"

Winter nodded, conceding the point. "Well, Esme, whatever you made smells amazing."

"I'm not as good as you, but I try," she replied.

Jae hugged his housekeeper and handed her an envelope, which Winter assumed was filled with money by her reaction to its weight. "Merry Christmas, Esme," he said.

She smiled and kissed him on the cheek. "Merry Christmas, Jae."

As Esme left, Winter's stomach let out a loud, unexpected growl, and Jae turned to her with a smirk. "Somebody's hungry... almost like you got a case of the munch—ouch!"

Winter punched him in his arm before he could finish the word. Miri, unphased by it all, rushed to the kitchen and grabbed a Body Armor.

"Do not drink my Kobe Bryant one, Miri, I only got one left."

"Too late," she said as she opened the purple bottle and gulped it down in one go.

Jae shook his head.

The three of them sat down to a feast of roasted chicken, garlic mashed potatoes, green beans, and fresh rolls—simple comfort food, but exactly what Winter needed.

They ate heartily, laughing and sharing stories. Miri seemed to be in better spirits, and even Winter felt a bit of the day's tension begin to lift.

Once dinner was over, they moved to the living room, where Jae set up their '80s movie marathon. *Coming to America* came on first, and the familiar scenes brought on a wave of nostalgia. Miri laughed until tears streamed down her face, but as the night wore on, her eyelids grew heavy. Before long, she was curled up on the couch, fast asleep.

Winter looked over at Miri, a soft smile on her lips. "She's out."

"Long day," Jae said, turning down the volume. "But she's tough, like her mom."

Winter rolled her eyes playfully. "You always know the right thing to say."

Jae got up and walked over to a small bar in the dining room, motioning for Winter to follow him. He pulled out a bottle of wine. "Remember this?"

"Reunite? Oh no, you didn't!"

"You know I had to."

He poured them both a glass. "We lived off this stuff in college."

"Yeah, before either one of us knew what good wine was."

"Hell, that was before we were old enough to drink. Don't even get me started on MD 20/20."

"Lord, you say that and I might get sick just thinking about it."

Winter took the glass from him and took a sip. "Damn, this is good."

"Sugar water."

The two laughed.

Winter sighed wistfully. "Damn, we had a good time in college. Where did the time go?"

"Well for me it was the NBA, and for you... well, it's over there on the couch sleeping."

She smirked at his response, a mischievous glint in her eyes.

She grabbed for the remote. "I feel like dancing."

Jae's eyebrows rose. "Dancing? Now?"

"Why not?" she replied, scrolling through his playlist until the smooth, nostalgic beat of Camp Lo's *Black Nostaljack* came on. "Let's go back to college for real. Remember this one?" she asked. As the beat came on, she started bopping her head from left to right. Winter laughed and posted at Jae, shaking her head. "You and your '90s hip-hop obsession."

He walked over to her, spinning her playfully. "Nah, college would've been this one." He took the remote and changed the song to Lil Keke's *Southside*, a Houston anthem.

Winter's eyes widened. "No, you didn't!"

Before she knew it, Jae started doing the dance that accompanied the song. "Throwin' up the deuce, and giving playa's dab."

"You know the Southside's acting bad on the slab!" she sung as she joined in.

As they danced, their laughter and banter flowed easily, reliving a different memory from college with each song that played.

"You remember the first time we did this one?" Jae asked. "It was at that party on the quad."

Winter grinned. "No, that wasn't it. It was marketing class freshman year. Everyone wanted to meet the great Jaden Carter, the savior of the basketball program."

"Chill out, Short stack."

"You know I'm telling the truth. It's probably why you didn't remember me," she teased.

"I was with Genesis then, that's the only person I saw back in those days. Till we split up that first time."

"I remember. Then when you got hurt and I was a trainer, you didn't want nobody to work on you but me, since Carla kept trying to grope you."

"Man, I forgot about her. She was a predator."

Winter laughed. "She was our age."

"I felt molested every time I went in there. You were the only one who didn't see dollar signs."

"You're right, I can't front," Winter said as she laughed. "Everyone thought we had a connection."

"Hell, even Genesis."

Winter paused for a moment, her voice softer. "Maybe they were right."

Jae's gaze lingered on her. "Yeah, but then you met Malik."

"You mean you introduced me to Malik. Pawning me off on your brother like that. That was dirty."

"It wasn't like that."

"Oh Really? Then what was it like?"

"It was… a long time ago."

They both laughed, the moment hanging heavy between them. Before it could turn too serious, Tamia's 'So Into You' started playing.

Jae's face changed, the playful smile replaced by something deeper. "Well, this is a switch," he said, his voice lower.

Winter stepped closer, looking up at him with a teasing grin. "What's the matter, Jae? You getting sentimental?"

Jae's eyes locked onto hers as he took hold of her hands, and they began to move slowly, swaying to the beat. "Maybe I am. College was special. Good times, you know."

"The best times."

The tension between them was palpable, a magnetic pull neither of them could ignore. Winter's heart began to race as she felt Jae's arms tighten around her waist, pulling her closer.

"You're a lightweight when it comes to wine," Winter teased, trying to ease the intensity of the moment.

Jae smirked. "You're one to talk, Ms. Edible."

They laughed, but the laughter faded into silence as they stared at each other, their faces just inches apart. Without thinking, Winter reached up and gently touched Jae's cheek. "You've always had my back, Jae. The restaurant. The day I found out about Daddy."

"Just like you had mine when Malik—"

"We had each other's backs that day."

"Double up." The two gave their high five to each other.

The air around them seemed to thicken, and in one fluid motion, Winter leaned up and kissed him. It was tentative at first, a soft press of lips that felt both familiar and brand new.

Jae's heart hammered in his chest as he kissed her back, his fingers tangling in her hair. The kiss deepened, becoming urgent and raw, filled with years of unspoken longing.

Jae pulled back suddenly, his breathing ragged. "Winter... what are we doing?"

Winter's eyes were heavy-lidded, her voice husky. "Something that feels... right."

She pulled him in again, their lips crashing together in a burst of passion.

They stumbled backward, knocking over a small vase on the side table. Jae caught it just in time, his laughter mingling with hers.

"Maybe this is a mistake," he whispered against her lips, his voice low.

With a seductive smile, she slowly peeled off her shirt, revealing the lace bra beneath.

"Maybe it's one I want to make," Winter replied, her eyes blazing with desire.

She stepped back toward the stairs, her eyes never leaving his, and gave him a look that left no room for misinterpretation.

"Are you coming?" she asked, her voice dripping with invitation.

Jae hesitated for a second, then his resolve crumbled. He followed her up the stairs, his eyes filled with desire.

WHEN THEY REACHED THE BEDROOM, Winter turned to face him, her body already buzzing with anticipation. Jae wasted no time, his hands exploring her skin with a mixture of tenderness and urgency. He pulled her close, kissing her deeply as they tumbled onto the bed.

Winter's fingers found the buttons of his shirt, fumbling in her haste to unbutton it. Jae's hands were on her waist, sliding up her back and unclasping her bra with practiced ease. The bra fell away, and Jae paused, his eyes tracing the curves of her body.

"Damn… I never realized how beautiful you truly are," he said, his voice thick with emotion.

Winter reached up, pulling him down to her. "Show me."

Jae's mouth found her neck, his kisses slow and deliberate as his hands explored every inch of her. Winter arched against him, her breath hitching with each touch. She felt a surge of warmth pooling deep within her, a hunger that had been building for years.

Clothes were discarded quickly, their bare skin pressed together as they moved in sync. Jae's touch was both gentle and insistent, his lips leaving a trail of heat wherever they landed.

"Jae…" Winter breathed, her voice filled with longing.

He looked down at her, his gaze intense. "Are you sure about this?"

"More than anything," she whispered.

With that, he entered her, the sensation overwhelming and yet utterly right.

His dick filled her, gratifying her immensely. It had been years since she'd been touch by a man in this way. But in a way, it felt like the very first time.

His stroke intensified as they moved together in a rhythm that was both familiar and electric, the years of friendship adding a layer of intimacy that neither had experienced before.

As they reached the peak of their passion, Winter's fingers dug into Jae's back, her breath coming in short, ragged gasps. He kissed her fiercely, and she felt a surge of emotion welling up inside her—joy, relief, and something that felt a lot like love.

"Do you want me to stop?"

"Never," she moaned.

Their passion increased, and she moaned with disregard for anyone. As her moisture saturated his rock hard dick, he responded with heavier, deliberate thrusts. She wanted—no, she *needed*—him in a way that only a woman who felt safe with a man she loved could.

She was finally able to let go of all the stress in her life.

They made love, exchanging orgasms like notes in class. His tongue found her nipples and bit on them, intensifying as his dick pushed all the stress out of her body.

It no longer felt like love. It *was* love.

By the middle of the night, his sheets were soaked with their cum, but neither one of them cared. They were right where they belonged, as one.

He rolled onto his back, never removing his dick from her moist, tight pussy. She moaned as he pulsated inside of her. "Damn, you're deep Jae," she whispered as his eyes met hers.

The moonlight kissed her skin, and he followed the traces of her divine beauty with his tongue. Their love-making went from sex to fucking, back to love-making without skipping a beat. He knew what she wanted, and she knew the same. It was the most natural experience she'd ever felt.

As she thrust her pussy on his dick with reckless abandonment, his eyes told the story of an orgasm that only helped her reach hers. They were going to cum one final time together.

"Fuck!" he moaned savagely as his cum erupted in her core. Feeling the heat of his nectar only made her explode with the same pleasurable ferocity.

"Oh God, I'm cumming again! Please don't stop! I'm cumming again."

He didn't stop, and she released her wetness as her orgasm flowed through her body, draining the both of them, collapsing in ecstasy.

A tear was in her eye as she fell next to him.

He gazed into her deep brown eyes, satisfied in a way no woman had done for him before. He took a deep breath, mustering the strength from the heavens to whisper, "That was... you are..."

She kissed him before he could finish his thought. There was nothing else to be said.

They both knew this night was perfection.

1 9

SLAM DUNK

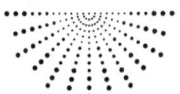

*W*inter slowly blinked awake, the soft gray of the early morning light filtering through the curtains. The room was dim, but there was just enough light to make out the familiar shape of Jae lying beside her. His breathing was slow and steady, his face relaxed in sleep.

She took a deep breath, the reality of the moment settling over her like a warm blanket. The events of the previous night flooded back— soft whispers, lingering kisses, the unmistakable rush of something long-suppressed finally finding release.

What in the hell have we done? she wondered, but the thought wasn't filled with regret. Instead, there was a strange sense of peace, of rightness, that wrapped around her heart.

The clock on the nightstand read 5:30 a.m. It was Christmas Eve, a day normally filled with holiday bustle. But here, in this quiet moment, everything felt still.

She looked over at Jae's sleeping form, a soft smile tugging at the corners of her lips.

Damn, that was good... she thought, her heart swelling.

She gently pulled the covers up to her chest, careful not to disturb him, and lay there quietly, unsure of what the day—and the new reality between them—would bring.

She wouldn't have to wait long for her answer.

"Morning, Short stack," he said, his muscles glistening as he rolled over and looked at her.

"Hey," she replied softly.

She wanted to know what he thought, but wasn't sure what to say.

As if on cue, he addressed the elephant in the room. "This is awkward."

Winter laughed at his words. It *was* awkward, but their friendship was intact, making it all feel natural in the moment. She nestled in his arms and smiled at the idea of what had happened. The idea had crossed her mind many times, though she'd tried to suppress them.

Her mind went back to the first time she'd felt curious about him in this way, in the rehab training room. Of course, that was before she'd been introduced to Malik.

Malik. Damn it, Wyn, out of all the men!

Guilt settled in her mind, running her joy off like a stray dog.

She sat up and looked at his fine frame. "This is crazy. We can't do *that* ever again."

"Wyn, you're the one who—"

"I mean, I was married to your brother. You're my brother-in-law."

"Wyn, if you just list—"

"You're Miri's uncle. It would just confuse her. I mean, how would I even begin to tell her about this…. about us?"

"Wyn!" he said firmly.

She fell silent.

He leaned over and reached for her hand, kissing her palm. "I feel you, and I feel the same way. Won't happen again."

She nodded, although slowly her guilt was being replaced with disappointment. She wasn't supposed to like it, but she was having a hard time not kissing him, even as he spoke. A part of her was dejected, although she wasn't sure why.

She looked down at the bedspread. His morning erection was poking against the lavender goose down comforter.

Damn, that's a big dick.

Something inside of her had awakened. She knew she should get up and get cleaned up before Miri woke, but she couldn't move. She didn't want to.

"What's on your mind, Wyn?" he asked, seeing that something was bothering her.

She leaned next to him. "I mean, we can never do this again."

Jae looked confused. "Right, we just said that."

"Then why is your dick hard?"

"I can't control that. It's a natural reaction, especially to good sex."

"So you liked it?"

He smirked, moving in closer to her. "It was incredible, but like you said, we can't do it again."

"Right. That's non-negotiable," she said as he put her hand on top of the cover where his bulge was.

"Exactly." He leaned closer to her and nestled his head between her neck and shoulder. Winter leaned into his lips and he kissed her on her neck, slowly arousing her.

He kissed her again as she whispered, "But like—and just hear me out on this—" she said as she tightened her hold on him.

"I'm listening, Short stack, but I gotta say, that's a step in the wrong direction."

"I know, but what if... I mean, we're both already naked. And you're clearly thinking about it..."

Jae pulled back playfully. "I'm thinking about it? Where is your hand?"

She rolled her eyes. "I'm just trying to be a good friend. I mean, I don't want you going days, weeks, and months thinking about all this goodness over here."

Jae chuckled. "Oh, please. You are literally making this harder."

"I'm just saying, we're already here. We already crossed the line. And we both liked it. I'm willing to make the sacrifice... as a favor to a friend in need."

Jae smirked. "You mean like a loan."

"Exactly! Just like a loan. You know, like you're my boy and if you needed, say, I dunno, some sugar or some eggs, I'd loan it to you."

"Right, and if you need a ride, even if it was out of my way, I'd do it, cause you're my homie."

"Now you're getting it. So, I mean, clearly you need some cheeks right now. I don't want to do it, but you're not gonna be able to function all day walking around with this in your system. And it is Christmas Eve. Miri won't wake up till at least nine."

"You're just doing me a favor."

"Cause that's what friends are for."

He ripped the covers off them and climbed on top of her, kissing her neck before slowly making his way down to her nipple. She moaned in pleasure, stroking his hard dick, rubbing it on top of her already-pulsating clit.

Suddenly she stopped. "But again, we can't tell Miri."

Jae rolled his eyes at the thought of telling his niece what he'd done to her mother. "I'm not telling her."

"Promise me, Jae."

"Wyn. You're making this weird."

"Okay, okay, double up." The two hit their usual handshake, then Winter laid back and said, "Now, come get this pussy."

"Oh, you feeling like that?"

"Yeah, don't be nice."

Without another word, she felt the weight of his dick slide deep inside of her pussy walls in a painfully pleasurable way as he remained there, waiting for her unspoken consent. As her eyes rolled to the back of her head, she nodded in agreement. He tightened his grip in her hair and thrust hard inside her, forcing her to squeal.

"Do that again," she moaned.

"You want to be punished?"

"Yeah, I've been a really bad girl."

He thrust in her again, this time as deep as he could go.

She looked in his eyes as she let out a high pitch yelp. It was perfect.

"You want to be fucked, don't you?"

She nodded desperately.

He began to drill her with precision. This wasn't lovemaking, this wasn't passion, this was fucking, as well as she'd ever been fucked. With the endurance of a high-end athlete, he moved inside of her masterfully. His dick was right up against her g-spot, not relenting until she submitted her body fully to him. The pleasure was overwhelming to the point her orgasm was already reaching critical mass.

"Oh, my... got... da...shit!" she yelled as her orgasm exploded out of her, saturating the sheets. She had never squirted like that before.

She dug her nails deep into his back, demanding more. Instead, he pulled out of her.

"Wait! What are—"

"I want to taste you."

Without another word, he buried his face on her hyper-sensitive clit, at first tenderly. His tongue forced an entirely new set of sensations to flood her body.

She moaned in a high pitch voice. "Get it. Get it for me, Jae."

He continued to suck on her pulsating clit. It was too much, alternating between the warmth of his tongue and his lips as he sucked and licked her. It was only when he slid two fingers inside of her, on top of his sucking motion, that she had another mind-blowing orgasm.

"Jaden," she moaned in ecstasy. He released her clit as she gasped for air.

Still panting, she said, "I don't ... I don't know if I can take any more."

He climbed up on top of her again, her nectar still dripping from his beard. "Let's find out," he said with authority as he slid inside of her.

She didn't care about their friendship, what Miri would think, what her mother would think. All she cared about was his next stroke and the orgasm it would inevitably bring.

She moaned loudly as he drilled her without mercy. "Fuck that pussy, papi!"

She was in college again, fulfilling a fantasy she'd kept in the back of her mind. The way she'd wanted to sleep with Jaden back then.

"You can't handle it, can you?"

She couldn't. It was too good. But her pride kicked in. *We're not tapping out*, she told her pussy. She started to thrust her hips at him.

"Oh, shit," he moaned. She wasn't just receiving. Winter was fucking him back. His dick rose to the challenge as she kissed him passionately.

"God damn," he moaned.

That's it, girl, work it.

With each thrust, the pair found a rhythm unlike either had ever experienced. Winter was giving as good as she was getting, and she had him. *Let's finish this motherfucker.*

She rolled him over on his back and pulled off him, moving down to suck his dick, engulfing him between her full, moist lips.

"Holy mother of God," Jaden moaned.

She salivated on him as her mouth got wetter, his pre-cum awakening her inner freak. Making him as hard as he could get, she climbed back on top of him, presenting him with her back, and rode his dick.

"Fuck!" he moaned as he slapped her bouncing ass with each thrust up and down.

If it weren't for the soundproof walls, there'd be no question that not only Miri, but the neighbors, would hear them.

She didn't care. She needed this, and she was loving every moment.

It wasn't long before she felt his dick swelled. "Fuck!" he moaned as his seed released uncontrollably inside of her.

She continued to ride his dick, reaching yet another orgasm of her own.

She collapsed on top of him and looked into her newfound lover's eyes. Both of them wanting to talk, neither one of them knowing what to say.

After a spell, Jaden finally said, "You nasty."

She laughed as she kissed his shoulder, thinking about how natural it all felt.

She examined him and the grin on his face.

"That was a hell of a loan," he joked with a breathless chuckle.

She looked over at the clock. It was 7:43 a.m.

Did we just fuck for over two hours?

It didn't matter. She had no guilt for enjoying herself.

"We need to shower before Miri wakes up."

She nodded as he grabbed her hand and led her to the bathroom, a sanctuary of sleek marble, warm lighting, and polished chrome fixtures. Jae's shower was the epitome of luxury: a spacious, walk-in rain shower encased in glass, with multiple showerheads lining the walls.

Water cascaded down like a gentle waterfall, the steam filling the room as Winter stepped inside, her skin prickling with warmth.

Jae joined her, the size of the shower allowing them to move freely, with enough room to comfortably fit two, maybe even three, people. Jets on the side walls provided a soothing massage effect, while rainfall showerheads mimicked a tropical downpour.

As water poured over them, Winter ran her hands along Jae's broad shoulders, tracing the muscles that were still firm beneath her touch. He leaned in, pressing a soft kiss to her wet hair, his hands resting on her waist, pulling her close. The steam surrounded them, blurring the glass walls and creating an intimate, cocoon-like atmosphere.

After rinsing away the remnants of the night before and the morning, they shared lingering kisses under the streaming water, laughter breaking through as they splashed each other playfully. Jae reached for a bottle of eucalyptus-scented body wash, lathering it onto her skin with tender, deliberate motions.

When they stepped out, Jae grabbed a pair of matching flannel pajamas from a neatly folded stack on his dresser. "Thought we'd need these," he said with a grin, handing Winter a set.

Wrapped in fresh flannel and the quiet intimacy of their shared morning, the reality of Christmas Eve felt warmer, simpler, and somehow just right. As Jae dressed, Winter continued to dry her hair.

She found herself searching Jae's eyes, a question forming in her mind. This was more than just the physical, and she wanted to know if he felt it too. "Jae..." she started hesitantly, the words faltering on her lips.

He turned, sensing her hesitation. "What's on your mind?"

But before she could answer, the unmistakable sound of a door closing echoed through the house. Jae tensed, quickly putting on the flannel pants and grabbing a t-shirt.

"Hold up," he muttered.

A notification buzzed on his phone, which sat on the bathroom counter. He glanced at the security footage on his screen, his expression shifting from relaxed to alert. "It's Miri," he said, his voice low. "She's awake."

Winter's heart skipped a beat as she fumbled for a towel, suddenly feeling exposed. "Already? She normally doesn't get up till 9 when she's out of school."

"Damn it," Jae muttered, suddenly remembering a conversation with his niece yesterday. "The Rockets are having a Christmas Eve shoot around. That's why she's up."

"Uncle Jae? Mom?" Miri's voice echoed through the house. She was getting closer.

20

CLUTCH TIME

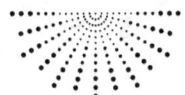

"**D**amn it, she's headed up here," Jae said.

Winter's heart pounded as Miri's voice grew louder, each step echoing through the hallway. Jae glanced over his shoulder at Winter, his face a mix of urgency and confusion.

As he dressed hastily, she whispered under her breath. "She can *not* catch us like this!" She scrambled to find her clothes.

"No shit, Wyn. What do you want me to do?"

"Uncle Jae? Mom?" Miri's voice echoed through the house. She was nearing the room.

Wyn turned to Jae. "She's coming upstairs! Hide in the closet."

"What? I'm a grown ass man. I'm not—"

"Hide!" Winter barked as she pushed Jae in the closet and scrambled for her panties and the Christmas flannels Jae had just handed her.

She had just put on the shirt when Miri opened the door. "Mom? What are you doing in here?"

"Hey baby, I was... um... looking for Uncle Jae, but he's not here. I found these flannels, though. Here are yours." She handed Miri the third pair.

She started to walk past her mom. "Well, good, I'm sore from the game yesterday and I want to use his massager, the good one he doesn't like to share. He keeps in it the closet."

Winter sprinted in front of her and stopped her. "No Miri, you can't go in there!"

"Why not?"

"Because, baby, um... isn't that it over there on the charger?"

Miri turned around and, sure enough, the charger was sitting on the nightstand.

"Oh, yeah... wait, why are you acting weird?"

Winter's face became flush as her daughter examined the room. "I'm not."

"Mom, I'm not stupid. You don't think I know what's going on?"

A wave of embarrassment came over her face. "Miri, baby, I can explain."

"You don't have to. I already know."

"Y—you do?"

"You're trying to cover for Uncle Jae because he snuck a baddie in last night and he's getting rid of her."

"Hold on, he did wh—"

"Yeah, he said he had a date yesterday, and clearly it went well. There's thot sauce everywhere." Miri pointed to the sheets which were saturated with her orgasm.

She wanted to die of embarrassment, but it would have to wait for another time. Winter saw her way out of this, and agreed with her daughter's assessment. "Right, you got me... I mean, him... I mean us. I mean—"

Miri laughed. "Mom, chill. I'm old enough to know these things. It's okay, I just can't wait to get to the stadium today to let some of the old players know that the Smoke still got it. Tag 'em and bag 'em."

Winter's jaw dropped open. She had to suppress a smile at the thought of Jae listening to this conversation from the closet. "Excuse me?"

"Something the guys on the Rockets used to say when I was a kid and Jae would me take up there. There were always women around. Wait, you didn't sit on the bed, did you?"

"No."

"Good because thot sauce is a woman's— "

"I know what it is, Miri. The question is, how do you know?"

"Look, Mom, just because your sex life is nonexistent, doesn't mean I plan on mine being the same way." Winter's eyes bulged as Miri raised her hands in defense. "I haven't done it yet, Mom, I'm saying when the appropriate time comes."

"That better be a long time from now."

"We'll see."

Winter punched her daughter in the arm, who chuckled playfully. "I'm just kidding. But not about Uncle Jae, take it from an athlete: we —I mean, *he*—can get it anytime he wants, and we'd never know." She knocked on the walls. "Soundproof walls, see? While we were asleep, he probably snuck her in and now he's kicking her out. You know how these ballers are."

"Yeah, you're on it. But let's get out of his room. I'm sure Uncle Jae would be embarrassed if he knew we were in here."

A combination of relief, guilt, and embarrassment flooded her as she tried to maintain her composure.

Her daughter was right. Jae *did* sleep with someone, but never in a million years could Miri imagine it was Winter. She needed to preserve that innocence and put on the full armor of Mom once more.

Winter nudged her daughter out of the door as the pair left the room. Unsure of how this would play out, since Jae was still in the closet on the second floor, at some point he'd have to come downstairs to a bevy of questions.

To her surprise, Jae was walking in the front door when they entered the living room, catching Winter entirely off guard. "Jae? How did you get down here—I mean, where are you coming from?"

"Yeah, Unc, where were you?"

Jae stammered as he struggled to find suitable response. "I, um... I went to take out the trash."

"But I took out the trash," Miri retorted.

Jae was startled by the response. "You did?"

"Yeah, it's the first thing I did this morning. Figured it was the least

I could do since Esme's off and I crashed so hard on you guys last night."

Jae nodded. "Right. what I mean to say was, I started to take out the trash, but saw you did it, then decided to head out for a quick lap around the block. You know, keep the blood flowing."

"In your pajamas?"

Jae's eyes bulged as he looked for an excuse. He took a breath. "Gotta stay active, even on Christmas Eve."

Winter forced a grin, trying to play along. "Yeah, he's really into, uh, spontaneous exercise. Some retired athlete thing he's trying."

Miri looked at both of them suspiciously. "You guys are acting weird."

"Who, us? No way." Jae moved to lean against a wall but miscalculated the distance and lost his balance.

Miri pointed to him. "Case and point, but you know what? It doesn't matter. I was trying to find you because I wanted to get to the Rockets' shoot around early to get some good photos for social media. Is that cool, Unc?"

"Yeah… yes, great idea. I'll get ready. Winter, are you gonna stay here, or no?"

Winter nervously responded. "You know what? I'll join you. Besides, I gotta go check on Nan-Nan to make sure she isn't spending all of Jae's money."

"Mom, you okay?"

"Yes, honey, why do you ask that?"

Miri examined her mother. "You never come to these things. You're always saying that basketball takes up so much of your life. Also, you're… very relaxed, which is odd for you. I mean, you were kind of a space cadet yesterday, but today you just seem like you're… I don't know."

Before her daughter could finish her thought, Winter walked over and put her hand on her daughter's back. "Honey, it's Christmas Eve. I'm just glad to be spending time with the people I love—I mean, not like that! I mean, I love you, and I like Jae. I really, really like Jae, but I don't love him. I mean, I love him but not like t—"

"And she's back," Miri said, cutting her mother's awkward response.

Jae stepped in and said, "Guys, let's just get dressed and head out. Is that cool?"

The trio agreed and went their separate ways to get dressed for the day. Winter couldn't stop thinking about the morning despite the current awkwardness. The drive to the stadium was quiet. Miri had her headphones on but would glance up from time to time, clearly confused by the silence between the two.

When they got to the stadium and got out of the car, she stopped the pair. "Okay, guys, before we go in, we need to talk. I know what's going on."

Apprehension flooded Winter's face as she stammered for a response. "Wha—what do you mean, baby?"

"Cut the act please, it's pretty obvious, Mom. "

Jae cleared his throat. "Miri, I before you jump to any conclu—"

"Save it, Unc, I'm not stupid. Anytime you and Mom are together, you're chatterboxes. And today, for the first time in my entire life, neither one of you said a word to each other on the way over here."

Shit, we're busted.

Winter glanced at Jae, who was clearly thinking the same thing. She took a deep breath. "Baby, just let me explain."

"There's nothing to explain. Like I said, it's obvious. I know I'm a kid and all, but it's pretty clear you guys had a fight, and if I had to guess, it's about this morning. You're mad at him for putting you in a spot where you have to cover for him. I get it mom but I'm not a kid. Look, I'm just asking, please don't let whatever it is ruin Christmas. Like it or not, we're a family. Mom, I know Unc has an ego the size of his big head, but you're the one that always says that anytime there's a gap to be filled, Jae's right there to step up and fill it with no complaints."

"Kid's got a point," Jae mumbled while scratching the back of his neck. Winter, catching the innuendo, punched him in the arm.

"Ouch!" he moaned. He looked at her as he held his arm, a tiny smirk on his face.

Winter turned to her daughter. "Baby, we're fine. We did have a disagreement about the new restaurant, but we sorted things out."

"Good, because I don't need any funny business between you two while I'm in here. After last night's game, there's gonna be a lot of press and I need to be on my A-game. I need you guys on yours as well."

Jae stepped in to put his hand on his niece's shoulder. "Don't worry, Miri, we got you. Go show them why you're the top talent in the nation."

As the trio walked in, the atmosphere at the Toyota Center was buzzing with anticipation as fans watched the players warm up.

Jae, Winter, and Miri made their way to the lower section, where they had access to the floor seats. The players ran drills, dunked, and shot three-pointers, while Miri watched intently, clearly thrilled to be there.

Soon it was her turn to get on the court, and as she ran her drills, Jae and Winter exchanged subtle, knowing glances.

Winter's phone buzzed, and she glanced down to see a message from Jae.

I thought we were busted.

Winter smiled and replied back. *Me too! I'm so tired.*

Probably shouldn't have been up half the night doing what you were doing.

I regret nothing.

Still can't believe you made me climb out of my own house.

Winter suppressed a giggle, replying, *Well, it was either that or deal with the firing squad and we both know you don't want that Smoke... see what I did there?*

Jae stifled a laugh, shaking his head as he sent another message. *You're lucky you're cute.*

But not everyone found their banter amusing.

Darren, standing a few rows behind them, noticed the intimate smiles and the constant phone checking. His face darkened, and it didn't take long for him to put two and two together.

Miri was busy running a fast-break drill when Darren made his move, sidling up to Winter while Jae was momentarily distracted by some fans asking for an autograph.

"So, I guess vandalizing my car wasn't enough, you want to rub it in my face that you were playing me the whole time?" Darren whispered harshly, his voice low enough to avoid Miri's hearing, but filled with bitterness.

Winter turned, caught off guard. "What are you talking about, Darren?"

"Don't play dumb," he said, his tone cutting. "I see the way you two are acting. I always knew you'd end up with Jae. Guess I was right all along, cause it didn't take long after we split."

Winter's eyes narrowed. "Darren, this isn't the time or place."

"Oh, of course not. Neither was the coffee shop when you smashed a cheesecake into my car," he sneered. "But you didn't think twice about doing this in front of Miri, did you?"

Before Winter could respond, Jae stepped in. "Hey, what's going on here?"

Darren's gaze snapped to Jae, the anger clear in his eyes. "You're what's going on, Carter. You're always what's going on. Cause every time I go after anything in life, you're the motherfucker standing in the way."

Jae's eyes turned cold. "What are you talking about?"

"You know damn well what I'm talking about," Darren hissed. "From the moment you got to campus, all you've done was take from me. First my friend, then my starting spot, and now Winter. You've always been waiting for your shot, Carter. Everybody knows it. So tell me why in the hell did you wait to shoot yours? Didn't occur to you until after I shot mine?"

Jae's jaw tightened, his voice low and controlled. "Darren, you need to chill."

But Darren wasn't done. "Let me tell you what your fans won't, Carter. You're a bitch, Choke. Can't even find your own woman, so you steal someone else's. But it's all good. Sometimes you gotta let a mutt be with a mutt. You two deserve each other."

"Darren, you need to pump your breaks, real hard. 'Cause first, I'm

167

not that kind of girl, and second, you're causing a scene," Winter warned.

Darren nodded as he stood courtside. "I'll back off, but you're wrong about one thing, Wyn, because by my count, that's Malik, me, and now Jae. Face it, you are that kind of girl."

That was the last straw. Before another word could be said, Jae's fist connected with Darren's jaw in a swift, controlled punch that left no room for retaliation.

Darren stumbled back, clutching his face in shock. Jae scanned the area. It happened so quickly that none of the cameras had time to react.

Winter's eyes widened, and Miri, now alerted by the commotion, ran over. "What happened?"

Jae quickly composed himself. "Just a misunderstanding."

Darren, still nursing his jaw, chuckled and looked at the trio. Jae could tell he wanted to retaliate, but he was in control of his temper.

He took out a napkin and wiped a trickle of blood from his lip. "Yeah, a little misunderstanding."

Jae looked at Miracle. "Miri, let's go get some fresh air. See you around, Darren."

"Oh, indeed you will, Carter."

As they walked toward the exit, Winter gave Jae a sideways glance, surprise and gratitude in her eyes.

"I know that wasn't all about me, but thank you," she murmured, her voice low enough for only him to hear.

"Yeah," Jae agreed, rubbing his knuckles slightly. "That's been brewing for a while, but there are lines you don't cross. And also, I really hate that fucking guy."

As they made their way to the parking lot, the air between them was charged with a mix of tension, relief, and something else entirely —an unspoken understanding that whatever had changed between them wasn't going to affect their friendship, but it also wasn't going away.

21
COURT VISION

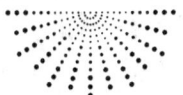

$\mathcal{A}$ s they left the stadium, the adrenaline from the day's excitement lingered in the air, but the tension from Jae's encounter with Darren hadn't quite faded. Winter cast a sideways glance at him as they walked toward the car.

"Did you really have to punch him?" she asked, a small smile tugging at her lips despite her best attempt to sound serious.

Jae shrugged, his expression unapologetic. "He was asking for it. Besides, you saw how he was talking to you. I wouldn't let him get away with that in college, and I wasn't about to let him get away with it today."

Winter shook her head, though there was a glint of admiration in her eyes. "You know, you're lucky he didn't swing back."

"Oh, please," Jae scoffed. "He wouldn't risk messing up his manicure."

They both burst into laughter, the tension melting away as they reached the car. Miri walked behind them smiling. Jae turned and said.

"Hey, Cupcake, I'm sorry we ruined the— "

"It's fine, Unc. If it were Shasha I would've done the same thing.

What I can't believe is that it took this long. You never punched him back in college, Uncle Jae?"

"Oh, believe me, I wanted to. Matter of fact, there's one practice I'll never forget. He knew I was coming for his spot after rehab. I came out and I was straight beast mode. I was scoring with my left and my right hand, there was nothing he could do against me. I went in for a layup, he gave me a hard foul to the ribs. Took the wind out of me. I got up, and I walked over to him, about to rearrange his face, and he just stood there. I cocked back to swing, and in an instant I realized, if I hit him, I'm gonna get kicked out the game, possibly benched. So, before I could get my hand past my face, I opened my fist and pretended to blow smoke. And that's how that move was created."

"No way, are you serious?"

"Yeah, it was the first time I did it. He laughed, but I went to drop thirty points on him after. It was like the smoke was blowing dead ashes on a player or a game, at least that's what it became to me afterwards. I wanted to break his jaw but instead, I broke his will. He never was a starter again."

Miri laughed at Jae's bravado. She patted her uncle on the back. "That's a crazy story, Unc. So admit it, it felt good to punch him today."

"You have no idea."

The trio laughed hysterically as they got in the car.

Just as Jae was about to start the engine, Winter's phone buzzed. She glanced at the screen, her face lighting up when she saw her mom's name.

"Hey, Mom," she greeted, still smiling.

Denise's voice came through the speaker, equal parts warmth and mischief. "Well, it's about time you answered, Miss Busybody. Guess who just finished putting the final touches on *the* restaurant?"

Winter's eyes widened in surprise. "Wait, already? I thought we had a few more days!"

"Do you think I'd let my daughter's opening look anything less than world-class?" Denise scoffed, but there was an unmistakable note of pride in her tone.

Winter, still stunned asked, "Mom, how did you put this toge—"

"I called in a few favors, had Esmerelda on standby, and worked a little of my magic. It's practically glowing, honey."

Jae leaned over, clearly listening in, and mouthed, "Told you so."

Winter chuckled, shaking her head. "Mom, you're a miracle worker."

Denise let out a triumphant laugh. "Damn right, I am. And you'd better remember that the next time you think about doubting me, Miss Chef Extraordinaire. Ain't nobody better than you, except maybe me," she joked, her voice carrying that familiar, playful pride.

Winter laughed, feeling a wave of warmth and gratitude. "Thanks, Mom. Really. I don't know what I'd do without you."

"Of course, baby. Now, don't keep me waiting too long. I want to see that look on your face when you walk in and realize just how amazing it is."

Winter could almost see her mom's proud, teasing smile through the phone. "We're on our way," she promised, catching Jae's amused expression as she ended the call.

"She's really something," Jae said with a chuckle.

Winter nodded, a glint of pride in her eyes. "She really is. I guess I get it from her."

As they pulled up to the restaurant, Winter felt a flutter of excitement and nerves. The building had been hers for a long time in her mind, a dream she and her father had once sketched on the backs of napkins. But stepping inside and seeing it fully realized was something else entirely.

Denise was inside, arranging the final touches on the tables and adjusting the lighting. The ambiance was breathtaking—a blend of cozy elegance, the kind that made people want to linger over their meals and enjoy the experience. Warm wood tones, exposed brick walls, and pendant lights gave it a refined yet welcoming feel.

Winter stepped through the front doors, her breath catching as she took in the space. It was as though every detail she'd ever imagined had come to life. The restaurant was a stunning blend of modern luxury and cozy warmth, with clean lines and sophisticated touches that made it feel both inviting and impressive.

The floors were a rich, dark oak, their polished surfaces reflecting the soft, ambient lighting that glowed from overhead fixtures—sleek, gold pendants hung at varying heights, casting a warm glow across the room. Along one wall, a series of floor-to-ceiling windows allowed natural light to stream in during the day and would offer a striking view of the city skyline at night.

Tables were set with simple but elegant stoneware plates, with subtle variations that made each piece unique. Delicate glassware sparkled beneath the light, and minimalist arrangements of fresh greenery added a touch of life to each table without over-whelming the space. In the center of the room, a long, sleek bar with a marble countertop ran almost the full length of the back wall. Its surface was a rich, creamy white streaked with veins of charcoal and gold, giving it a luxurious yet grounded look. Behind the bar, shelves made of matte black metal and warm walnut wood held an array of artisan liquors and finely crafted glassware.

To one side, a small lounge area featured low, comfortable seating in warm, earthy tones—a place where guests could unwind with a drink before their meal. The walls were adorned with art pieces that leaned toward the abstract, each one a conversation starter in its own right, adding an air of sophistication to the space.

Winter could hardly believe her eyes. She felt as though she were standing in a dream—the culmination of years of hard work, vision, and heart. It was exactly as she had hoped: modern, timeless, and uniquely hers.

She looked around, letting the reality settle over her, a mix of pride and gratitude filling her chest. Her mother's voice broke through her reverie, filled with both pride and a teasing edge.

"Pretty spectacular, isn't it?" Denise said, a gleam of satisfaction in her eyes. "I told you no one would do it better."

Winter nodded, unable to keep the wide smile from her face. "It's perfect. Every single detail."

Denise's eyes softened, and she placed a hand on Winter's shoulder. "Just like you deserve, baby."

Winter's eyes sparkled as she took in the scene. "No, really, Mom, it's… it's beautiful," she whispered, genuinely moved.

Denise turned to Jae, a knowing smile playing on her lips. "Couldn't have done it without him," she said, patting Jae on the shoulder. She gave them both a look, one Winter couldn't quite decipher, and then went back to her work, humming under her breath.

Jae caught Winter's gaze, a grin spreading across his face. "What do you think, Short stack? Does it measure up?"

Winter laughed, feeling her heart swell. She marveled at the sheer brilliance of *her* restaurant. "More than measures up, Jae. It's perfect."

Just then, Miri's phone buzzed, and she looked down at the screen, her eyes widening. "Oh my god, it's Coach Matthews from UConn!"

She held up her phone, showing them the incoming video call.

Winter and Jae crowded around as Miri accepted the call, her hands shaking with excitement. The screen lit up, showing Coach Matthews' friendly face.

"Miracle Carter," the coach began, smiling warmly. "I know it's Christmas Eve, did I catch you at a bad time?"

"No, Coach, it's fine. How are you?"

"I'm good, listen I don't want to hold you long. We love the fire that you play the game with, and our starting point guard is graduating next year. You're going to have many suitors after the Texas high school playoffs, so I wanted to beat them all to the punch. I'm pleased to officially offer you a full scholarship to join us at UConn."

Miri's face broke into a huge grin as she let out an ecstatic scream. "YES! Oh my God, YES!"

Winter and Jae cheered, hugging her as she practically bounced in place. As the call ended, Miri's phone buzzed again, messages flooding in from teammates who had also received scholarship offers to various colleges.

"Mom, can I go celebrate with everyone?" Miri begged, her eyes bright. "It'll just be a kickback at Ella's place. Please?"

Winter hesitated, still processing everything, but Denise stepped in, patting Miri's shoulder. "I'll take her. Go have fun, honey—you deserve it."

Miri threw her arms around her mom and Jae, and then she and Denise headed for the door, leaving Winter and Jae alone in the quiet, warmly lit restaurant.

Winter turned back to look at Jae, her heart still racing from all the excitement. "This feels surreal," she murmured, her voice soft. "It's like… everything is coming together all at once."

Jae stepped closer, his gaze intent. "You've worked hard for this, Short stack. You deserve every bit of it."

They stood in the middle of the dining area, an unspoken tension building between them. Jae reached out, tucking a strand of hair behind her ear, his touch lingering. Winter felt her breath catch. The space between them charged. She smirked.

"I told you that you'd be thinking about it."

"About what?"

"This morning." She placed her hand on his chest before turning and walking away, playfully looking back to check he was playing his part in this cat-and-mouse game.

She turned as he leaned against the wall, trapping his elusive prey. He looked at her with unquestioning intent.

She smiled coyly. "You think you 'bout to get some because you bought me a restaurant?"

"I can think of worse things, but to be clear, I didn't buy you anything. We're business partners, remember?"

"Is that right? So, I guess I should give you my half of the payment for this place, partner?"

"That depends on what you have in mind."

"Well, I thinking, I'm going to need that loan from this morning paid back immediately."

"Oh really."

"With interest."

"Right now?"

"The longer you wait the higher the penalty." She smirked.

His looming six-foot-seven figure towered over her. For the first time, she took in her best friend as a man—the tall, sexy, broad-shoul-dered man he was. He wasn't lanky Jae anymore. The stubble of his beard was desirable. The fullness of his lips was calling to her. He was magnetic, and his eyes bore a hole in her spirit, looking to be reunited since this morning.

Without another word, she leaned in, her lips meeting his in a kiss that was gentle at first, then deepened, slow and searching. The world around them seemed to fall away as they moved in perfect harmony, their years of friendship lending an intimacy to each touch, each whisper.

Jae pulled her closer, his hands exploring the curve of her back as he moved to push her against a nearby table. She felt her heartbeat quicken, a warmth blooming in her chest.

They stumbled together, laughing breathlessly as they moved through the restaurant, knocking over a chair in their path.

"Still such a lanky, clumsy kid," Winter teased between kisses, her voice a playful murmur.

Jae chuckled, his voice husky. "I'm skilled in the right places."

Winter arched her eyebrows, surprised by his bravado. She liked this side of him. She kissed him again. "Show me."

They made their way into the adjoining bakery, the familiar scent of flour and sugar filling the air as they became lost in each other. There, amidst the tools of Winter's craft, the passion simmered into something slower, deeper. Every touch felt like a promise, every kiss an affirmation of something they'd both felt but never voiced.

She leaned against the counter and, without another word, he slid down her tights and inside of her.

"Damn, you are so wet."

She huffed at the fullness of his manhood pulsating inside of her and bent over, allowing him to go deeper. "Go deeper, daddy, fuck me like you did this morning," she moaned.

He wasted no time, thrusting deep inside of her with all the force he could muster.

She welcomed every inch of his dick. Years of repressed animal attraction was being released by their union, each thrust with less regard than the one before it.

"More!" she demanded as he began to build a sweat. "Oh, shit, right there. Don't you dare quit on me, Smoke, I'm close."

Jae obeyed and continued to drive his dick deeper and harder into her core until her legs began to shake. "I'm cumming!" she screamed. "Don't stop."

He obliged as he pushed all of his manhood deep inside her sweet pussy, the orgasm flowing through her body as he continued. She was immensely satisfied. Noticing this, he slowed down his pace.

"How are you still hard?" she gasped, surprised by his stamina.

"I'm an athlete?" he mocked.

He wasn't satisfied, and neither was she. "You want more?" she asked seductively.

He couldn't talk, he was still inside of her.

She pulled away and turned around to face him. She slid her tights off all the way and hopped in his arms, locking her ankles together behind his back. He wasted no time picking back up where he left off, sliding inside of her again.

She could feel the warmth of his girthy dick inside of her, and it only aroused her more as he lifted her up and down on his shaft. She looked into his eyes and, in an instant, something changed. This wasn't sex anymore. There was a strong attraction, but there was much more sensual passion than she'd realized.

They kissed and touched each other as she allowed him to enter her at his discretion. Their eyes locked as they kissed, the two spirits finding each other and refusing to let go.

He pressed her body against a nearby wall to get deeper. She moaned in pleasure, digging her nails into his back. It didn't stop him, nor did she want it to. Their passion had transcended sex. This was something different, though. Winter dared not call it by name. She wanted to live there forever, yet eternity would be short-lived as it was replaced by the ecstasy of their combined orgasms.

He huffed, losing strength with each explosive surge of his hot, sweet load inside of her. Their dance in the heavens had come to a blissfully intense conclusion.

Still holding her with what strength he had left, he settled them both on the floor.

When they finally pulled apart, breathless and slightly dazed, Winter leaned against his shoulder, straddling him, feeling a strange mix of joy and vulnerability. She could feel the quiet shift between them, something that had changed—perhaps forever.

They sat together on the floor of the bakery, Winter's head on his shoulder, the silence between them comfortable and familiar.

She took a breath. "That was…that was…"

Without a word, Jae extended his hands, and they hit their double up.

The pair laughed as naturally as they ever had before. Winter thought about the times before Malik, when they were somehow closer.

After a moment, Winter broke it, her tone teasing but with a hint of something else. "You ever think about college?"

"All the time. After I left school, I basically became a business, which was cool, but in college I got to just be Jae, not Smoke Carter or anyone else."

"I feel you, but I mean, like… us, in college."

Jae looked to her, then to the heavens, and nestled his muscular arm behind his head as he let out an exhaustive sigh. "I think about us. We were the cool kids, you know. After me and Genesis broke up was a confusing time, a lot happened real fast. I was focused on getting to the pros, and you and Malik decided to get married, then Miri was born, then Leek was gone. At the same time, I had every camera from here to New York asking me if I could take the Rockets to the play-offs. There were a lot of things I never got to process or say."

"So, do you think some of this was there back then?"

"Where is this coming from?"

"I don't know, just thinking."

"What about you?"

Winter shifted and hesitated to be honest. She wanted to tell him the truth, but instead gave him an opening to validate the thought she wouldn't dare utter. "You know, there was Malik, and me and you... well, we were genuine friends."

"Are friends. These lovemaking sessions mean nothing."

Winter bit him on the nipple as he groaned, and the pair laughed.

"Then you got back with Genesis, which was kind of surprising when you guys broke up not much longer after getting back together. You know, we never talked about it. Why did you and Genesis break up the second time?"

The subject created instant tension as Jae shrugged. "Who knows? It ran its course."

"Does that work on the girls you date?"

"What?"

"You lying through your teeth?"

Jae laughed softly, his hand tracing gentle circles on her back.

Winter persisted. "I'm serious. I know you loved her. What happened?"

"Yeah, she was..."

"A bad bitch," Winter smirked as Jae chuckled and continued.

"She had her charms," he admitted, a smile playing on his lips. "But if I'm being honest, she wasn't exactly 'forever' material."

Winter's gaze softened, her mind drifting back. "You know, I remember that night when we were all supposed to meet at Cougars. It was the night after the big game and you said you wanted to talk, I thought maybe... maybe you and I had something. But then you introduced me to Malik and left with her."

Jae's expression grew thoughtful, his eyes searching hers. "It wasn't like that. I did want to talk to you about something, But Malik was there, and you were already on his radar. And you know him—when he wanted something..."

Winter nodded, a sad smile tugging at her lips. "He always got it."

She looked up at him, their faces inches apart, a mixture of amusement and regret in her eyes. "Well, here we are now."

Before he could respond, Jae's phone buzzed on the floor beside them, cutting through the intimacy of the moment. He glanced at the screen, his expression shifting to concern.

"It's your mom," he said, handing Winter the phone.

Winter's heart skipped a beat as she took the call, her fingers trembling slightly. "Mom? What's going on?"

Denise's voice came through, calm but urgent. "Winter, honey, when we got to the kickback, Miri had an episode. She's passed out. I called 911, and they're on their way to the hospital."

Winter's hand flew to her mouth, her breath hitching. "Oh my god... Is she—"

"She's stable, but they're taking her in as a precaution. We'll meet you there."

Winter felt a rush of panic flood her system, but Jae's hand on her shoulder steadied her. She met his gaze, the shock and fear in her eyes reflected back at her.

"Let's go," he said, his voice calm and steady, grounding her in the chaos.

They stood up, and Winter clutched Jae's hand as they dressed and hurried out of the restaurant, the memory of their tender moments left behind, replaced by a single, overpowering thought: Miri.

22
BROKEN PLAYS

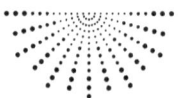

"**G**o faster."

"I'm already punching it, Short stack." Jae barked as they raced down the highway, the weight of Denise's voice still ringing in Winter's ears.

She clutched her phone tightly, her thoughts spiraling with fear and memories she'd tried to bury for years. Jae, steady behind the wheel, kept one hand on the steering wheel, the other reaching over to squeeze her hand.

"Winter," he said firmly, pulling her from the edge of panic, "we're taking her to my clinic. Dr. Mason specializes in exactly what Miri's dealing with. He's world-class, and I trust him with my life."

Winter's voice was barely a whisper. "Jae, this is…"

"I know what this is, Wyn,"

"Then promise me that this doctor is the best, that he's seen this before."

He nodded, his gaze fixed ahead. "He is. I spent years researching specialists after… well, just trust me. Dr. Mason's the best. I've spent millions getting the resources he needs. That's what this clinic I've opened has been about. I thought we'd have more time, but I know he's close."

"Close isn't good enough. Jae."

"It's the best we've got, Wyn. You just have to trust me."

She wiped the tears from her eyes and nodded as he drove well past the speed limit.

They arrived at the clinic, rushing through the doors with Denise close behind, her face a mask of worry. They were ushered down sterile hallways that blurred in Winter's vision until they reached a private treatment room, where Miri lay pale and unmoving, hooked up to monitors and IV lines. The room was quiet except for the steady hum of machines and the soft beeping of her heartbeat, the sound punctuating the heavy silence.

Winter stumbled forward, nearly collapsing as she saw her daughter's face so still, her skin alarmingly pale against the white hospital sheets. The same haunting image she'd seen years ago with Malik. She felt herself unraveling, as if the edges of her world were fraying beyond repair.

"Oh God, Jae..." Her voice cracked, and she felt herself sink against him, her sobs wracking her body. Jae's arms wrapped tightly around her, his embrace firm, grounding her in the chaos.

"Winter, look at me," he said, his tone unyielding, almost commanding. "She's not going anywhere. I promise you that. This isn't going to end like before. Not this time."

His words cut through her panic, a lifeline she clung to. She looked up at him, her eyes full of fear, but in his gaze, she found a spark of determination, a belief she hadn't had the strength to summon.

Dr. Mason entered, his face set with a professional calm. He took Winter's hand, giving her a reassuring squeeze. "My name is Dr. Mason. I wish I had time to give you the details of the science, but I'm afraid we need to move quickly. Your daughter is in critical condition, but there's a treatment plan we're ready to start. We just need your consent to begin."

"You have it. I'll sign whatever you want."

"Okay, that's good. A nurse will be with you shortly with all the paperwork. We'll also need a transfusion, and since we have Jae's bloodwork on file, I can confirm he has the matching blood type."

Jaeden didn't hesitate. He walked towards the doctor. "Let's do it."

Winter watched, her heart shattering with each passing second, as they led Jae into another room to draw the blood. She wanted to follow, to be everywhere at once, but she couldn't move. She was frozen, her mind a mess of anguish and half-formed prayers.

As she sat in the waiting area, scenes of Malik's last days played in her mind—his labored breathing, the way he'd looked at her, helpless yet resigned. She remembered every last moment, the ache that had settled deep in her chest and never quite left. Now, watching her daughter lie there, teetering on the edge of life, that same pain clawed at her, as if her very soul was fracturing.

"Not again," she whispered, her voice choked with grief. "Please, God, not again."

Denise sat next to her. "Baby, I know this is hard. But you named that child Miracle for a reason. If there's anyone who can pull through this, it's her."

Winter nodded, squeezing her mom's hand. "I'm glad you were there, Mom, thank you."

"Baby, you never have to thank me. I love you."

"I just wish you were around more."

"Winnie, now's not the time for this."

"I'm drowning. Mom. We need you. *I* need you."

Before Denise could respond, Jae returned, with a slight pallor to his skin but determination in his eyes. "Am I interrupting something?"

"No," Denise insisted. "I was just about to get some fresh air. She's all yours."

Winter scoffed. "Try not to find a plane ticket to Cabo while you're outside."

Denise stood in silence, then looked at Jae. He understood what was happening.

As Denise walked outside, he sat beside Winter, wrapping his arm around her shoulders, grounding her in his steady presence. "Man, we've been around a lot of doctors," he said, trying to break the tension in the air.

Winter nodded, unmoved by his statement.

He continued. "I was just thinking about the first time I came to the rehab center on campus. I was nineteen when I ruptured my hamstring. I didn't think I'd be able to jump again, let alone play ball. They assigned my recovery to the best trainer, who assigned you, a kid who didn't want be in sports medicine anymore, to their best athlete. I thought it was over, but you surprised me."

"Hell, I surprised myself," she chuckled.

"You were damn good at it. You helped me get my form back, and even made sure that my vertical was higher than it was before I left. Each time I wanted to quit, you reminded me I wasn't going through it alone, and I never felt like I was, because with every setback, every hurdle, you were right there till I got back on the court."

He pulled her in closer and said, "You're not going through this alone, Winter," he murmured, his voice soft but certain. "We're getting her through this. She's a fighter, just like you."

Winter leaned into him, closing her eyes as he held her. His steady hand rubbed circles along her back, soothing her even as she felt herself teetering on the brink. The world around them felt surreal, as though the walls and lights and sounds were all part of a nightmare she was desperate to wake from.

The hours dragged on, each minute stretching unbearably as they waited for news.

It was Christmas Eve, but nothing about the sterile hospital waiting room felt like the holiday season. The dim lights hummed softly overhead, casting cold shadows across the walls. Outside, the sky was a steely gray, the world darkened by the weight of winter. And in that stillness, time seemed to stretch endlessly.

Winter sat slumped in a chair, staring blankly at the worn pattern on the carpet, her mind spinning with memories of Malik's last moments and the bleak possibility that she might lose Miri, too. She ran her fingers over her phone, glancing occasionally at the endless stream of notifications: ESPN, Twitter, messages from friends, family, teammates—all filled with concern and speculation.

Jae sat beside her, his hand holding hers tightly, never letting go, as if his grip alone could keep her tethered to hope. They exchanged glances, both worn and drained but refusing to let go of the belief that Miri would make it through.

Hours passed. A nurse came by periodically with updates: they had administered Jae's blood, her vitals were stable but low, they were monitoring her closely. Each snippet of information seemed just enough to keep them holding on, yet never enough to ease their fear.

The evening slipped into night, and Winter found herself drifting between memories and reality, her mind replaying all the moments she'd had with Miri—her first steps, her first words, her smile lighting up every room she walked into. And now, here they were, fighting to keep her from fading away.

Around midnight, Dr. Mason came out, looking more exhausted than before. He gave them a brief update: Miri's condition was still critical, but she'd made it through the transfusion. They had administered the experimental drugs, and now it was a matter of waiting.

"Her body has to respond," he said gently, his voice low. "The next few hours are crucial."

Winter nodded numbly, the weight of his words pressing down on her like a vise. She leaned back into her chair, closing her eyes as fresh tears slid down her cheeks.

Jae leaned over, gently placing a hand on her shoulder. "Winter, listen to me," he murmured, his voice a steady anchor in the storm. "She's a fighter. You raised her to be one."

Winter looked up at him, her eyes searching his. "I'm terrified, Jae. I don't know how to do this again. Not after Malik."

He took her hand, his grip firm, grounding her in the moment. "You're not going to lose her. This is different. And you're not alone this time." He brushed a tear from her cheek, his gaze unwavering. "I won't let anything happen to her."

Somewhere in the early hours of Christmas morning, Winter drifted into a restless sleep, her head leaning on Jae's shoulder. The waiting room was silent, the quiet hum of the building the only sound. Outside, the first rays of dawn began to break through the heavy clouds, casting a pale light across the world.

Winter stirred, blinking her eyes open as the dull ache of exhaustion settled into her bones. She glanced around, disoriented for a moment before reality crashed back over her. She sat up, her heart racing as she remembered where she was and why.

"Jae?" she murmured, her voice barely above a whisper.

He stirred, waking slowly, his arm still around her shoulders. "Morning," he said softly, his voice thick with exhaustion.

Just then, Denise walked in, her eyes red-rimmed but her expression calm as she took in her daughter's face. She sat down beside Winter, wrapping her arms around her in a tight hug.

"Merry Christmas, baby," Denise whispered, her voice trembling.

Winter let out a shaky breath, clinging to her mother. "It doesn't feel like Christmas," she murmured, her voice barely audible.

Denise pulled back, looking into her eyes. "I know it doesn't. But you have to hold on to hope. Miri's tough. She's got you and Jae here, and she's fighting with everything she's got."

Just as Denise finished speaking, Dr. Mason appeared at the doorway, his face unreadable. Winter's breath caught as he approached, his gaze meeting hers with a mix of compassion and gravity.

He cleared his throat, glancing at Jae and Denise before focusing on Winter. "We've done everything we can. Her body's responding, but it's weak. The next twelve hours are critical. If she can make it through today, there's a good chance she'll pull through."

The weight of his words settled over them like a blanket, both heavy and fragile. Winter felt her chest tighten, a painful glimmer of hope sparking in the depths of her heart. She clung to Jae's hand, the faintest spark of belief flickering within her.

"Thank you," she whispered, her voice breaking.

Dr. Mason nodded, giving her a reassuring squeeze on the shoulder. "I'll be back with updates as we have them."

As THE DAY WORE ON, the hours blurred together in a haze of hope and fear. Winter and Jae remained by Miri's side, each monitor beep and movement a reminder of how fragile life could be. Occasionally, Denise would bring them coffee or food, coaxing them to eat even when the taste of everything felt like sandpaper against their throats.

By late afternoon, there was still no word. Jae spent most of the day fielding questions from all the local sports media. He even spoke to the small vigil gathered outside the facility and signed autographs.

He walked in and sat down next to her, clearly exhausted from the barrage of questions. Winter instinctively leaned on his shoulder as he wrapped his arm around her. With her face resting against his chest, she asked, "Does that ever get old?"

"What exactly?"

"Always saying the right thing."

"I've been media trained since I was eighteen. But yes, it's draining. Any word on Miri?"

"Hell, I was hoping you got word. What's taking so long? It's been over twelve hours."

"We just got to let Dr. Mason do his work. He's the best in the world."

"I just want to know what's taking so long." Winter said. She shifted up.

Denise, who was sitting in a chair next to the two of them, shook Winter's leg.

"Looks like you won't have to wait much more to find out." She pointed to Dr. Mason who had just walked into the room. "Mrs. Carter?"

"Yes," she answered.

As she was about to stand to her feet, the doctor stopped her. "You might want to stay sitting down."

♡

23

CRUNCH TIME

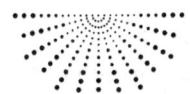

"*D*octor, how is she?"

"She's doing well, and that's what I wanted to talk to you about." The doctor leaned back as Winter tensed with apprehension. "As you know, we know very little about this particular strand of sickle cell, but our research has been results driven since before we partnered with Mr. Carter and—"

Winter raised her hand and leaned forward, exasperated. "Doc, I'm not trying to be rude, but it's been a long twenty-four hours. Is my baby going to be okay or not?"

The doctor leaned in closer and placed his hand on top of hers. "Forgive me for burying the lead. Your daughter is fine. In fact, for all intents and purposes, she is cured."

Winter sat in the hospital waiting room, her heart pounding from the doctor's words. *Cured.* The word echoed in her mind, a promise she had dared not hoped for. Her knees buckled as she let out a trembling breath, leaning into Jae's steadying arms.

"My baby is cured," she whispered, almost as if saying it aloud would make it real. She glanced up at Dr. Morgan, expecting him to confirm it again, to somehow explain the miracle unfolding before her.

Dr. Morgan looked back at her with a gentle but resolute expression. "Yes, Mrs. Carter, Miracle's body has responded beyond anything we could have anticipated. The advanced therapy, combined with the transfusion from a genetically-compatible paternal donor, it allowed her immune system to replace defective cells with healthy ones. We saw strides well outside of the parameters of our testing. The compatibility between her and her father's blood type was key in helping her recover so completely."

Winter's face lit up as she hugged Jae, joy surging through her... until Dr. Morgan's words sank in fully. *Paternal donor.*

She froze, the joy in her heart turning to confusion, then to a gnawing sense of dread. Winter's brow furrowed. "Wait. Did you just say...'paternal donor'?"

The doctor nodded, seemingly unfazed. "That's right. The compatibility came from her biological father's unique genetic profile. It's what allowed for this miraculous recovery."

Winter felt her stomach drop. She pulled back, looking up at Jae, who now wore an unreadable expression. "But... but Jae's not her father."

The doctor paused, his brow dimming as he exchanged a look with Winter. His face softened as he seemed to realize the implication of her words. "I... I'm so sorry. I thought you understood. The genetic compatibility tests confirmed it. Miracle's father—biologically—is Jaden."

Winter stumbled back in the chair, clutching the paperwork Dr. Morgan handed her, staring at the numbers and percentages that confirmed it, undeniable in cold, hard text.

Paternal match: 99.9% compatibility.

She processes the words. All of it, her daughter's cure and the scientific fact of Jae being her father.

"I'll give you both a moment." Dr. Morgan excused himself, leaving them in a silence heavy with revelation and disbelief.

Winter rose to her feet then turned to Jae, who also stood, her voice barely a whisper. "What in the hell is he talking about, Jae?"

Jae took a deep breath, his eyes heavy with the weight of the secret he'd carried for years. "Winter... let's go somewhere private. I'll explain everything, I promise. But right now, there are too many eyes, and we need to focus on Miri."

"I don't give a damn about these people, Jae," Winter said firmly, the shock quickly turning to anger. "I want to know *right now*."

"I'll tell you, but you don't want the optics."

"No, *you* don't want the optics, because you have to plan everything you say and do. I don't give a shit." She started to shake with anger, and let out a slight chuckle as she read the paperwork again. "I know this is Christmas Day, but I ain't Mary, and Miri isn't Jesus, so tell me Jae, how in the hell I ended up with a kid who's biologically yours when, until this week, we'd never had sex?"

Jae's face tightened as he struggled to gather his thoughts. Finally, he looked her in the eyes and began. "After you and Malik got married, that's when he got really sick, Winter. And when the doctors told him he'd never be able to have children—even with IVF—it crushed him. You know Malik, not willing to take no for an answer. All he wanted was to be a father, to give you the life you both dreamed of."

Winter's face twisted with confusion, anger, and something else—hurt. "We needed IVF, yes, but we agreed to try everything. He didn't say anything about that part of the diagnosis. I thought we were still trying..."

"He didn't want to tell you. I used to take him to all his appointments, and I'd just been drafted," Jae said softly, his voice thick with emotion. "He asked me to... to help. To be the donor. He knew he didn't have much time, and he didn't want you to live without the child you both wanted so badly."

Winter stumbled backward, her hand flying to her mouth. "So... you're telling me... Malik *asked* you to father our child?"

Jae nodded, his voice breaking. "I refused at first. We fought about it for weeks. But then he said, 'When have you ever been there for me when I needed you most?' and the truth was, I'd never been there. I wasn't around enough. It was a low blow, but he was my brother, Winter. He was dying. I couldn't say no."

Tears streamed down Winter's face as she tried to comprehend it all. She remembered those dark days after Malik's death, when she'd found out she was pregnant, and felt as though a part of Malik had come back to her, a gift of love and hope. And now she was learning that the child she'd believed was Malik's last connection to her was, in truth, Jae's.

"I can't believe this," she whispered, her voice thick with betrayal. "You... both of you... kept this from me?"

Jae's face crumpled, guilt and pain etched into every line. "I wanted to tell you. So many times. But you were already grieving, and then you were dealing with morning sickness, but it didn't really hit me, what I'd done, until Miri was born. When you looked at her, you were happy for the first time in months. I couldn't bring myself to shatter that. So, I stayed in the background. I became 'Uncle Jae' because... because that's who I thought you needed me to be."

Winter closed her eyes, reeling from the weight of the truth, her mind whirling as she tried to make sense of everything. "You looked me in my face, knowing the truth, and kept it from me for years."

"I'm not making excuses, but I was twenty-two years old. Up until I found Malik, I didn't have any family. He was my big brother, and he was dying. I kept his secret the same way you want me to keep from Miri that we're sleeping together."

"That is *so* different. Our situation was a one-time thing."

"Really? You're not counting the bakery? The other morning? From where I sit, I'm the only one sacrificing for the people I love."

Winter was about to respond when a voice broke through the silence. "Wait... you're my dad?"

They turned to see Miri standing at the doorway, her face pale and eyes red-rimmed, her expression a mixture of shock, anger, and heartbreak.

"Miri...how long have you been standing there?" Winter began moving toward her, but Miri stepped back, her gaze never leaving Jae's.

"You're... thot sauce?" She looked at her mother, who stood

motionless. The embarrassment of it all told Miri everything she needed to hear.

Winter wanted to hug her daughter, whose mood had soured. "Miri, honey, listen, it's not—it's complicated."

Miri put up a hand, her face a shade of horror. "No, actually, it's not complicated, Mom. It's just… gross. You're telling me you two finally decided to… and then this?" She shook her head, a shiver of revulsion running through her. "I didn't need to know that."

Jae stepped forward, hands outstretched. "Miri, we never meant for you to find out any of this this way, and I know it's a lot to process—"

"A lot to process?" Miri cut him off, looking between the two of them. "My uncle is actually my dad, and he's sleeping with my mom. That's a shit ton to process."

"Miri, honey, just—"

"No! You guys have been lying to me my whole life. And now on the day I get the best news of my life, I find out you're actually my dad? All while you two are apparently… screwing each other?"

Winter's face flushed with embarrassment, but she tried to keep her composure. "Miri, it's more complicated than that. We were just—"

"—just keeping secrets, like always," Miri finished for her, her voice filled with bitterness. "Seems like that's the only thing this family's good at."

Before they could respond, Miri turned and stormed out of the room, leaving them standing there, the weight of her words hanging heavy in the air.

Winter let out a shaky breath, her shoulders sagging.

Just as she gathered herself to go after Miri, she caught sight of a flash outside the window—a news crew with a camera, clearly filming part of the heated exchange.

Winter's stomach dropped.

"Oh my god, Jae," she whispered, nodding toward the camera crew. "They're filming this."

Without a word, Jae bolted toward the door, bursting outside and charging toward the crew. "Turn that off!" he barked, his tone steely and unyielding.

The reporter, unfazed, took a step back. "The public has a right to know—"

Jae glared, taking another step forward. He snatched the camera and smashed it on the ground.

"My camera!" the cameraman shouted in protest.

"If you don't get out of here right now, you'll be dealing with more than just a broken camera. Now *leave.*"

The crew reluctantly backed away, and Jae watched them go until they were out of sight. Only then did he turn and head back inside, his face tense with anger and frustration.

As he walked back toward Winter, Denise intercepted him, her expression a mix of disapproval and protectiveness. As he stood there, trying to process it all, he felt Denise's hand on his shoulder. "We'll get through this, honey," Denise said softly. "But you need time. And so does she."

There was nothing else that needed to be said. Jae walked out, glancing back, only now realizing the true depth of his brother's request.

24

IN TRANSITION

$\mathcal{T}$he morning light filtered through the blinds as Winter paced her living room, phone in hand, barely registering the news anchors on the TV.

"Breaking news on the recent confrontation between former NBA star Jaden Carter and Houston Rockets GM Darren Bailey," the anchor announced. "Sources say the altercation stemmed from personal matters involving Carter's newly-confirmed paternity of high school basketball prodigy Miracle Carter. Jaden's attorney has confirmed that he was merely a donor for his brother, former Cougar, Malik Carter, but the family decided to keep it confidential. Jaden's attorney wasn't available for additional comments. In other sports news, UConn has decided to rec—"

Click.

Winter turned off the television. Denise turned around and said, "Hey, I was about to watch that."

She walked over and handed her mother the remote, who turned it back on.

"Damn it, Winnie, they've moved past the story."

"Don't worry, I'm sure it will come back on. This is the second time they've run the story about Jae this hour."

Winter shook her head as the screen showed grainy footage of Jae smashing the camera at the facility, followed by shots of Jae brushing past reporters on his way out of the Rockets gym.

She switched off the TV again, disgusted with the vultures circling her family's pain. "This is insane. They're twisting the entire story."

Her mother sat at the kitchen table, sipping coffee with a steady gaze. She set her mug down, breaking the silence. "You know, Jaden was just a kid himself back then. Trying to be there for you."

"Mom, why are you always defending him? He's not putting you in his will."

"Wyn, I had a wonderful husband, God rest his soul, and two sons that hung the moon. Now, don't get me wrong, there's a lot to be desired with the state of our men, but I've been blessed and so have you. This man has made something of himself, and is always trying to do the right thing. Someone's gotta advocate for 'em. Jae isn't perfect, but he's good."

Winter nodded and looked out of the window. "I know, but I trusted him. I mean, he's my best friend. How could he look at me for years and just say nothing?"

"The same way you could tell him to lie about you two bumpin' uglies. Momma's proud of you, by the way."

"See, this is the bull I be talking about."

"Girl, hush, I saw that coming years ago. I'm just happy it finally happened."

"You know, what bugs me is, I look at Miri every day. I mean, I just didn't see it. Hell, Miri looks more like me and Malik's momma more than anybody. And there would be times she'd move like him on the court, and I thought, okay, it just runs in the family. But now... now I can't unsee it, and I feel so stupid."

"You were stupid, Winnie, but so was he, and that's the point. Jae loved his big brother more than life itself, and he made a decision that he could never really understand the implications of. Sometimes you get into a situation you don't know how to get out of, and you think the best thing to do is not rock the boat. And I'm not saying it's right, I'm just saying I've been there before. But let's be honest, that's not where we should place the blame. Let's not forget this was your *husband's* idea."

Winter threw her hands in the air. "Oh, here we go."

"Winnie, I'm just saying, there's plenty of blame to go around. You're throwing all the blame on Jaden, but he was trying to *help* Malik, rest his soul. Malik was the mastermind behind this."

"I don't even know why I expect anything different from you," Winter said as she walked towards the kitchen.

Denise followed her. "And what is that supposed to mean?"

"Mom, be real. You always had a problem with Malik."

"And you've always found a reason to defend him. Even in this, you're blaming Jae. Not the man who had the plan."

"Mom, I'm not stupid. You wanted me to be with Jae because he had money. You never liked Malik. You never even bothered to see what I saw in him."

Denise put her coffee down, grabbing her daughter's hand. "Baby. I need you to understand something. I love Jae, and it ain't got a damn thing to do with his money. Do you want to know why?"

"Sure, let's hear it. I'm all ears," she huffed.

She was halfway through an eye roll when she noticed her mother's face. It carried a sternness that disarmed Winter's defensiveness. She had seen that look at different points in her childhood, and while she couldn't think of a specific moment, she knew her mother meant what she was about to say next.

"I never truly got a chance to grieve your father. I was too busy trying to hold all of you together. I know your daddy meant the world to you, and to lose him like that... Well, I thought I'd never see you smile again. We all had the same reaction then, try to hold each other up to get through it, you know. You were going to school, moving through the motions, putting on a brave face, but you weren't Winnie.

"Then, about nine months later, almost like God's timing, I heard something I'll never forget. You giggled, and it wasn't any kind of giggle; it was the same kind of giggle I let out the day I met your daddy, and it wasn't long before this tall, lanky, handsome young man started showing up, and every time he came around, you were smiling. He did the same thing for you when his brother died. That's why I love Jae."

Denise let her daughter's hands go and wiped a tear from her eye, only for it to be replaced by another. "Listen, I know you and Jae want to remember Malik as a saint through the lenses of your rose-colored glasses, but I didn't wear any glasses. I saw him for who he was, and I liked pieces of him. But there were pieces of him, like all people, that weren't so shiny."

"Momma, what are you talking about?"

Denise threw her hands in the air. "So you just gonna make me come out and say it, huh?"

"That would be nice."

"Okay, you want the truth. Here goes: Malik was a selfish user who would have bled his brother dry had he kept living."

"Momma! I can't b—"

"Baby, tell the truth and shame the devil. I was there back then, Wyn. I remember when you and Jae were on the phone, you just talked about life and your days and what happened on campus. But when you started talking to Malik, most of your conversations somehow went back to Jaden's money. "

"What? No, I—it wasn't like that."

"Child, quit lying to yourself. I know you liked Jaden before then."

"That was just freshman year, and you're making it sound worse than what it—"

"I'm telling you how I saw it. Whether you knew it or not, you liked Jaden, and Jaden liked you, and then one day this Malik was in the picture. He didn't like the idea of you two being friends. I heard him say it with my own ears in my house. He never had a problem going to his little brother for a few dollars to buy you something nice. He was cock-blocking then, and he's cock-blocking from beyond the grave now."

Winter was beyond offended by what her mother was saying. "I won't have you talk about my husband and the father of my child that way."

"That's the point, honey, he's not the father of your child. Jaden is, and from where I sit, he's been a damn good one. You're mad at Jaden when you should be pointing the finger at Malik."

"Momma, that's enough—"

"Like hell it is. I'm slapping some sense into you today, Winnie. I'm so sick and tired of people turning into saints once they pass. Let's put some truth to light. Malik Carter was a user, and he was selfish. A charming user, but one nonetheless. He had flaws, like all of us. It was *his* plan, Winnie. You couldn't see it, and neither could Jae, but the man was conniving. He was a good man. He probably would've grown out of it, but he was young. You just have to accept it."

"Why do you care about any of this?"

"Because I want you to be happy, Wyn, and when Jaden's around, that's when you're the happiest. That's always been true. Even when Malik was here. At least from what I see."

"When you're around," Winter muttered.

Her mother cocked a brow. "And what's that supposed to mean?"

"Nothing, Momma. It meant nothing at all."

"Girl, you've been beating around the bush with something you've wanted to say since I been in town. Either speak your mind, or hold your tongue, but I won't do all this passivity."

Winter's face twisted with frustration. "Well, maybe if you had stuck around more, I wouldn't feel so... alone. Now, Miri's caught up in all this, and I'm stuck cleaning up the mess everyone left."

Denise shook her head. "Winter Elise Villery-Carter. You are being selfish. You know the other thing I didn't tell you in that story earlier, was when you and your siblings were out living your lives, that's when I was finally able to grieve your daddy. He wanted to do two things: open Villery's so you could own it one day, and travel the world. Now you got the restaurant, and I got a ticket to Spain. We're both doing what we feel is right. I need to live out his dream for him, and I think I'm owed as much."

Winter hung her head. Her mother had a way of making her feel small with her insight. She nodded as her mother continued. "You act like you're an island when you're not. When your father died, it was just me and four kids. I didn't have a Hall of Famer multi-millionaire best friend to call on. Have you even thanked him for the countless ways he's stepped up? And I'm not just talking about his money, I'm talking about his time. Your daughter is about to attend one of the best schools in the nation because he taught her the sport she loves."

"Like I said, you always find a way to defend Jae," Winter bristled, grabbing her purse from the counter. "Thanks, Mom. Real supportive."

Her mother's words stung, regardless of how true they were. She needed to end the conversation.

Denise shrugged in concession, but as Winter moved toward the door, Denise called after her, a wry smile on her face. "Oh, by the way, those papers you're going to sign with Christina? That whole deal to get Villery's? That was Jae's handiwork, too. So, what you call defending, I call setting the record straight."

Winter paused, her mother's words sinking in.

She left without another word, but her mind buzzed with the realization that Jae had quietly set the stage for her restaurant to open after all, even amid their chaos.

She drove over to the bakery and parked outside. She decided to take the entrance to the restaurant, using the key Jae had given her for Christmas.

Once inside, she took a moment to take in the restaurant. It was better than she'd imagined it.

The tears formed in her eyes. Her life wasn't in shambles, but it felt like it.

She caught a glimpse of Christina at the entrance. Turning her face, she wiped her tears and got herself together as her ex-friend walked in.

"Thank you for coming on time, Christina."

"I'm always on time, Wyn. You're the one that runs behind."

Winter sighed. *So this is how it was going to be.* "I didn't mean anything by that."

"I know how you meant it. I'm just clarifying to you who I am."

There was an awkward silence.

Christina hovered as she took in the ambiance of the restaurant.

Winter found a slight dip in the tension between them when she said, "Your place looks nice."

"Thanks."

"I would've gone with a teal, cream and dark oak look, but I guess I'll have to start out with a food truck since that's all I can afford after Jae's *generous* offer."

Winter shook her head. She needed to defuse the situation. "How did we get here Chrissy?" she asked her friend, exhausted from the fight.

Her friend glared at her. "No, Wyn, you don't get to do that."

"Do what?"

"Act like you didn't snap at me in front of Jae and your momma, then sent your pit bull after me to strong arm me."

"I'm not strong arming you. And I didn't send Jae."

"You do it so much you can't even help it... showing up late with a whole batch of excuses while I'm busting my ass getting the bakery open in the mornings. "

"So I'm a few minutes late? Between this business, Miri, and—"

"You don't get to do that either."

"Do *what*?"

"Be... you. I'm so sick and tired of hearing you complain about everything that's right with your life. You have a daughter smart enough to graduate two years early and get a scholarship, you have a momma who taught you how to bake and a dad who taught you how to cook so good you're gonna get paid for it, and let's not forget about your fairy God-Uncle Moneybags. Did Jaden tell you he threatened to ruin me if I didn't sign over this property? And what am I gonna do, fight a multi-millionaire? With what money? It's just me out here, Wyn. I don't have nobody but me. You'll never know what that feels like."

"Chrissy, since you've known me, I've done three things: be a wife, be a mother, and run this bakery. I can't be responsible for you not wanting to stick with something longer than a weekend."

"Oh, here we go," Christina huffed as Winter walked around a table, growing in anger.

"You wanna go there?"

Christina crossed her arms in defiance. "Let's go there."

"Fine, I said I have to carry you because I do. You've had fifteen different careers in ten years. First you wanted to be a chef, then a real estate agent, then you want to be a nurse, and each time one of those got hard, you'd need a place to stay, or a job, or whatever you needed, and I was there for you. "

"I ain't gotta explain my choices to you."

"But you sure as hell had no problem sitting on my couch crying about it. And don't even get me started on the men."

"Oh, we going there?"

"You took it there Chrissy, I'm just showing up. I've seen you discard perfectly good men for no other reason than you were bored with them, and you did it for years."

"Kiss my ass, Wyn—"

Winter began ticking them off with her fingers. "Rodney, cause he was boring. Raheem, for clipping his toenails. Avon, for breathing too loudly after sex."

"So what?"

"So, they were good men, but you're a runner. You say you want to be married, have kids. You could've married either of them and been down the line, because they're all great husbands now. But you wanted Big Dick Davion, Kujo Rich, and put those men through hell trying to get them."

Christina hung her head and closed her eyes as Winter continued. "And what was Big Dick Davion doing, Chrissy? Cheating every chance he got. How many baby mommas did he make while you were chasing behind him? Four? Six?"

"We can't all have a Jae!" Christina shouted.

Silence filled the room.

After a while, Christina out pulled the paperwork and signed it as a tear fell from her eye and dropped onto the page.

As she was about to leave, she stopped. "One last act of friendship." Christina wiped a tear from her eye. She took a breath and spoke. "I'll admit. I may have been low down with this move right here," she gestured to their surroundings, "but what you're doing to Jaden is far more sinister, because you don't want him, you just don't want nobody else to have him. You're hovering close enough to him that he can't make room for another woman. I feel sorry for the both of you, because you're scared to live, and you won't let either of you move past college. He'll never find happiness outside of you, and what's worse is, you're doing it with a smile."

As Christina opened the door, Winter wiped a tear from her eye and said softly. "Christina."

"Yeah?"

"You're fired."

Winter refused to look at her, but from her periphery she could see a hand in the air as Christina walked out the door. She assumed she had flipped her off.

She let the tears fall, processing the fight that just happened, torn between accountability for her part in the betrayal, and Christina's own betrayal.

She was juggling with each emotion when her phone rang. "Hey, Momma."

"Hey, baby, you sound upset, but I need to tell you something."

Winter wiped her tears as a chill ran down her spine. "What is it now? Is Miri okay?"

"Honey, that news that you cut off about UConn was about Miri. They rescinded her offer letter because they weren't informed about her medical issues."

"Damn it. Where is she?"

"That's why I called. I went to go check on her, but Miri's gone."

25

POST-UP PRESSURE

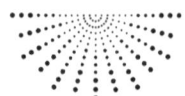

*J*ae was sitting on his couch, staring blankly at a stack of papers he'd been meaning to go through. The last few days had been a whirlwind, every piece of his life somehow exposed and dissected for the public, and the weight of it all was starting to press down on him. He ran a hand over his face, trying to clear his mind

He missed his girls. There hadn't been a day since Miri was born that he hadn't talked to one of them. He wondered how quickly things could turn from such a blissful high to the nightmare he was now navigating. He looked at the pile of papers again.

"Time to get to it, Carter," he huffed. He picked up the first envelope in the pile when his phone buzzed beside him.

It was a text from Winter. He opened it, and his eyes felt heavy looking at her message.

Hey, have you seen your niece?

Immediately, something felt off. Why would she be asking him that out of the blue?

A second message came almost instantly, and his heart dropped when he read it.

Sorry, I mean your... your daughter. She's missing, Jae.

He sat up straight, adrenaline kicking in as he read the words over again. *What?* He typed back quickly, fingers shaking slightly. *What happened? Is she okay?*

The reply came fast, each word worst than the last. *She found out UConn pulled their offer. My mom said she took off. I've looked everywhere and... nothing.*

Jae's mind went blank for a moment, and then the panic hit, sharp and immediate. Miri was missing? Out there somewhere, feeling hurt, betrayed, alone?

His response was automatic, his fingers moving on their own. *Go home. I'll find her.*

He wasn't sure if Winter would listen, but he couldn't waste another second. He grabbed his keys, already knowing where to start looking.

As he bolted out the door, he felt the weight of everything he hadn't said to Miri bearing down on him. The truth he hadn't been able to tell her, the moments he'd lost as her father, the anger and hurt he knew she'd been carrying all alone. And now, in her moment of pain, he hadn't been there. *Not this time,* he thought. He was going to find her, no matter what it took.

The drive was a blur as Jae tore through familiar streets, his mind racing as he thought of every place Miri might go. He knew her habits, her favorite spots, and he trusted that she hadn't strayed too far, but she wasn't at any of her usual hangouts.

McGregor Park, he thought to himself. It was a long shot, but that place had always held a piece of her heart. She loved its open spaces, the memories they had there together, and watching all the legends that had played there over the years. If she was anywhere, it would be there.

He pulled into the parking lot, cutting the engine and scanning the area, his heart pounding. At first, he didn't see her, but then, on a bench near the far end, he saw a small figure hunched over, her shoulders slumped in a way that made his chest tighten.

He pulled out his phone and sent a text.

Found her. I'll make sure she gets home safe.

Thank you, Jae.

He put his phone back and watched as Miri got up from the bench and headed to the court to start shooting the basketball. Relief washed over him, but it was quickly replaced by the sharp sting of seeing his daughter like that, alone and visibly hurting. He approached slowly, wanting to give her space but also needing her to know he was there.

"Miri?" he called gently as he got closer.

She looked up, her eyes narrowing when she saw him. There was no relief in her gaze, no comfort. Just hurt, mixed with a spark of anger that took him aback.

"What are you doing here?" she demanded, her voice icy as she started to shoot the basketball.

Jae stopped a few feet from her, hands in his pockets. "Your mom told me you were missing. I was worried."

Miri let out a bitter laugh, shaking her head. "Figures that she'd call you instead of looking for me herself."

"She has been looking," Jae said softly. "Your mom's worried sick. She didn't want to leave any stone unturned."

"Right," Miri muttered, looking away. "Everyone's so worried about me now. Funny how that happens *after* they ruin my life."

Jae felt a pang in his chest, but he forced himself to stay calm. "Miri, I know you're hurt. And you have every right to be. But disappearing… that's not going to fix anything."

Miri's gaze snapped back to him, fierce and defiant. "What would you know about it? I worked my whole life for this, and because of your public spectacle at the hospital, now it's all gone. UConn was my dream, and you and Mom took it away from me."

Jae's heart broke at the accusation, but he nodded, acknowledging her pain. "I know UConn was important to you. And I know you feel like everything's falling apart right now. But this… this is just one setback. It doesn't define who you are."

"Doesn't define who I am?" Miri laughed, but it was hollow, her voice trembling. "You don't get it, Jae. My whole life, you and Mom lied to me. And now I don't even know who I am. Or who you are."

Jae took a deep breath, the guilt weighing on him like a stone. "I wish I could change that, Miri. I wish I could take back all the secrets. But I can't. All I can do now is try to be here, to be someone you can trust, moving forward. Starting right now, I'll answer anything. Whatever you want to know."

She said nothing, but continued to dribble the basketball and work on her shot. Jae walked over to her as she shot the ball and it went in. He picked it up and tossed it back to her as she took three more dribbles and shot again.

"Miri?"

"What is there to talk about, Unc?"

"Well… there's a lot to talk about."

"No shit."

"Miri, come on now, I know you're upset, but I'm still your—"

"My what? My coach? My dad? Or my uncle? 'Cause I'll tell you right now, at least one of those is a goddamn lie!" she yelled as she threw the basketball against the fence. A tear fell from her eye.

Jae watched his heart break in front of his eyes at the true level of his deception. The pain forced tears from his eyes. He didn't want to stand, but he couldn't move. He could only watch the daughter he'd let grow up alone.

Miri composed her sobbing, took a breath. "You know, my whole life I wondered if I could beat my dad one-on-one? I think every baller wants to know if they can. I'd ask you about Malik, and you used to say he was so much better than you. I never believed you, though. You were an NBA prospect, and he wasn't. Now I know two things: one, how it feels to play against my dad."

"Miri, please just list—"

"And two, he's a goddamn liar."

"I'm so sorry, Cupcake. You gotta believe me."

"Sixteen years, Uncle Jae?" she screamed with tears flowing from her eyes. She fought to control her pain to continue. "For sixteen years, I wondered what it would be like to have a dad, and I had one the whole time." The silence between her words was deafening. She looked towards the sky then chuckled as if recalling a memory.

"I remember I used to have sleepovers, and I'd tell people you were like a dad to me. But you were nothing like a dad. Because a real dad wouldn't lie to his daughter!"

"I know, Miri… it was complicated—"

"I don't give a damn how complicated it was! There's nothing in the world that should've stopped you from telling me that I'm your daughter."

She was right. No matter what he thought, deep down she was right.

"Do you know how many sleepless nights I stayed up, praying just to have a conversation with my dad?"

Jae hung his head in shame. "Maybe not all of them, but I do know that some of those nights you called me, and every one of those nights I listened."

"Then why didn't you tell me? I get why you didn't tell Mom, as messed up as that was. But why didn't you tell me? When you knew how I felt. Why wasn't I good enough for you to tell me the truth? I thought you were supposed to love me?"

She sobbed uncontrollably. They both did as the tears were flowing freely from Jae's face. He walked closer to her and grabbed her chin. "I need you to know something. I love you more than life itself, and you have always, always been more than good enough. Never doubt that."

"Then why didn't you tell me?"

"I fucked up, Cupcake," he said as he tried to regain his composure. He wiped the tears from his eyes, took a deep breath and said, "I'm not making any excuses, but I was twenty-two years old. All I had done with my life was try to find Malik and play basketball. I was new to the league, and the brother I'd spent half my life trying to find again, was dying. He asked me to bring you into the world. I said no at first, but he cut me off and I had already lost enough time. I couldn't loose anymore with him."

He took a breath as he wiped the tears, still freely flowing from his face and continued,

"You might not see it now, but twenty-two-year-olds have a lot more in common with sixteen-year-olds than they do thirty-eight-year-olds. I had no idea what I was doing, I just wanted him to be happy. I wanted everyone to be happy, even if that meant I wasn't happy. It wasn't until you were born, and I looked in your eyes, I realized what I'd actually done." His knees nearly buckled as the weight of his confession bore on him. He steadied himself and continued. "You are still the most beautiful creature I've ever seen in my entire life. The first time I held you, I saw you had my hands—not Leek's, mine— and I knew I'd made a terrible mistake, but I didn't know how to fix it. So, I just... became Uncle Jae, and I hate that with all my heart and soul."

He took a deep breath, reflecting on the years of agony. He bit his lip as the tears fell. "But I swore to myself that every decision after that would be the best thing for you. That's why I never took a contract to leave Houston. That's why I coached your AAU league teams. That's why I saw you every week of your life, because I put you in this position, and I had to make sure you were going to be fine as best I could. You have been the reason I've done everything I've done."

"It wasn't enough!" she yelled, not bothering to check the tears that rolled down her eyes. Jae sat silently as her fury rose. "I needed you. You! My dad. Not some uncle that bought me nice things and lived across town. I just gotta know one thing: if this hadn't gone down the way it did, were you ever gonna tell me?"

Jae wanted to respond, but could say nothing. He hung his head in disappointment as she continued. "What? Ain't got nothing to say? I guess you really do choke in the clutch, Choke Carter."

Miracle walked over and picked up the basketball which had rolled near the bleachers. She took a few dribbles and sunk the shot from thirty feet away.

As the ball sailed through the net, she chuckled, shaking her head. "At least I know now why I'm so good at basketball. Don't come to my game, Pops, you're not invited. Tell your baby momma she can stop worrying. Her bastard is on her way home."

"Miri, if you would just let me—"

It was too late, she was already walking away.

26
SHUTOUT

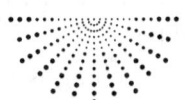

inter stood in front of the mirror, adjusting the strap of her dress for the alumni gala. The gown was elegant, midnight blue with a subtle shimmer, but her heart felt anything but light. This event was supposed to be a celebration, a step toward launching her father's dream restaurant, yet she couldn't shake the heaviness in her chest. She glanced at her daughter, Miri, slouched in the corner with her arms crossed, her expression closed off and distant.

"You don't have to look so miserable, you know," Winter said gently, trying to catch Miri's eye in the mirror. "This could be a good thing for us."

Miri didn't respond, just looked away, her gaze fixed somewhere far from the present moment. The silence stretched between them, the air thick with words left unsaid.

Winter's mother, Denise, stepped into the room. She took in Winter's outfit. "Baby, you look fantastic. Almost as good as me at that age. Lord, I do good work." She strutted over to examine the gown closer. She stopped midway and noticed Miri's dejected face.

Folding her arms with a knowing look, she pointed to the both of them. "You two are going to have to deal with this tension at some point. You think I haven't noticed?" she asked, raising an eyebrow at Winter. "If I didn't know better, I'd say you two were more alike than either of you will admit, but I'm just gonna mind my black-owned business over here."

Winter rolled her eyes, but her mother's words hit home. Denise wasn't one to sugarcoat things, especially when it came to her granddaughter. She kissed them both on the cheek and left the room.

Winter took a deep breath and turned to face Miri fully, crossing the room to sit down next to her.

"Miri," she began softly, searching her daughter's face. "I want to apologize about UConn. I know it meant the world to you, and if I could change how all of this happened, I would. But baby, you're a hell of a basketball player who scored the most points in state history, and just 'cause UConn can't see that does not mean other schools don't. Stanford, Clemson, and South Carolina have all called about your intent. You got options, is all I'm saying."

Miri's eyes softened slightly, but the guarded look stayed in place. "It's not just UConn, Mom. It's everything. It's like my whole life changed overnight. I thought I knew who I was, but now... I don't know. I don't know anything."

"Hey, look at me. You are Miracle Ja'nae Carter. And you are an awesome, awesome person. That will never change."

"Okay, Mom."

Miri forced a smile, but it was obvious she was doing it for her mother's sake.

Winter's heart ached, hearing the pain in Miri's voice. She reached out, placing a gentle hand on her daughter's shoulder. "I can't imagine how confusing this must be. I know how much you loved Malik, and how much, in your heart, you looked up to him. But Jae... he's not trying to take Malik's place in your heart. He's just trying to be there for you."

"But that's the thing, Mom," Miri said, her voice wavering. "All my life, Jae was the one who felt like my dad. Dad—I mean... Malik —he's just this... stranger I wondered about. I spent years filling in the blanks with every story you guys would tell. And now I don't know if I want anything to do with him. It's like he was never really mine."

Winter felt her throat tighten, her own memories flooding back. She took a deep breath, choosing her words carefully. "I understand, honey. I really do. I'm gonna tell you an unrelated story but I hope you see the relation."

She said as she sat next to her daughter and held her hand. She took a long pensive pause to truly process her words before saying. "You know, I never talk much about Grandpa—my dad—but he was everything to me when I was your age. I loved him more than anything. He'd just become the head chef at a new restaurant downtown called Perry's, and I was so proud, mainly because he was so excited. He worked back of the house, which is basically anybody in the kitchen, and was always working, and analyzing everything at his job that was good and bad because he was getting ready to open his own restaurant, and he wanted it to be successful."

Miri looked at her, surprised by the shift in conversation. Winter continued, her voice soft but filled with emotion. "One day, he was finishing his shift... and a fire broke out in another building nearby. Well, my dad was always the kind of man to do the right thing, no matter what, it was just his way. There was a mother with her children trapped on the second floor. I remember everyone saying how brave he was to run into that building. But if I'm being honest, it was the one time I wish he'd been selfish... because I'd never see him again. He survived the fire but died of smoke inhalation, and just like that, he was gone," she paused, swallowing back the pain that had never truly faded. A tear fell from her eye as she bore the gravity of her words. She pressed on. "I found out hours later, too late to even say goodbye. He never got to see the restaurant he dreamed of, and so I made it my personal mission to honor him. That's what tonight is about, see? Villery's was going to be the name of your Grandpa's restaurant."

Miri's eyes shimmered with unshed tears, her own defenses cracking. Winter took her hand gently, squeezing it. "For a kid, your father —good or bad—leaves an impact on you. That's why I'm opening this restaurant. It's a way to keep his dream alive, to honor him and, most importantly, to move forward and keep dreaming. It's what he would've wanted. Which is why I'm going to help you protest this thing with UConn. Once we show them a clean bill of health, it should be no problem for you to get where you're going."

Miri sat up. "You're... you're gonna help me?"

"Of course, baby, because that's your dream, and it's time I recognize that you have dreams of your own. I'll do all I can, but we both know Jae is the right man for the job, and I'm sure he'll help, too. Maybe that's not something you want to think about right now, but I'll say this, Miri: if I could have one more moment with my dad, I'd give up anything except for my daughter. You have Jae, right here, right now. You may not have had the time you wanted, but you've been given a new lease on life, and you have the chance to build something real with your father. One who, despite how it feels right now, we both know loves you very much."

Miri looked down, her fingers tracing the pattern on her dress. Winter leaned closer, her voice soft. "It would be a shame if you let that go to waste, baby. Sometimes, we have to make the best of what we're given, even if it wasn't what we planned."

Miri was silent, her head nodding slightly as she absorbed her mother's words. Winter could see the internal struggle in her daughter's eyes, the slow acceptance that perhaps, just maybe, this new reality could be something worth embracing.

She walked out of the room and joined her mother in the kitchen, who was reading a book she'd picked up along the way. Winter was still wiping the tears from her eyes when Denise looked up.

"You okay, honey?"

"I was telling Miri a story about Daddy and it made me realize something. I haven't grieved him either."

Winter broke down in tears in her mother's arms as Denise held her and calmly rubbed her back.

She eventually pulled back. "You know, the reason I became a chef and a baker was because the day he was taken from us was the last day all of us were ever together as a family. We had made Sunday dinner, and the boys were watching football, and Nene faked like she was sick again so that left me to help the two of you cook and bake for everyone else."

"I remember the day. You came home early, all my babies back in the house for the holidays. You were helping me with the cakes and pies, and him with the brisket."

"I loved every minute of that day, until he said he had to run to work real quick, and my life changed," she said as she wiped the tears in a futile effort.

She continued. "I think, when I was young, a part of me thought that if I could just open up this restaurant, maybe he'd come back, but I know that's not possible. So that's why I've been dragging my feet."

"Honey, I know how hard change, is believe me."

"I didn't have time to say goodbye, Momma." She began to sob again profusely, as Denise held her tightly and wiped away tears of her own.

She touched her daughter's face and said, "Baby the one thing I know about Floyd Villery is that he was full of life. He was always looking for an adventure. When you graduated high school, he started planning the restaurant. The most ambitious man I'd ever met."

"I had an amazing husband; he was a hell of a father and provider. And he wanted you, all of you, to live life on your terms. That's why I travel the world, baby. Not to punish you, but to honor your father. That's what we were going to do together. I go to all the places Floyd told me we were gonna go. And sometimes I cry, but most times I laugh and smile and live. You don't have to live in that day, Winnie. If you don't want any of this, you can walk away from it all right now, starting with this soft-opening gala, and I'll be the first in line to snatch a heffa's wig if someone got anything to say. But if this is what you, and only you, want, then enjoy it. Live in your purpose, Winnie, not for me or Miri or anyone else. Live your life."

Her mother hugged her.

Miri came out and saw the two of them hugging and called out, "Awww, now I want in."

Denise waved her over as the three generations of beauty and strength and resilience bonded in a loving restorative embrace that lasted what felt like an eternity.

Finally, being restored, Winter separated the hug and said, "Thank you, guys, but now I have to go show a room full of people why I'm the best damn chef slash baker this side of the Mississippi. "

"That's my baby!" Denise said.

She hugged them both again and went to refresh her now-ruined make-up.

She looked at herself in the mirror finally able to accept some truths about her journey. It was time to put all her talents on display.

It was time to live again.

27

NO LOOK PASS

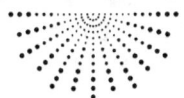

*W*inter headed to the alumni gala at her restaurant later that evening, finding herself surrounded by familiar faces from her college years, people she hadn't seen in ages.

The event was lavish, the restaurant decorated in twinkling lights, and the hum of laughter and conversation filled the air. But there was a part of her that felt incomplete, a longing glance she kept throwing toward the door, as alumni gathered in celebration. As full as the room was, she knew there was someone missing.

She wasn't sure if Jae would show up. They hadn't spoken to each other since he'd found Miri a few days ago, and though they had texted briefly, there hadn't been any deep conversations or apologies. She wondered if he was avoiding her or simply giving her space. She missed him, and the absence gnawed at her.

As she sipped her drink and scanned the room, her eyes landed on someone she hadn't expected to see: Genesis Monroe. Stunning, poised, and exuding a confidence that made heads turn, Genesis was the kind of woman who commanded attention effortlessly. Winter had always thought of her as *that bad bitch* from their college days—a title she hadn't relinquished in the slightest.

Genesis caught Winter's eye and raised an eyebrow, her lips

curving into a smirk. She sauntered over, her heels clicking against the marble floor as she approached. "Well, if it isn't Winter Carter. The moment I tasted one of the cinnamon rolls, I knew you were behind the event," Genesis praised, her voice smooth as silk. "Still as poised and as beautiful as ever, I see."

Winter froze, her confusion turning into a reluctant smile. "Genesis Monroe. Of all the people I expected to see tonight..."

Genesis tilted her head, her gaze flicking over Winter's dress with a critical, yet approving eye. "Let me just say, you are wearing that dress."

Winter gushed. "You... you like it?"

"Honey, that's fire."

"Thank you. I mean, you're so fashionable on the news. I—" Winter took a moment to compose herself mid-sentence. "I'm sorry. I'm just having a fan girl moment. I've been wanting to tell you since college that you're a bad bitch."

Genesis chuckled, her pearly white teeth giving the perfect chuckle.

"Thank you that's so sweet, but not as sweet as these red velvet cinnamon rolls. U of H colors? You go girl. I could see why all the boys were crazy about Winter Villery-Carter."

Winter continued. "You... I didn't think you knew who I was."

Genesis laughed, flipping her long, flawless hair over one shoulder. "Girl, don't look so shocked. It's a small world, especially for bad bitches like us." She gave Winter a once-over, her expression approving. "You're looking good, Wyn. Like, really good."

Winter chuckled despite herself. "Thanks, Genesis. You're not doing too bad yourself."

Genesis stepped closer, her aura magnetic. "So, I heard this restaurant is opening to the public soon. Making all of us proud with those desserts of yours, too. Go Cougars."

Winter felt her cheeks warm under the compliment. "It's been a journey, that's for sure."

Before Winter could respond, Genesis glanced around the room, her tone shifting slightly. "You know, I never thought I'd see you like this. Owning the room. Back in college, you were always so focused, so ambitious. But now, it's like you've finally arrived."

Winter smiled, though she sensed there was more she wanted to say. "Thanks, Genesis. That means a lot."

Genesis tilted her head, a knowing glint in her eye. "I noticed Jae wasn't here. That surprised me, considering you two have always been peas in a pod it's kind of shocking."

Winter's heart skipped a beat, but she kept her face composed. "Jae's... around," she said, hoping the lie would be enough.

Genesis raised an eyebrow, clearly unconvinced. "Around, huh? Funny, I don't see him. You know, we used to come to these things together every year. Of course, that was a long time ago, back when he and I were... an item. I just figured I'd see him in your restaurant tonight."

Winter's polite smile grew strained, but she maintained her composure, trying to shift the conversation. "Right. You and Jae, back in the day. You guys were relationship goals."

Genesis looked at her, a glint of curiosity in her eyes. "Hardly, but you know, we actually had something good going. But sometimes, people want different things. Or they're too busy chasing dreams to hold on to what they have."

Genisis was about to leave, but before she could, Winter's curiosity got the best of her. "Why did you two break up, if you don't mind me asking?"

Genesis paused and let out a low laugh, her gaze drifting across the room as if recalling some long-lost memory. "Jae and I were intense, both of us ambitious, both a bit selfish. I think we were both so busy trying to be the best that we forgot to actually be there for each other. And then once he got injured, well, he started spending more time rehabbing. Between that and him following Malik around like a lost puppy, it was too much. That's why we broke up. But if I'm being honest, the second time around, was because I also didn't realize how much time he was spending with *someone else*."

Winter's heart skipped a beat, her mind racing back to those college days when she and Jae had been inseparable. They'd been friends, just friends... or at least, that's what she'd told herself. But there had been moments, glances, the feeling of something *more* just beneath the surface.

Genesis seemed to read her thoughts, a knowing smirk playing on her lips. "You know, Winter, people always said Jae looked at you like... well, like you were more than just his friend. I used to think it was just friendship. But now I know better. After all these years, seems like I'm the only one who does."

Winter's cheeks flushed, and she quickly glanced away, trying to ignore the flurry of emotions Genesis's words stirred up. "We were just friends, Genesis. That's all."

Genesis's smile widened, her eyes glinting with mischief. "Oh, I know... 'cause like you said, I'm a bad bitch."

"Facts," Winter grinned, examining the flawlessly-fit bombshell.

Genesis continued. "But it was enough to make me insecure, if only for a minute back then. I felt it was almost karma, since I started that rumor about me sleeping with Brandon Hightower." The words stunned her. She shook her head in confusion and raised a hand to pause Genesis momentarily.

"So you didn't sleep with Brandon Hightower?"

Genesis took a sip of her champagne, then let out a low laugh. "Hell no! I told Jae I slept with him to get his attention. And when Jae found out, he broke up with me. Clean, no drama. That was his style."

Winter felt a flicker of old anger, but she tamped it down. "So, you just let him think... what? That you were with Brandon?"

Genesis sighed. "Pretty much. It didn't matter at that point. What did matter was that Jae and I were on the rocks anyway. He was spending more time with Malik, and then... with you. So even when we tried again, it was pretty much over."

Winter stiffened. "I promise we were just friends. I respected your relationship."

Genesis smirked, her voice softening. "Maybe. But friends don't look at each other the way Jae looked at you. I wasn't blind, Wyn."

Winter started to protest, but Genesis raised a hand to stop her. "I tried to hold on, though. When you and Malik got engaged, Jae was distracted. He had the worst game I'd ever seen him play. That was the night *Choke* Carter was born, and for a while it made sense. Anyone who knew Jae knew how much he idolized his brother. But then one day, I found these notes at his apartment—affirmations, thank yous. They were so heartfelt, so beautiful. Thirty days' worth. I thought they were for me, and for a while, I convinced myself they were. I thought it was the most romantic thing a man would ever do for me, and I was determined to work it out."

Winter felt her stomach twist. "So... what... what happened?"

"I realized," Genesis said, her voice quieter now, "they weren't about me. They were about you."

Winter's breath caught, her chest tightening. Genesis smiled faintly, reaching into her clutch. "Well, of course I was furious, and though you guys never crossed a line, I gave you an opening by playing games in the first place." Genesis said as she reflected on her youth. Suddenly her eyes flickered with excitement as she reached in her purse.

"I kept one of the notes. It was so beautiful, I couldn't let it go. I carried it with me until I met my husband. I needed to know what real love looked like before I said 'yes' to anyone else. But seeing that we're right here, right now, it's only fitting I give it to its rightful owner. Here."

She handed Winter a small, folded piece of paper, worn down from the years, but still intact. She opened it, and Jae's handwriting was unmistakable. Hesitant, Winter opened it, her hands trembling as she read:

"Day 12: Thank you for reminding me that love is not perfect, but it is constant. That laughter can heal even the deepest wounds, and that the quiet moments—the ones where words aren't needed—are where we find the truest connection. You make me better, even when you don't know it. And for that, I'm grateful."

Winter's eyes filled with tears as she folded the note back up, her mind reeling. "He wrote this?"

Genesis nodded. "And twenty-nine more just like it. That's when I knew Jae was in love with you, Wyn. And I wasn't the kind of woman who could settle for being second. So I let him go."

Winter looked at her, overwhelmed by the weight of the revelation. "Genesis, I... I don't even know what to say."

Genesis smiled, a genuine softness in her expression. "You don't have to say anything. I've moved on. I have a husband who adores me and two beautiful kids. My life turned out just fine. But you? You've got a chance to figure out what you want. Don't waste it." She leaned in, her voice dropping to a conspiratorial whisper. "Jae's a good man, Wyn. Always has been. Just... don't let fear get in the way."

With that, Genesis stood, her heels clicking softly against the floor as she walked away. Winter sat there, clutching the note, her thoughts swirling. For years, she'd buried her feelings, told herself they were just friends. But now, faced with the undeniable truth, she couldn't ignore it anymore.

Winter was left speechless as Genesis walked away, her words echoing in her mind. All those years of friendship with Jae, all those shared dreams and quiet moments... had there been more to it than she'd allowed herself to see?

Her gaze drifted back to the door, wondering if Jae would walk in, if he would meet her gaze and somehow reassure her of everything she couldn't quite put into words. The music swelled around her, the night unfolding, but Winter's mind was far from the glittering restaurant.

The world seemed to shift around her, and as the evening wore on, one thought consumed her.

Maybe it wasn't too late to find out.

28

ONE-ON-ONE

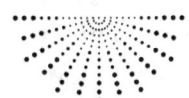

"And the high school scene is buzzing now that Miracle Carter has been cleared to play after making a remarkable full recovery from a rare form of sickle cell. Rob, let me ask you, did UConn move too fast?"

"Absolutely they did, Bill. Miri has been a phenomenon all season long, and it was a knee-jerk reaction."

"If she wins the state title tonight, she will be able to cap off a season for the ages."

"That's right, Bill. Let's be honest, with UConn pulling out, there's a good chance the University of Houston could land this five-star recruit, giving her a chance to do what her uncle—excuse me, father—did and revitalize the women's program."

"That's right. When you're talking about the greatest Houston basketball players, the list is short. Hakeem 'The Dream' Olajuwon, Clyde 'The glide' Drexler, and Jaden 'Smoke' Carter, and now his daughter Miracle Carter could join the ranks."

Click.

Jaden turned off the radio. He hadn't talked to Winter or Miracle since their discussion at the court. He wasn't sure what to say.

He wanted to be at the game tonight, but was certain he wasn't invited. He decided to take some time to leave his head and go to the quiet place he fell in love with basketball.

The Rockets stadium was packed because of the game, but the practice facility the players used right behind the stadium was empty. From the moment he got out of his car, he felt odd.

They are going to play zone defense. She needs to concentrate.

He proceeded into the facility, the rhythmic echo of the basketball hitting the hardwood court reverberated through the empty Rockets gym as he practiced. Jae was deep in thought, the ball's steady bounce his only solace. He aimed for another deep three-pointer, the swish of the net doing little to ease his mind.

She can kill them on the edges with her shooting range, soften the defense up.

The radio he'd escaped in his car was blaring in the background over the stadium loudspeaker, and it wasn't helping. Every station seemed to be buzzing about the state championship game. Miracle Carter, back after a medical scare. Her talent undeniable, but her resilience questioned. Words like "rusty" and "pressure" cut through the air, adding weight to Jae's already heavy heart.

Jae missed his third shot in a row when he'd had enough.

"Can someone turn that off?" he yelled out.

Someone from the maintenance crew mumbled, scrambling to change the station.

Jae's sharp glance made them quicken their pace.

"Messy motherfuckers," he muttered under his breath, bouncing the basketball a little harder against the court this time.

He took another shot and missed.

Frustration boiled up in him, but instead of releasing it, he sank into his thoughts.

Miri, the girl he hadn't ever truly known as a daughter. Malik, the brother he'd idolized but now felt he barely understood. Winter, the woman who'd been a constant in his life but had always seemed just out of reach. The past weeks had been chaos, a tidal wave of revelations and emotions that left him drowning.

He didn't notice Darren until the ball was snatched mid-dribble.

"What the hell are you doing here, Bag Boy?" Darren asked, spinning the ball on his finger.

Jae grabbed it back, the force of his hand enough to stop the spin. "Minding my business. You might run the Rockets front office, but these banners? My name's on them. I can come here whenever I damn well please."

Darren folded his arms, unfazed. "That's not what I'm talking about, Carter. What are you doing here *now*? Don't you have a game to watch? You know, state championship? Miracle Carter, your—" Darren caught himself, smirking. "—niece."

Jae ignored the jab, turning back to the hoop. "Not in the mood, Darren."

Darren let out a low laugh. "Damn, Bag Boy, you haven't changed since college. Always choking when it matters."

Jae's shot ricocheted off the rim, the clang louder than it should have been. He turned to face Darren fully, his jaw tightening. "What in the hell is your problem with me, man? You want me to apologize for taking your spot in college? I won't. I was better than you as a freshman, now and always, because I was made for the league and you were made to sit on the sidelines."

"If you think that's what this is about, then you're even dumber than I thought, which was an incredibly low bar," Darren said, stepping closer. "You're supposed to be at that game, Jae. But no, you're here, wallowing in whatever the hell this is. And you know what? You've always been like this. Self absorbed."

Jae let out a humorless laugh. "That's rich, coming from you. You tried to smash your dead best friend's wife."

"And the irony," Darren shot back, his voice dripping with sarcasm, "is that you actually *did*."

The words landed like a punch, but Jae didn't flinch. Instead, he closed the distance between them, his voice low and dangerous. "Watch yourself."

"Why?" Darren snapped. "Because you'll swing on me? Go ahead, Choke. Prove me right. Show me that you're still the guy who folds when someone applies a little pressure."

Jae's fists clenched, but he didn't move. "What's your deal with me, Darren? You say it has nothing to do with the court, but you've been on my ass since college. Always got something to say, always fucking with me."

Darren's eyes narrowed as he scoffed. "You really don't get it, do you?"

"Get what?"

Darren paced and lifted his hands in the air. "You had everything, Jae," Darren said, his voice rising. "I mean everything. The girls, the news. You came from money and still got even more money in college, about to sign for even more money the day you left campus. I beat my meat to Genesis Monroe at least twice a week and she's your leftovers," Darren huffed, crossed his arms and continued. "And that was fine. I promise you, I'm not a hater, but you walked around like you had nothing, and as a person who actually had nothing, that has always pissed me off. You came into college with a chip on your shoulder, acting like the world owed you something, while the rest of us were out here fighting for scraps."

"Speak for yourself, D. Don't try to lump anyone else in this by saying *us*."

"Well, then, how bout *we* motherfucker? Cause more than me felt this way."

"So now you want to lie on the team?"

"I'm not talking about them."

Jae shook his head, confused. "Then what are you even talking about?"

Darren took a deep breath, his tone softening but losing none of its edge. "Malik. He loved you, man. You were his little brother. But... he also resented you, too. And honestly? I don't blame him."

Jae froze, the words hitting harder than any punch. "What? Man, what are you even saying, you gonna lie on your best friend no—"

"Just shut the fuck up for a second, Jae," Darren said, cutting him off. He nodded, his gaze steady. "When your pops left, Malik had it rough. You were, like, four, but Leek was seven. And he just found out that the man he thought was his dad wasn't his dad."

"Wait, what?"

"You wanted the real, I'm bringing it. Apparently your mom had an affair, which resulted in Malik and that was too much for your dad, so he took you and left. Malik was devastated and he was angry, but your mom was sick. He had to become an adult fast. But as far as he was concerned, you all abandoned him, you feel me? He had to be that way, he grew up over in Sunny Side. That's not Houston, that's H-Town."

"What does that have to do with anything?"

"It means he had to grow up fast, bringing in money, you know the thing they just hand you 'cause it's Tuesday. You didn't know your mom, but I did. I saw what Malik went through. Most nights, they didn't have food. And whatever money he made, he gave it to her. That's why he was always bucking authority, and before he met you, getting in trouble with the law. He didn't have a choice, Jae. And then you show up, fresh out of nowhere, with a bankroll bigger than any of us ever saw, talking about reuniting with your 'long-lost brother'. Of course he resented you."

Jae took a step back, shaking his head. "You're lying."

"I'm not," Darren said firmly. "H-town's a tough place, and Malik… he saw you as a mark at first. That ain't me making it up. That's just the truth. Maybe he changed over time, and I know he loved you in the end, but don't act like he was some saint. He played you, Jae. In more ways than one, if you ask me."

Jae sat in silence. He didn't want to believe Darren, but the look on his face told the story he'd secretly wondered from time to time himself. Darren wasn't lying.

"Played me how?" Jae's voice was barely above a whisper, but the anger in it was palpable.

Darren cocked his head and let out a disappointed smirk. "With Winter, Jae," Darren said, cutting straight to the heart of it. "From the jump, he knew you liked her. Hell, we all knew. But he used that 'sick card' every time he wanted something from you, and you gave it to him. You always did."

Jae's vision blurred, his hands tightening into fists at his sides. "Why are you telling me this?"

"'Cause I'm an adult, and I don't have to like you to do the right thing. And you're a dumbass that's never gonna fix your life when all the pieces are right in front of you. You don't want to hear it, but it's the truth, and it's time you knew it," Darren said, stepping closer. "And if it's worth anything, maybe Malik felt guilty in the end. Maybe he even loved Winter. But don't stand here and act like he didn't see you as a walking checkbook when he needed one."

For a moment, neither of them moved. The gym was silent, the tension thick enough to cut.

"You're full of shit," Jae finally said, his voice trembling with barely contained rage.

"Maybe," Darren said with a shrug. "But deep down, you know I'm right."

Before Jae could respond, Darren turned to leave. But just as he reached the door, he stopped, turning back with a smirk. "One more thing," Darren said, his tone casual but pointed. "You might've been better than me on the court, but off it? You've got a lot to learn."

And then, without warning, Darren swung, his fist connecting with Jae's jaw. The impact staggered him, but Jae didn't go down. He steadied himself, glaring at Darren, who shook out his hand with a grimace.

"Now we're even," Darren said, his voice calm.

Jae watched him leave, his mind spinning. Darren's words, the punch—it was all too much. But deep down, something in him shifted. The truth hurt, but it was undeniable. For the first time, Jae wondered if maybe, just maybe, he'd been living in a lie of his own making.

29

CHAMPIONSHIP MOMENTS

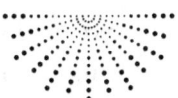

The gym was electric, packed with fans and reporters. The Jack Yates Lions, led by Shasha Wilcox, had already set the tone with their aggressive play. The energy was palpable, but not in Miri's favor.

She stepped onto the court, the bright lights shining down on her, amplifying the sweat forming on her brow. The murmurs from the crowd were already getting under her skin. She adjusted her jersey and glanced up at the stands, scanning the rows of faces. She saw her mom and Denise sitting together, they're nervous clapping a poor attempt to mask their own anxiety.

But Jae's seat? Empty.

The ball tipped, and it was immediately clear this wasn't going to be a fair game. Shasha Wilcox and her squad didn't just come to win; they came to embarrass.

From the opening play, the Lions swarmed Miri. Shasha shoved her shoulder into Miri's chest during a screen, and no whistle blew. They double-teamed her at every touch, grabbing at her jersey, tangling their arms with hers. One of Shasha's teammates smirked after Miri missed her first shot.

"You missed that? Thought you were supposed to be the big star. No wonder UConn dropped you," the girl sneered.

The crowd roared every time the Lions scored, and Miri felt the weight of their eyes on her every move. The whispers from the stands weren't whispers anymore.

"Look at her—she's off tonight."

"Is that the Miracle Carter everyone's been hyping up? What a joke."

"Guess sickle cell runs in her game, too."

Miri clenched her fists. She wanted to block it out, but the words cut deep. Her chest tightened.

She looked over at the bench, hoping for a nod of encouragement from her coach, but he was barking orders at the other players. No reprieve there.

She missed another shot, the ball bouncing hard off the rim. The Lions grabbed the rebound and sprinted down the court. Shasha pulled up for a three, draining it effortlessly.

Miri glared at her but said nothing. She couldn't let Shasha know she was getting to her, even though her stomach churned.

By the end of the first quarter, Miri was rattled. She hadn't made a single shot, and the Lions were up by fifteen. Every time she tried to pass, the Lions closed in, cutting off her options. Her teammates hesitated to give her the ball, and when they did, the Lions were ready, pulling at her arms and swatting the ball away.

"Where you at, Carter?" Shasha taunted, getting right in her face after another turnover.

Miri shoved past her, trying to keep her composure, but her movements were stiff, her decisions rushed.

At the start of the second quarter, the Lions ramped up the physicality. One girl grabbed Miri's wrist during a drive, yanking it hard enough to make her stumble. The ref blew the whistle, but instead of calling a foul, he signaled a travel.

Miri heard someone laugh from the crowd. Her eyes darted toward the sound, but she couldn't pinpoint who it was.

"She's looking like a sophomore out there," the announcer said, his voice booming through the gym.

Miri's cheeks burned. The laughter from the stands felt louder, harsher. She could feel every pair of eyes on her, judging her, doubting her.

Midway through the second quarter, Miri got her chance. The Lions defense loosened just enough for her to make a break. She drove hard to the basket, rising for a layup—only to have Shasha swat it out of bounds with a vicious block.

"Is that all you got?" Shasha said, her voice dripping with mockery.

Miri's coach called a timeout. She trudged to the bench, keeping her head down. Her teammates avoided eye contact. Even her coach seemed hesitant to address her directly.

She glanced up at the stands again. Still no Jae.

Her heart sank further.

The timeout ended, but things didn't get better. The Lions doubled their lead, and Miri continued to struggle. Every missed shot, every turnover, every taunt chipped away at her confidence.

Shasha stole the ball from her with ease on one possession, laughing as she jogged back down the court. "Y'all see this? Miracle Carter's disappearing act," Shasha said, grinning at her teammates.

She jogged past Miri on the way back down, her voice low but sharp. "Guess you got more in common with your pops that we thought, Baby Choke."

Out of frustration Miri pushed Shasha, instantly earning a technical foul, giving the Ballers more points at the free throw line.

Shasha clapped toward her before sinking both free throws.

Miri's chest tightened again. She glanced at her mom and Denise, who were cheering despite the disaster unfolding on the court. But her eyes kept drifting to that empty seat.

The half ended with the Lions up by twenty-five.

The buzzer sounded, but instead of heading to the locker room, Miri lingered on the bench for a moment, staring at the scoreboard.

This is my choke game, she thought bitterly.

She wiped her face with a towel and stood, her legs feeling like lead. The whispers, the taunts, the laughter—it was all too much. And the person she wanted to see most still wasn't there.

Miri trudged off the court, her shoulders slumped. She didn't know what she needed, but she knew she couldn't find it on her own.

As she walked into the tunnel, her coach's voice echoed in her ears, laced with frustration.

"Carter, I don't know what the hell is going on with you, but you better figure it out fast."

Her chest tightened again. But just as she was about to step into the locker room, she heard a familiar voice from behind her.

"You're really gonna let them do you like this, Cupcake?"

She turned sharply. There he was. Jae stood in the tunnel, arms crossed, his eyes steady but full of challenge.

Miri froze, a cocktail of relief and anger bubbling to the surface. She wanted to yell, to cry, to ask him where the hell he'd been. But all she could do was glare at him, the weight of the first half pressing down on her like a ton of bricks.

Without another word, she stormed past him, her mind a whirlwind of emotions.

In the locker room, Miri sank into her seat, tuning out her coach's tirade. Her head throbbed, her heart raced, and her stomach churned. She didn't know if she was angry at Jae, Shasha, or herself. Maybe all of the above.

She sat in the locker room, drowning in frustration and self-doubt. Her coach was already there, pacing, face red.

"Carter, what the hell are you doing out there?" he barked. "You're getting clamped! You're supposed to be leading this team, but instead, you're—"

"I know, Coach!" she snapped, her voice cracking. "I know."

The team fell silent as Miri's emotions spilled out. She grabbed a towel and threw it over her face, slumping into the corner. Tears pricked her eyes as she tried to steady her breathing. She felt overwhelmed, humiliated, and angry—not just at Shasha, or her teammates, but at herself.

A knock interrupted the tension. The door cracked open, and Jae poked his head in. "Coach, can I have a minute?"

Coach grumbled but waved him in. "You've got two. Make it count."

As the team left, Miri felt her heart twist as Jae stepped inside, closing the door behind him. He stood there for a moment, leaning against the wall, arms crossed. His eyes were calm, but the weight in his gaze was unmistakable.

"Miri," he said quietly.

She didn't look up. "What do you want? To tell me I suck? I know that already, Dad. Or is it Uncle Jae? Or is it Coach?"

Jae nodded and walked closer. "I'm not here to talk to you as your dad. Or your uncle. Or even your coach. I'm here as a baller."

She lifted the towel slightly, peeking at him through swollen eyes. His tone wasn't sharp, but it wasn't soft either. It carried weight—one she couldn't ignore.

"I'll tell you the truth. There's only one thing I hate more than not being there for you as your dad." He paused, his voice lowering. "It's the fact that the name 'Choke Carter' was born the minute I did what you're doing right now."

She sat up, confused. "What do you mean?"

Jae took a breath, dragging a hand over his face. "The night of my infamous choke game, my agent tried to spin it as if I just had a bad game. But the truth is, I did choke. My mind wasn't in the game. You know why? Because I'd just found out Malik and your mom were going to get married. And it wrecked me. Because I wasn't honest enough to tell myself that I was in love with her. I let my personal shit mess with my game. And because of that, I didn't just lose the game—I lost myself."

His voice cracked slightly, but he pushed through. "If you go out there and play like you did in the first half, win or lose, you'll second-guess yourself for the rest of your life. Trust me. I know."

Miri looked up at him, a tear sliding down her cheek. "You... loved my mom?"

"Always have, Cupcake." His voice softened, but the emotion was raw.

"What's the point, anyway? We're getting blown out. We're down twenty-five points."

"Not gonna lie to you, kid. For the Houston Lady Nets to win this game, it's gonna take nothing short of a miracle. Luckily they have one."

Miri sat up, vulnerable. She sniffed, wiping her face. "I... I'm scared."

Jae crouched down, meeting her at eye level. "I know. But you don't have time to be scared. So play ball. *That*, you can do better than anyone in this gym, including me."

"They're fouling, double teaming me. I can't get a shot off."

He stood, glancing toward the door. "Decide if you're hurt or injured. If you're injured, come out the game. If you're hurt, get back in the damn huddle."

Miri blinked, processing his words. Slowly, she stood, her posture straightening as determination hardened her features.

Jae continued. "They're supposed to play dirty. You're a great player, they gotta throw everything, including the kitchen sink, at you. Play ball. You want to be great, Miri? This right here is your moment. No one climbs to the top of a mountain without scars to prove they made the climb. So go out there and get your damn trophy."

She nodded, her face now expressionless but her eyes burning with a newfound fire. Without a word, she walked past him and out of the locker room. The steel-cold determination in her eyes spoke louder than anything she could've said.

The third quarter started, and the energy in the gym shifted. Miri was different. She wasn't just playing; she was orchestrating.

She walked the ball up the court and before the defense could set up, hit a long three-pointer from nearly half-court.

She looked at Shasha and said, "Twenty-two."

The Lions had possession. Miri rushed up the court, cutting off the pass and stealing it with a quick swipe. She zipped a laser-like pass to an open teammate, who drove in for an easy layup.

"Twenty," Miri muttered under her breath as she turned back to Shasha.

On the next possession, Miri intercepted an inbound pass, feeding another teammate for a wide-open three.

"Seventeen."

The crowd roared as the deficit shrank. Miri's vision was sharper than ever, finding the open player every time the double team came her way. She turned her precision into momentum, and the Lady Nets clawed their way back.

By the end of the third quarter, the lead was down to ten. Miri dribbled up the court, scanning the defense. Shasha pretended to double-team, but hesitated. Miri faked a pass, darted through the gap, and made a no-look pass to a trailing teammate who sank the shot.

"Eight."

The crowd erupted, and the Lions coach called a timeout. Miri walked to the bench, her expression unflinching. She glanced towards the empty seat now occupied by her father, Jaden Carter. He nodded once, his message clear.

Job's not done.

She understood his message. They were down by eight at the start of the fourth. Shasha was less confident as she walked over, her gaze locked in. "Playtime is over, Baby Choke. You wanted me, you got me."

Miri ignored her and called for the ball as she scanned the defense for the inbound pass.

The fourth quarter began, and Shasha took it upon herself to guard Miri one-on-one.

Miri smirked. "Big mistake," she whispered.

Shasha lunged as Miri hesitated, biting on the fake. Miri blew past her, laying the ball in with ease.

"Six."

The crowd erupted. It was her most confident shot, a moment that would defined the rest of the game. It didn't matter if they fouled her or not. She could shoot it from anywhere. They simply could not guard her.

Shasha came back down the court, trying to overpower Miri with her speed, but Miri stayed with her. When Shasha went up for a shot, Miri blocked it clean, sending the ball flying into the crowd. Shasha picked up the ball and threw it at her, hitting her in the back. She turned around and balled up her fist and was about to swing but saw her father out of the corner of her eye. Before the referee could stop her she turned her hand and used Jae's signature move. She blew smoke on Shasha. The referee separated them. For the first time all season Miri was in Shasha's head and there was nothing she could do.

"You wanted the smoke?" Miri shot back, her voice ice-cold. "Can't handle it now, can you?"

"Shut up and play ball, hoe," Shasha spat.

"Hey, you asked for this," Miri shrugged, jogging back to the other end.

With the ball in her hands, she took a deep breath. One sharp crossover, a step back, and the ball soared from beyond the arc.

"Three."

The crowd roared. The announcers rose to their feet. Shasha looked clearly rattled.

None of it mattered. Her team was down by three, and with a minute and a half left in the game, she needed to even the score.

They trapped her with a double team, but she made the pass easily to one of the sharpshooters on the team, who hit a wide open three-pointer. The game was now tied.

The gym was thunderous, the crowd split between chants of "Defense!" and "Let's go, Nets!"

The score was tied, and Miri Carter felt every bit of pressure on her shoulders. The Lady Nets had fought tooth and nail to bring themselves back into this game, and now the fate of the state championship rested in her hands.

Miri dribbled up the court, her eyes darting between her teammates and Shasha Wilcox, who was practically glued to her hip. The

Yates Lions had tightened their defense to a suffocating level. Every step Miri took felt like navigating a minefield.

With less than thirty seconds left, Miri made her move. She crossed over, feigned a drive to the right, and cut left toward the basket. Shasha anticipated her, closing the gap, but Miri was quicker. She spun away, rising for a shot just as Shasha reached out.

Chirp.

The ref's hand shot up, signaling a foul. Shasha's hand had made contact with Miri's wrist, sending her off-balance. Miri crashed to the floor, her heart pounding.

The crowd erupted in chaos.

"That's all ball!" Sasha screamed, stomping toward the ref. "Are you kidding me? That's CLEAN!"

The ref signaled for her to back off, his hand hovering near his belt, warning her silently. Shasha's coach pulled her aside, hissing in her ear to calm down.

Miri pushed herself up, her breath ragged. She stared at the ref, then at Shasha, who glared daggers at her. The weight of the game was crushing her chest. Her teammates clapped and cheered her on, but their voices sounded distant, muffled by the pounding in her ears.

At the free-throw line, Miri tried to steady herself. She took the ball, bouncing it three times before exhaling slowly.

Clang. The first shot rimmed out, the crowd groaning loudly.

Miri wiped her palms on her shorts, her heart racing. She closed her eyes for a brief moment, blocking out the noise.

Swish.

The ball cut through the net cleanly, and the scoreboard flipped. *72-71, Lady Nets.*

With twenty seconds left, the Lions inbounded the ball. Miri's teammates scrambled to apply pressure, and the gym felt like it was vibrating with tension. The ball found Shasha, who barreled up the court, determined to seal the game.

Miri sprinted to intercept, planting herself in Shasha's path. Shasha smirked, driving hard to the basket. Miri went up, arms outstretched. Their bodies collided midair, and the whistle blew again.

"Foul on 32."

The crowd erupted into boos and cheers as Miri fell back, landing hard on the floor. She slammed her fist against the hardwood, furious with herself.

Shasha stepped to the free-throw line, the gym pulsing with anticipation. Her first shot swished in effortlessly. Tied again.

She lined up for the second shot, smirking at Miri. She sank the second shot.

73-72, Yates Lions.

Miri's team inbounded the ball, the clock ticking down. Fifteen seconds. The coach didn't call a timeout, trusting his team to execute.

The ball found its way to Miri's hands. She crossed half-court, her teammates spreading out on the floor, giving her room to operate. The gym felt like it was holding its breath.

She sized up Shasha who was guarding her tight, her feet planted, daring Miri to make a move. Miri dribbled twice, then made a hard drive left. The defense collapsed on her, and she stepped back, rising for a three-pointer just beyond the arc.

Clang.

The ball bounced off the rim. Gasps rippled through the crowd, but her teammate grabbed the rebound, immediately kicking it back out to her.

Five seconds.

Miri reset, her heart pounding. Shasha closed in again, but this time, Miri didn't hesitate. She stepped back further, planting her feet and letting the ball fly from deep.

The gym went silent, the ball arcing high and spinning perfectly toward the net.

Swish.

The buzzer blared, the crowd erupted, and Miri's teammates stormed the court.

75-73, Lady Nets.

Miri was swarmed, her teammates lifting her into the air as the gym roared with celebration. She glanced toward the stands, her eyes locking onto Jae, who had stood quietly throughout the chaos. He didn't cheer or jump—he simply gave her a small nod, his expression filled with pride.

Job done.

For the first time all night, Miri allowed herself to smile.

30

OVERTIME

The championship game was over, the echoes of the roaring crowd still bouncing off the walls of the stadium. Miracle Carter had cemented her place in history, her game-winning three-pointer the kind of moment people would talk about for years to come. But while the celebration was in full swing on the court, Jae Carter was making his way through the dimly-lit hallways, heading for the exit.

He moved quietly, his head low, his mind racing with a tangle of emotions he didn't yet have the energy to untangle. Miri had done it. She'd risen to the occasion in a way he never could back in college, and she'd proven herself on the biggest stage.

Yet the weight of everything—their relationship, his place in her life, and the turmoil with Winter—was heavier than he wanted to admit. He also didn't know what to say to Winter. They hadn't spoken during the game because Miri was down and in her head. But now...

"Smoke!" a voice called out sharply.

He stopped in his tracks, turning slowly to see Winter standing at the end of the hallway.

Her heels clicked against the tile as she strode toward him, her expression somewhere between anger and determination.

"What's up, Wyn?" he said, trying to keep his voice light, though his shoulders were tense.

"What's up?" she shot back, her voice dripping with sarcasm. "You were about to sneak out of here without saying a word to me or Miri. That's what's up."

Jae sighed, running a hand over his face. "She doesn't need me hovering. She's got her moment, and she earned it. As for you… well, I wasn't sure you were ready to talk."

"Cut the crap, Jae." Winter stepped closer, pointing a finger at his chest. "She was out there looking like someone I knew back in college. You know who I'm talking about?"

Jae's lips curved into a faint smirk, though his eyes stayed serious. "Yeah. I know."

"Exactly." Winter's voice softened, the tension in her shoulders loosening. "Before you got here, she kept looking at your seat. I know what that look meant. It meant she needed you, even if she didn't say it. And then you showed up, like you always have for her."

Jae nodded slowly, letting her words sink in. "She played like hell tonight, Winter. She played like she had something to prove. She didn't need me, she didn't need anyone."

"Sounds like her father." Winter's tone was gentler now, and she folded her arms, tilting her head as she looked at him. "She's got your fire, Jae. And yeah, she's got some of Malik's swagger, but when it comes to guts? That's all you."

He let out a low chuckle, his eyes dropping to the floor for a moment. "I can't front, she made me proud out there."

"She makes us both proud." Winter's voice wavered slightly, and she took a step closer. "But I'm not letting you leave without talking about what's between us. I need to say something, and I need you to listen."

Jae met her gaze, his expression unreadable. "I'm listening."

"Someone told me I haven't been a good friend lately."

"Was it Christina?"

"Wha—why would you say that?"

"You only got two friends, Wyn."

"Boy shut up and let me talk." Winter took a deep breath, steeling herself. "Back in college, this night went a totally different way for you. I didn't see it then, but you were looking over at the bench the same way Miri was. I was so caught up in Malik and the proposal, in trying to make the most of however much time we had left, that I didn't notice you—not like I should have. And then, the other night, someone reminded me of that."

She reached into her bag, pulling out the folded note Genesis had given her.

Jae grimaced as she handed it to him, her hand trembling slightly.

He unfolded the paper, his eyes scanning the familiar words. It was one of the affirmations he'd written years ago, words he thought he'd buried along with everything else he'd felt back then.

"How did you...get this?" he asked, his voice low, almost a whisper, somewhat confused.

"Genesis kept it," Winter admitted. "She thought it was for her, until she figured out it wasn't. And when she showed it to me, Jae... It was like a puzzle piece I didn't even know was missing, clicking into place."

Jae looked up at her, his nerve hardening. "What are you saying, Winter?"

She hesitated, her eyes locking with his. "I'm saying, I see you now. I see you in a way I didn't let myself see before. If I'm being honest, I've been scared to let you in like that, because every man I've ever loved has left me in the most painful way possible. I don't think I could live if something happened to you. So, anytime something rose up in me, I'd kill it before it could take root." She said as a tear rolled from her eyes. "But I don't want to be scared anymore. I just need to know. Do you still feel like this? Do you love me?"

Jae folded the note carefully, slipping it into his pocket. He felt the weight of pressure on him. But this time he wasn't going to choke.

He stepped closer to her, their faces inches apart. "Winter, you're my best friend. You've always been my best friend. But if you're asking for the truth, I've loved you since the first day you handed me one of those terrible practice muffins you made back in college."

She laughed, tears forming in her eyes. "They weren't that bad."

"They were awful," he teased, his voice softening. "But I ate every single one because it meant spending time with you. They say a man gets three great loves in his life. I have mine. Miracle Carter, basketball and you, and that will never change."

Winter bit her lip, her heart pounding. "So what now?"

Jae leaned in, brushing a strand of hair from her face. "Now, we stop pretending we're anything but perfect for each other. And we take it one step at a time."

She smiled, a tear slipping down her cheek. "One step at a time sounds good."

They leaned into each other, their lips meeting in a kiss that felt like years of unspoken feelings finally breaking free. It was slow and deep, filled with the kind of emotion neither of them had dared to name until now. Love.

She hugged him and kissed him again, leaning back to look in his eyes. "In case it was unclear, we're fucking tonight."

"No argument there."

The pair extended their hands for a Double up as they joined their daughter in celebration.

Back in the gym, Miracle stood in the middle of the court, holding the championship trophy high as ESPN cameras surrounded her.

One reporter stepped forward, mic in hand. "Miracle, congratulations on a game for the ages. I'm sure they'll be talking about this for years to come."

"Thanks Rob. It means a lot to me."

"You may not know this, but UConn announced they want you again. So the big question is, what's next? Are you sticking with UConn now that they've renewed their offer?"

Miri grinned, her eyes scanning the crowd until they found her mom and dad walking hand-in-hand toward her. "No," she said firmly. "It was always a dream of mine to play for the Huskies, but dreams change. I'm not going to UConn. If they'll have me, I'm going to the University of Houston."

The crowd gasped, the gym let out a roar of excitement. The

reporter blinking in surprise. "Well, let me be the first to say, I'm sure they'll welcome you at U of H. Can you explain to the audience why?"

Miri nodded, her voice steady. "This season I've been through a lot, and sometimes it didn't look like anything was going to work in my favor. But a wise person taught me that anyone trying to climb to the top of a mountain is going to have a few scars to prove they made the climb. For me, this isn't just about basketball, it's about legacy. My dad built his here. My mom's building hers here. And now, I want to build mine here, too."

She turned toward her parents, holding the trophy out to them. "Mom! Dad! Come celebrate with me!"

Winter and Jae exchanged a look, their smiles wide and full of pride. Together, they walked onto the court, wrapping their arms around Miri as the cameras flashed.

Shasha Wilcox approached, her expression subdued but respectful. She extended a hand to Miri, who shook it firmly.

"Good game," Shasha said quietly.

"Good game," Miri replied, a small smile tugging at her lips.

In that moment, rivalry or scores were meaningless. It was about respect, family, and the strength to fight for what truly matters. And for the first time, Winter, Jae, and Miri felt like a complete family, ready to face whatever came next—together.

AFTERWORD

Every story has a journey, not just for its characters but for the writer and the readers who follow them. Winter: A Love Story began as a tale of resilience and love, but it became so much more—a story about family, legacy, and the delicate balance of past and future.

Winter, Jae, and Miracle taught me that life is rarely neat. It's messy, full of unexpected turns, unspoken truths, and second chances that feel both terrifying and exhilarating. Through their struggles and triumphs, I wanted to explore what it means to truly fight for love— not just romantic love, but the love that binds families, inspires dreams, and gives us the courage to face ourselves.

To anyone who has ever felt the weight of the past or the fear of the future, this story is for you. It's a reminder that even when the odds feel stacked against you, there's always a way forward—if you're brave enough to take the first step.

As I wrote, I found myself thinking about the legacies we inherit and the ones we leave behind. Whether it's a dream passed down from a parent, a promise we keep for someone we've lost, or the marks we make on the lives of those we love, we're all shaping the stories that will outlive us.

Thank you for letting me share this one with you. I hope Winter's story inspires you to chase your dreams with unrelenting passion, to forgive even when it feels impossible, and to love fiercely—even when it scares you.

Because, in the end, love really is the greatest legacy we can leave behind.

Until the next story,
   NL

ABOUT THE AUTHOR

Norian Love is a best-selling author, screen-writer, songwriter, and poet, whose character rich storytelling and creative world building is swiftly setting him apart as one of the top writers in the black romance genre. His breakout release, Autumn: A Love Story, was the recipient of the Association of Black Romance Writers 2021 Book of the Year Award. It was also winner of the 2024 International Impact Romance Book award. Autumn's complementary poetic journal, Blue: Love Letters to Fatima, also became a number one best-seller, giving him the unique distinction of having number one releases across multiple genres. He was a finalist for the 2021 Black Authors Rock, Author of the Year Award, as well as a finalist for the 2022 Romance Slam Jam Best Erotic Romance EMMA Award. He is working on completing the highly-anticipated Money, Power, & Sex series and is currently serving as the head screenwriter for the University of Houston HIV Awareness campaign.

Penning the hashtag, #blacklovematters, Norian has been garnering accolades for his work from his reviewers, fans, peers, book clubs, and several podcasts. His books are sold worldwide and are published in print, eBook, and audio formats.

To learn more, visit www.norianlove.com or follow him across most social media outlets at @norianlove.

f X ⊙

ALSO BY NORIAN LOVE

Money, Power & Sex: A Love Story

Seduction: A Money, Power & Sex Story

Donovan: A Money Power & Sex Story

Autumn: A Love Story

Marcus: A Money, Power & Sex Story

Gibson: A Money, Power & Sex Short Story

Code Name: Soucouyant

Ronnie: A Money Power & Sex Story

Poetry

Theater of Pain

Games of the Heart

The Dawn or the Dusk

Blue: Love Letters to Fatima

Music

Autumn: A Love Story: The Soundtrack

Winter: A Love Story: The Soundtrack

Coming Soon

In the Case of Alexandria Hughes

Seduction II

Money, Power & Sex II: The Scent of Deceit